Crossing River Jordan

by

ML Barnes

FLYING TURTLE
PUBLISHING

Hammond, Indiana

Flying Turtle Publishing
Hammond, IN

This book is a work of fiction. Any references to historical events, real people, or real locales are used fictitiously. Other names, characters, places, and incidents are the product of the author's imagination, and any resemblance to actual events or locales or persons, living or dead, is entirely coincidental.

The publisher does not have any control over third-party websites or their content.

All scriptures are KJV.

Crossing River Jordan copyright © 2012
by Mari Lumpkin Barnes

Edited by Karen Rodgers (http://critiqueyourbook.com)

Cover by Balázs Lorinczi (http://balakin1.deviantart.com)

All rights reserved, including the right of reproduction in whole or in part in any form, without written permission from the author.

The text of this book was set in Georgia.
Manufactured in the United States of America

ISBN- 978-0-9851492-0-8

If you purchased this book without a cover, you should be aware that this book is stolen property. It was reported as "unsold and destroyed" to the publisher, and neither the author nor the publisher has received any payment for this "stripped" book. Please do not participate in or encourage piracy of copyrighted materials in violation of authors' rights.

The RIVER JORDAN Books

Parting River Jordan

Crossing River Jordan

ACKNOWLEDGEMENTS

To Michael Henry Barnes, My Honey:
The "He Is" who holds my heart.

This couldn't be done without the Alpha Readers:
Brandi Horton, LaDonna Burks
Carol Donovan and Simone Compton.

1

Dee Ramsey pulled into her garage and sighed. *I should have bought a house with an attached garage. That way, I could avoid neighbors I don't want to see.*

Sure enough, by the time the garage door had lowered, the neighborhood's most prolific gossip was hurtling her way, pushing a baby carriage. Mrs. Dorn had a preference for pink and Dee could have seen the woman coming from a mile away. Today, she wore a small white baseball cap and shocking pink jogging suit. Dee thought she resembled a bottle of Pepto Bismol.

Dee hoped that if she kept the conversation focused on the baby, she wouldn't have to listen to Mrs. Dorn trash any of the neighbors.

"Hey, Ms. Ramsey, how you doing today," Mrs. Dorn puffed. "I don't suppose you heard all that noise coming out of the Bakers' house yesterday?"

"No, I was away from home until late last night." *Oh, I probably shouldn't have told her that.* "Well, I'll see you..." Dee moved backward, reaching for her door.

Her neighbor rattled on. "It was awful! I couldn't tell if he was beating her or she was beating him. Nearly woke the baby!"

Desperate now, Dee honed in on Mrs. Dorn's newest addition. She cooed, "Oh, how precious. That's such a cute little outfit! And look how fast he's growing!" Dee tried to think of something else to say, but she was running out of clichés. Miraculously, the baby yawned.

"Looks like someone is ready for a nap," Dee added, hopefully.

Luckily, Mrs. Dorn agreed, but she offered a few more observations on the state of the Bakers' marriage before she moved on. Deanna exhaled in a *whoosh* as she closed the front door behind her. She just needed a few hours of peace and quiet; she planned to turn off the phone and enjoy some time with her feet up. She had a date with a great old Robert Montgomery movie, the *Lady in the Lake*. Dee loved the old mysteries. Her sister, Daisy, who preferred more modern films, often teased Dee about her taste for black and white suspense and "bloodless" murder movies.

Daisy wasn't her sister by birth, but as children they had formed ties that ran deeper than biology. Long ago, one of the venerable church Mothers had declared them "not birth sisters, but earth sisters," and no one—not even their own parents—had ever disputed the fact. As they'd shared more than 50 years of each other's lives, there were few people still living who knew that the sisters weren't blood relations.

Since retiring from her nursing career, Dee had found herself busier than ever. She didn't understand those people who complained about retirement because they "didn't have anything to do." She couldn't *stop* finding things to do.

She and Daisy were active in the hospitality and quilting ministries at River Jordan Full Gospel Church as well as being active in JAM, the Jesus in Action Ministry that began shortly after their young pastor arrived. There'd also been a boatload of things to do after she had single-handedly—well, almost single-handedly—solved the mystery of the attacks on the church.

A lot had gone on that she didn't know about at the time —like Deacon Uttley taking those horrible pictures and invading everyone's privacy and teens smoking marijuana in the church basement—but she *had* helped the police uncover the conspiracy that threatened the church.

Things hadn't slowed down after that. The decision to split into two separate churches that shared the same building had been the catalyst for some of the terrible things that had happened—had it only been five months ago? Even after choosing to reunite, there were still hurt feelings to soothe, ruffled feathers to smooth and hundreds of details to be ironed out.

Shortly after River Jordan tore down the dividing wall and became whole once more, the only full-time secretary moved to Atlanta. Keisha Peak, who had been Pastor Darnell's interim secretary, had gone back to school and was only available part time. Now, Keisha, and her surrogate mother, Daisy, were fully occupied with Keisha's impending nuptials. This meant that the secretarial duties were being shared by anyone willing to step in. For the past few weeks, Dee had shouldered much of the work.

Crossing River Jordan

At least she didn't have to worry about Mother Jessup and the Taylors. Nearly all the River Jordan elders—the entire Mothers Board and several deacons— had gone on a mission trip to Haiti, accompanied by many of the musicians. It was unfortunate that the trip coincided with Keisha's wedding. But after months spent wrangling red tape in the wake of Haiti's devastating earthquake, the opportunity arose for them to travel as part of a larger group and the Mothers wouldn't be denied. They had joined the annual mission conducted by a group of covenant churches. The safety in numbers made the River Jordan members feel better about their beloved elders making the trip.

"We *are* old," Mother Jessup admitted. "That's why we have to get while the gettin' is good! Besides, we get to have a party for the newlyweds when we get back!"

■

River Jordan Full Gospel Church was the religious equivalent of O'Hare Airport and Deanna felt long overdue for some self-indulgence. She had been wildly busy with marriage and bereavement counseling sessions, and wedding rehearsals being scheduled—all in addition to the regular church programs. The June weekends filled up with weddings fast and late-comers scrambled to fit their events into any day that was available.

She'd kicked off her shoes and hung up her jacket when the phone rang. "Brandon? Hi, sweetheart, how are you? I was just talking to your mom the other day...what? You haven't seen my mother since when? No, I wouldn't worry about that."

Officer Brandon Pink was the youngest son of Miranda Todd Pink, one of Dee's oldest and best friends. Brandon was on the police force in Three Rivers, the town where Dee's mother, Birdie Lee Streeter, had lived for nearly 50 years. When Brandon volunteered to keep an eye on her mom, Dee had accepted gratefully.

Birdie Lee had been mentally ill for most of her life. In fact, there'd been a continual string of sociopathic symptoms on the Streeter side of the family, stretching back generations. Her Grandma Streeter had disciplined her adult sons by shooting them with buckshot. Grandpa Streeter was a regular brawler whose jailhouse visits were so frequent that the small town sheriff's wife would regularly send him to work with Grandpa's favorite biscuits and syrup on Sunday mornings.

Dee figured she had barely escaped the family "curse," thanking the Lord for the dip in her father's gene pool.

"Wu saa," she would say, cupping a fist in one hand and bowing. "My father's kung fu was strong!" She never failed to giggle at her own silliness.

Dee dropped onto the couch and rubbed her ankle—darned arthritis was flaring up everywhere: knees, shoulders, ankles. "You know, she has that little cabin up at Piney Lake. She takes off and goes there without saying a word to anyone. I'll just give the resort rangers a call. They'll know if she's there. I'll call you back."

Brandon was a wonderful young man. Birdie had known the officer's mother since Miranda and Dee had been young girls, but Dee still got the occasional call from Birdie complaining: "that young cop is trying his best to date me, but I just can't go out with someone that young! I can't be one of them bobcats, no sir! What would people think?"

"It's 'cougar,' Mama, but you're right. You can't let anything ruin your reputation." *As the craziest old lady in the state of Michigan*, Dee thought, but didn't say aloud.

Birdie *had* gone to Piney Lakes. Slightly reassured after speaking to the ranger on duty, Dee pondered what she was going to do about her mother. Birdie was getting too old to drive and she wasn't fit to make the two-hour drive from her home to the cabin. Keeping the cabin was draining Birdie's finances, too. She was only able to visit a few times a year and the taxes and up-keep fees were steep, but every time Dee suggested that her mother sell the place, Birdie fought back fiercely.

"You don't tell me what to do! You want to take everything I own. You always were a selfish, greedy child!" Every attempt Dee made to care for her mother was like trying to *push* a car up a hill with a rope.

After sending Brandon a "thanks, she's fine" text, Dee turned off her phone and took a hot shower, determined to have the mini-vacation she'd promised herself. She collected her snacks—artisan crackers, a small wedge of Wisconsin

Crossing River Jordan

cheddar, sliced apples and a few grapes—and arranged them on her prized Wedgewood plate. She poured a glass of sparkling Riesling, settled on the couch and snuggled beneath a soft chenille throw.

She was searching for the remote to begin the movie—*how does that thing always lose itself?*—when she realized that the bottoms of her fluffy bunny slippers were wet.

Moaning, "Oh Lord, what now?" Dee retraced her steps to the kitchen. She spotted the puddle of water in front of the sink.

"Okay, I didn't spill anything. I was only at the sink to wash the fruit." Dee spoke to the empty room. When she opened the cabinet doors beneath the sink, she found a soggy mess among the paper bags and cleaning products she stored there. A leaky pipe? Well, that was all she needed. It wasn't enough that she had worked her tail off all week; now she had to spend her weekend searching for a plumber!

■

Detective Langston Hughes was in big trouble. It seemed his personal life had suddenly become much more worrisome than his job with the Chicago Police Department. At the moment, he was lying on his back, wedged in the cabinet beneath Dee's sink, holding a wrench in one hand and a cell phone in the other.

"Okay, I see it. Now what do I do?" He listened for a few seconds. "Wait, Steve I've got to put you on speaker."

Steve Kent's voice came through loud and clear. "It's simple, Lang. You'll be done in no time."

"Just talk me through," he said. "One thing I'm good at is following orders."

He knew both his lieutenant and his partner would have died laughing. Following orders was the thing Langston did *worst*.

Langston was not a small man. There was no graceful or easy way for him to maneuver around the pipe he was trying to replace. Much wriggling, muttered cursing and one bumped head later, he extricated himself from the cabinet, clutching the old metal pipe in his hand. He was triumphant!

He took a moment to imagine the smile on Dee's face when he showed off his handiwork.

■

Detective Langston Hughes was one of three boys born into a hard-working, middle-class family. His truck-driving father spent a lot of time on the road and his mother had been a secretary at the local high school. She had dreamed of teaching English literature at a college, but raising a family changed her plans. Still, her love of literature placed on each of her sons the burden of growing up with literary names. Langston and his younger brother, James Baldwin, were hassled less for their names than their older brother, Lord Byron. For the three brothers, fighting at school was a frequent occurrence.

As the middle child trying to carve out an identity for himself, young Langston fought more than most. Early on, Langston decided that since Lord was the mature one and Jimmy was the family clown, he would be the Big Bad. At 12 years old, he stood half a head taller than most of his classmates. He was on his way to becoming a legendary bully, when a coach for the local Pop Warner football league spotted him terrorizing some kids at a park.

Before Langston knew what hit him, *everyone* was hitting him. The coach had him testing his toughness playing one position after another. Getting his bell rung in game after game, often by boys even bigger than he was, gave Langston something serious to think about.

He decided to try out for quarterback after his coach challenged him. "Lang, a quarterback is a leader; he's the field general. He's got to know where everybody is and where they're going. He's always thinking of what might happen and what happens after that. Can you do it?"

It turned out Langston could and did. He led his team to the city finals two years running. He played through high school, but to his football-loving father's dismay, Langston wasn't interested in football as a career. Instead, he followed in the footsteps of his hero and coach, Officer Eli Segal. With two years of college under his belt, Langston Hughes became a cop.

Deanna had given him a laundry list of reasons why they shouldn't or couldn't be a couple, chief among them was the fact that she was eleven years older. That his job was dangerous and her heart couldn't stand the worry. And that he was used to being a swinging single and she was set in her ways.

Langston countered each reason: he didn't care about the age difference and she was beautiful. Because he worked in fraud, his job was no more dangerous than hers had been when she was in nursing. And finally, that his single hadn't been swinging for a very long time.

As for being set in her ways, Langston told her, "Teach me your ways and I'll show you mine. I'm sure we can meet in the middle."

Dee and the detective had been spending a lot of time together since they'd first met —when he'd kidnapped her the previous December. At the time, he had called it "protective custody."

Langston had been working undercover, building a case against corrupt building inspectors. The case had turned into extortion, arson, and conspiracy to commit murder. Because it involved River Jordan Church itself and one of its deacons, Dee had found herself in the thick of things when she stumbled onto the plot.

The first feelings Lang remembered having for Dee were amusement and admiration. She drifted in and out of roles like a seasoned actress. Watching her work reminded him of working with his partner, Javier Solis. Both Javi and Dee could put on a personality like it was a change of clothes and use it to their advantage.

Dee had been playing the "damsel in distress" as she snooped around, following Deacon Batt to discover what he was mixed up in. She'd accidentally overheard enough to be worried, but not enough to get police interested in her suspicions. At that time, Detectives Hughes and Solis had been deep undercover. When Dee met Langston, she thought he was one of the criminals.

Langston had chained her to a bed in his loft because he wasn't sure of her involvement in the case. Things were moving fast and needed to keep her out of the way. She *appeared* to be a harmless lady, so he was surprised by her ferocity as she fought against the restraints. He'd been afraid that she was going to injure herself and just a bit concerned that if she got loose, she might do some damage to him.

When they gathered in the office of Lieutenant Sean DeLuna, Langston's and Javier's superior, Dee revealed yet another side. She became a Queen, royally proclaiming the heroism of the detectives. More importantly to Langston, she hadn't divulged that he had used chloroform on her. She'd saved his badge.

Now, trying to scrub the dirt and rust from his hands, Langston wondered, *why am I chasing the woman so hard? Is it because I really want her or just because she's running?*

2

*S*he said no. Every time he closed his eyes, Pastor Darnell Davis relived the most humiliating experience of his life. His "church family"—the full congregation—and many visitors had all been there to witness the pastor's embarrassment. Georgia Beem, the other half of his heart and soul, had turned him down flat, in front of God and everyone. It was *"The Beem Bomb,"* according to Darnell the Cool, the pastor's frequently present inner child.

Pandemonium had followed the pastor's impromptu proposal, but awaiting her answer, the church became still. Darnell was positioned on one knee, smiling up at Georgia when she'd snatched her hands from his.

She said no. More accurately, as Darnell replayed it countless times in his mind, she'd burst into tears and yelled, "Darnell, I can't! I'm sorry; I just can't!" as she ran down the center aisle and out of the building.

The sanctuary was so quiet; Darnell was sure he would have heard his own heart beating if it hadn't stopped. Time had also stopped, but no matter how hard he prayed in those endless seconds, he did not suddenly become unconscious, disappear or wake up.

Crossing River Jordan

He could see everyone in the church staring at him. He saw triumph in the eyes of those members who considered him a young upstart—now getting his just desserts for usurping what rightfully belonged to Reverend Albert Beem. Adding to his emotional trauma, Darnell watched as the people who loved him suffered with him. He couldn't decide what was causing him the most pain.

He saw the confusion on the faces of guests who had come to the church to help celebrate the reuniting of River Jordan Church—Blessed River Jordan and Greater River Jordan coming together after months of rancorous separation. Darnell cursed his timing.

He still couldn't remember how that service ended. He supposed the Mothers Board, the deacons and the ushers had taken over. The choir would have rushed to provide appropriate music, perhaps *I Love the Lord; He Heard My Cry* or *Tears of a Clown*. The pastor had a dreamy memory of standing at the sanctuary doors shaking hands and receiving pitying hugs from the steady stream of people leaving the church. Finally, blessedly, he was in his office on the couch and Keisha was giving him tea.

"Earl Grey, two sugars. Just the way you like it, Pastor." Then she left, quietly closing the door behind her.

He'd begun taking catnaps on the couch in his office; he could hardly stand to be in his own bed. The bed where, only once, he'd shared a miracle with the woman he loved. Now the thought of making love with Georgia Beem burned his heart to ash. There was nothing pleasing in his world. Even his job, the work for which he had been called by the Lord, held no joy for him now.

She'd said no. Georgia's voice, choked with tears, echoed in his head. For a while, he didn't think he would ever be able to hear another sound.

"Earl Grey, two sugars. Just the way you like it, Pastor."

He experienced an uncomfortable moment of déjà vu. Fearing that he'd gone completely insane and was trapped forever in the memory of the Beem Bomb, Darnell sat up to find Keisha Peak extending a cup of steaming tea.

He rubbed red, sleep-starved eyes. He shook off the White Sox stadium blanket that was usually folded and kept on the back of couch.

"Pastor, you need to go home," Keisha fussed.

"I was working on the sermon and I needed to rest my eyes for a minute."

Keisha felt a stab of guilt because she was so happy. Everyone knew that Pastor Darnell hadn't been sleeping much—or eating much or smiling much. His usually energetic, inspirational sermons had become filled with dire warnings of hell-fire and damnation.

It was all Georgia Beem's fault! Imagine turning your back on someone like Pastor Darnell—you couldn't find a better man—other than her Steve, of course.

Noticing he wore one black sock and one blue, Keisha shook her head as the pastor swung his feet to the floor. His navy blue slacks were bunched and wrinkled; there was a small gravy stain on his rumpled white shirt. A blue and gray tie peeked out of a bundle of navy blue cloth on the floor by the couch.

She walked over and picked up the bundle, shaking out Darnell's suit coat and scolding, "Pastor, you can't keep this up. You need to go home and get in a real bed and get some real sleep."

"Too much to do," he mumbled, rising from the couch and stretching.

"I know what you have to do, but the Mothers would pitch a fit if they saw you looking like…"

Deanna interrupted when she walked into the office.

"I hope you're feeling rested now, Pastor Darnell." She glanced at the small notebook in her hand. "You've got two counseling sessions today—both for funerals…"

"And don't forget the wedding rehearsals!" Keisha chimed in. "You've got two of those scheduled for today. You need your energy, Pastor. Don't forget, my rehearsal is Wednesday— and you promised you'd join us for the dinner!"

The pastor gave a weary smile as he took his tea. "I wouldn't miss your rehearsal dinner for anything in the world." He told Dee, "Just give me a few minutes and I'll be right there."

Crossing River Jordan

"Oh, I've got to make some calls!" Still talking, Keisha rushed from the room, her mind on pre-wedding errands. Keisha was over-the-moon about her upcoming wedding to church caretaker, Steve Kent. She didn't realize how much pain the mere thought of weddings caused her pastor.

Her voice trailed off as the pastor padded to his office restroom and closed the door. The image in the mirror over the sink startled him.

Man, you look like five days' worth of hard nights, said Darnell the Cool. The Cool was that small voice in his head, offering immature insights and influence that the pastor still sometimes found himself fighting. *You gotta shake this off. All this drama over one girl. Man, you are ruinin' my rep!*

Darnell ran his hand over the stubble on his face before deciding that shaving was just too much trouble.

When he came back into the office, Dee took in every move. Their vibrant young pastor carried himself like an old man! Years of nursing had trained Deanna to pay attention to body language. She noted the way Pastor Darnell often held his arms locked across his body as if trying to hold himself together. Lately, he rarely maintained eye contact before staring at the floor or off into space.

I know we're on Your time, Lord, Dee prayed silently, *but could You give this man a little push, please?*

"I expected Rev. Beem to be involved in some of these duties now that he's back. Any idea where he is?" He could handle any kind of funeral service that grieving relatives might request, but Darnell wished that Beem could officiate at every wedding ceremony and couples counseling session.

Dee looked away, pursing her lips as if she'd just bit into a whole lemon. Nearly six months had passed, but Reverend Albert Beem's exploits had left a sour taste in the mouths of many River Jordan members. Whispers still abounded about Beem in compromising positions with various women, even though the majority of the congregation had never actually seen the photographs.

Many members wondered how much the reverend had known about Deacon Batt's gambling addiction and dirty dealings with the church funds. Batt had nearly caused the church to be destroyed! *After all*, the tongues wagged, *the deacon is Rev. Beem's best friend and when you lie down with dogs, you get up with fleas.*

These days, Beem's services weren't as well-attended as those conducted by Pastor Darnell, despite the pastor's grim sermons. The young pastor was being requested three times as often for all ministerial duties—from christenings to burials and everything in between. The congregation knew their pastor could use the help of an associate minister, but few believed that Beem was the right man for the job.

Deanna was all for Christian forgiveness and turning the other cheek. She shook her head, thinking, *but, Lord, You gave us only two!*

■

Rev. Beem's return to the church had been a spectacular event. The Sunday after Easter, Rev. Beem, flanked by former deacons, Uttley and Batt, joined the line moving to the front of the church for the alter call. When they got to the front, Batt and Uttley joined the kneeling group, but the reverend turned and faced the congregation.

The choir had been quietly singing, *God Is*, but the reverend's voice carried above all the other sounds.

"Brothers and sisters in Christ, I come before you in the Lord's house to confess before you and Our Heavenly Father. I have sinned against you all!"

He extended his arms to include the two ex-deacons. "*We* have sinned against you all!" He fell to his knees with his head in his hands.

When he raised his head, tears streamed down his face. "Between the three of us, there are very few sins in the Holy Bible that we haven't committed. There was a time when the only result we could expect would be stoning. The members of our community would have stood before us, hurling stones and cursing our names until our broken, bloody bodies moved no more!"

Deanna tilted her head; the reverend's actions seemed so familiar. After thinking for a moment, she whispered to Daisy, "He must have been on You Tube for days. Every movement is just like the apology that televangelist made on *his* show. Watch, now he's going to put his hand over his heart!"

Beem grabbed a fistful of his jacket over his heart. "But brother and sisters, who could cast the first stone? Which of you is without sin?"

Half of the congregation was mesmerized. The other half began rolling their eyes and muttering. From someone behind her, Dee heard, "Oh, here we go again!"

Uttley hunched his skeletal frame over his knees, making a low moaning sound. Even Ray Batt managed to send a single tear coursing down one cheek.

Dropping to his knees, Beem shuffled toward the pew where his wife and son stared with open mouths. "I know my actions have injured my wife and damaged my impressionable young son. If they can find it in their hearts to forgive me, couldn't the rest of my family in Christ do the same?"

He leaned over, dropping his head to Vanessa's shoes, and grasped her ankles. She stared at him as if he'd just grown a tail. The congregation gaped.

"You can lift this lovely foot and crush my head like the worthless snake that I've been. I would deserve no less, but I ask you to remember that our Lord instructed us to forgive 'seventy times seven.' How will you honor God?"

Cory, the reverend's 14-year old son, drew his legs up on the pew, fearing that his father would clutch at his ankles next. Beem sprang to his feet and whirled to face Pastor Darnell who quietly had continued praying with the few members who managed to ignore Rev. Beem's display. Darnell thought it was important to attend to those people who were *really* standing in the need of prayer. He knew Beem needed prayer too, just prayer of a different kind. *I wonder if the priests at St. Margaret's would loan us an exorcist,* he thought.

"Pastor Darnell Davis was very nearly a member of my own earthly family," Rev. Beem continued. "He was going to marry my only daughter and I would have welcomed him with open arms. Pastor, will you receive me today? Will you open your arms and your heart to three repentant sinners?"

Moving toward the minister, Darnell winced with every mention of the wedding that had never been. Anger bubbled in his chest. Everyone knew that Albert Beem had been dead-set against the marriage. Beem was standing in the Lord's house lying, even as he begged forgiveness for other offenses!

Beem threw himself against Darnell's chest. The pastor had to wrap his arms around the minister or fall backwards. At that, Batt and Uttley jumped up and surrounded the pastor yelling, "Glory to God! God bless you, Pastor Davis. Thank you, thank you!"

Baffled, a few church members began to applaud. In fits and starts, clapping came from other parts of the sanctuary. Eventually, the entire congregation stood for a bewildered ovation.

Immediately after the service, the Mothers Board met with both clergymen.

"Exactly what do you see when you look in the mirror, Albert Beem?" asked Mother Marva Jessup, the long-time president of the Mothers Board. She sat with her hands folded atop her cane and squinted up at the reverend as if studying an interesting new specimen.

That she was tiny, elderly and plain-spoken might have fooled most people, but Rev. Beem was always mindful of the bruises he got from bashing against the stone wall that was Mother Jessup. Sometimes, she mixed her metaphors, but her meanings were eventually clear and sharp.

This time, Beem wasn't sure he'd understood, "Excuse me?"

"Do you see a leader or a learner?"

Aware that he was on treacherous ground, the reverend chose to tread lightly. "Well, I like to think of myself as a leader who's willing to learn." He smiled, pleased with how he had handled her question.

She sucked her teeth and tapped her cane sharply on the wooden floor. "Do you see a senior minister who leads by his example or do you see a man who needs to learn how to lead by example?"

"Well, uh, that's what I meant..."

She cut him off. "Pastor Davis, could you work with this man?"

Darnell knew he had to be careful, as well. There were members who considered Rev. Beem to be the victim of a man-hating Mothers Board and a greedy young pastor. The church had only been reunited for a short time. The pastor didn't want to be the cause of any renewed tension.

Plus, it was important to live the Lord's words. Pastor Darnell didn't just believe *in* Jesus Christ, he *believed* Him.

"Mother Jessup, I believe that everyone can take a wrong path and everyone deserves a chance to make a u-turn. Rev. Beem got lost, but, I believe that with our support..."

"And guidance," interjected Mother Alma, another long-time Board member who was also Pastor Darnell's aunt.

"Yes, with the Lord's guidance," the pastor continued, "Rev. Beem could be a blessing to River Jordan Church." He hoped his words conveyed more faith in Beem than he really felt. "What kind of example would we be setting if we didn't reach out to those who honestly seek forgiveness?"

The decision was made. At the service the following Sunday, Uttley, Batt and the reverend would be formally welcomed back into the bosom of their church family. Deacon Uttley and Raymond Batt would no longer be deacons, but they could choose other ways to serve the Lord.

Commenting on the irony of "Deacon" being Uttley's first name, Mother Jessup said, "My folks could have named me 'Harley,' but that wouldn't have made me a motorcycle."

It was suggested that Uttley have nothing to do with the audio-video ministry. Of course, Batt, who had been the church's comptroller, would stay far away from the church finances forever.

Rev. Beem would be brought back to the pulpit, sharing the designation of associate with Pastor Darnell. Because Darnell wouldn't accept the title, there would be no senior minister.

"I prefer not to elevate one man over the other. Rev. Beem and I will work together for the glory of God."

Rev. Beem missed the end of the conversation, his thoughts on other things. He was back! As an added bonus, the young pastor's words about honestly seeking forgiveness had set off a rocket in the Reverend's busy mind. Forgiveness, that's the ticket!

3

Rev. Albert Beem straightened his tie again. *Maybe I should have worn the striped one. No, the solid gray looks good with this blue suit.* He'd become entirely too dependent on Vanessa's helping him choose his clothing. No one could say the woman didn't have excellent taste.

She'd thrown him out of his own home—all because of that little misunderstanding about the pictures. It was all that fool Uttley's fault, hiding cameras all over the church and taking pictures of people in private moments!

Rev. Beem had tried to tell his wife that all those women were before her time, but she was too angry and wouldn't hear him. He was sure that all those self-righteous biddies from the church sat around gossiping, adding fuel to Vanessa's fire. He'd hardly had time to grab his toothbrush and razor as she began tossing his clothing out on the front lawn.

Well, he couldn't think about that now. He checked himself in the mirror—perfect haircut, nothing stuck in the teeth. He stroked his mustache, took a deep breath, releasing it slowly. As he walked toward the set where the camera crew was waiting, he sipped from a bottle of distilled water.

"Nothing to worry about fellows," he told the crew. "You'll all be home before you know it. We'll get this in one take, maybe two."

Eleven attempts later, he finally read the tele-prompted copy perfectly.

"Brothers and sisters, are you experiencing the agony of anger? The horror of hurt feelings? Are you stuck in a time warp because you can't get over what she did to you or what he said about you? Do you hate yourself for things you did to someone else?

"Well, I'm here to tell you that your life can become a peaceful, painless journey if you just learn how to forgive. The Lord Jesus has already paid the price for you. If God can forgive you, then you ought to be able to forgive yourself.

"And what about forgiving others? Would you hold yourself higher than God? If we are to walk in His ways, is it not our duty to forgive others and to honor the passion of the Christ, who died that we might all be forgiven?

Crossing River Jordan

"Join me at River Jordan Full Gospel Church for the Forgiveness Festival, an afternoon packed with lectures, workshops and intercessory prayer sessions. You know you need to get right with God and get right with each other. No one knows the day nor the hour when the Son of Man shall come. Make peace with yourself, your family and your friends. You owe it to the Lord!

"Call 773-555-1855 right now, to reserve your space at this life-changing event. But wait, there's more! The first 100 callers will also receive a bottle of Heavenly Bath Salts, handcrafted by my lovely and talented wife, Vanessa. They will soothe your skin, just as the Forgiveness Festival will soothe your soul!

"Call the number on your screen today!"

The weary crew gave him a round of applause before they began to pack their gear and the reverend took a deep bow. He felt pretty good about himself and considered the pitch for Vanessa's bath salts a stroke of genius! She would feel grateful that he'd been supportive of her little business efforts. Part two of his master plan to win back his wife and his rightful place as head of River Jordan had gone well.

Now he had to hurry home to dinner with Ray Batt. Ray whined like a little girl whenever the reverend was late for a meal. The ex-deacon had been his friend since college and his right hand at the church until the separation had started all that trouble. Now, Batt was working as an assistant manager at a Chucks Clucks Chicken restaurant. He and the reverend shared an apartment over a funeral home on the corner of 80th and Ashland.

■

A few miles away, a trembling hand mashed a button to silence the television and then dashed the remote to the floor.

Forgiveness? He's going to teach forgiveness? If they knew the truth—what he was really like and what he'd done—no one would ever forgive him. That man should have protected me; he should have avenged me! Instead, he hid the truth. He sheltered the Evil and gave it a dark place to hide and grow.

Beem and the Evil had taken everything and now Beem grinned from a television screen. It was time—well *past* time for both of them to pay! Neither of those men had the right to live.

Well, the plan had always been there, simmering just below the surface. Now, it boiled over the top. *Maybe, if I do this right, the Lord will forgive me. Maybe then I can finally find some peace.*

■

Wearing a strange look, Keisha poked her head into Pastor Darnell's office. "Pastor, I've found Rev. Beem, sort of."

"Well, ask him to please come in here. He's needed." Not believing he had actually said those words, the pastor pulled on his jacket.

"He's not here; see, he's on television..." Confusion was all over Keisha's face.

They walked around the short wall that separated the secretary's office from Pastor Darnell's. Keisha had brought in a tiny television so that she could follow television classes as part of her first semester course work.

Rev. Beem's voice blared from the small set, "Join me at River Jordan Full Gospel Church for the Forgiveness Festival, an afternoon full of lectures, workshops and intercessory prayer sessions. You know you need to get right with God and get right with each other..."

"Forgiveness Festival? Did anyone know about this?" Pastor Darnell spoke in his "Quiet Voice." Everyone knew that meant he was tamping down fury. "He neglected to mention his plans to me. Did he bother to discuss this with *anyone*?"

■

It was a good thing that people were sharing the job of church secretary. Keisha Peak was so distracted by her upcoming wedding that she was making a lot of mistakes with the church paperwork. Dee spent hours re-checking Keisha's filing, data entry and message taking.

Keisha talked a blue streak as she collected her things. She swept a textbook, notebook, pens and highlighters into a large red backpack. "Auntie Dee, thanks so much for taking over for me. Steve's taking the kids home after school—all seven of them—and he'll stay with them until Aunt Daisy gets Uncle Carl from at the airport. I'm meeting a couple of girls to study for the literature final."

"Tiffany called. She's on her way." Dee reported.

"She's got the last two hours here for me and then we're studying together, too."

"It's good that you and Tiffany share some classes."

"It's better than good. Tiffany is really smart about most things, but she doesn't do math as well as I do. I help her with math and she helps me with everything else," Keisha laughed.

She struggled a bit under the weight of the pack, wiggling to get her arms through the straps—*God only knows what that girl has in there*, Dee thought and then she focused on her own problems. Deciphering Keisha's phone messages was proving to be quite a challenge.

The young woman swooped down and pecked Dee on the cheek. "You'll be at the rehearsal, right?"

"Nothing could keep me away," Dee assured her and then Keisha was gone in a rush of air from the open door.

No one could blame Keisha for being scattered. She'd discovered that the love of her life had always been in plain sight at the church. Steve Kent was more than the caretaker of the church. He was the chief maintenance engineer in charge of everything from the carpentry and grounds to the electrical work and plumbing. When it came to the inner workings and the outer beauty of River Jordan Full Gospel Church, Steve was the Man with the Plan. His engineering expertise had made it possible for the church to be divided by a single wall, and made it relatively simple for that same wall to be taken down.

Like many other women at the church, Keisha had her eyes on Pastor Darnell from the moment that the young pastor had arrived. But Steve had set *his* sights on Keisha, in spite of the fact that at 25 years old, she had three children and had never been married. He saw that Keisha downplayed the sweet, capable, intelligent woman she was inside because it was easier to be the stereotype than to fight it.

With Steve, Keisha found that the sexy package might have caught his attention, but the real woman kept him coming back. And miracle of miracles—he loved her children! Who wouldn't love Hope, the sweet, shy eight year old? But Wisdom and Knowledge, ten and seven year old boys, well, they were more than a notion. Thank God, Steve had a heart big enough for all of them.

Keisha also shared the responsibility for helping her twin brother, Kendrick, raise his three girls. The older ones, Kiana and Kiera were no trouble, but the baby was a different story. Kensha had entered the "terrible twos" with a vengeance. Screaming tantrums were the order of every day and "no" was her favorite word.

The twins and their children lived with Daisy Franklin and her husband Carl in a sprawling, four-flat building. Daisy and Carl had acted as mother and father for most of the twins' lives. The Franklins had recently invited Tiffany Steele and her infant son, Tremain, to stay with them. They had only been members of the household for a few months, but Tiffany and Tremain were treated with the same love and concern as all the rest. Carl called Tremain "Lucky" because he brought the total number of children to seven.

Dee was transferring the messages into a list for Pastor Darnell when she caught the mistake: two weddings and two funerals all scheduled for the same day! Both within minutes of each other; there was no way that Pastor Darnell could handle everything. She checked again—the Ogilvie funeral was at the Roberts Funeral Home at 8:30 in the morning, right on the heels of the Pettaway/Burks sunrise wedding on the beach.

Unless he had a helicopter, the Pastor could never travel from the Indiana lakefront to the west side funeral home in time. To make matters worse, another funeral was planned for the Lawnvale Cemetery, at noon, followed by the Salter/Rush wedding at River Jordan at 2 p.m. The Forgiveness Festival began just two hours later. The schedule was a disaster!

As much as she hated to disturb the pastor, he had to know what was going on. He'd left early, complaining of a headache. They were all worried about him; he hadn't been the same since Georgia Beem had walked out on him. He hadn't been taking very good care of himself; he seemed to be disappearing before their eyes.

Crossing River Jordan

The pastor had to be alerted to the scheduling conflicts. Though it was late and she was tired, Dee would stay and help with whatever needed doing. Dee tried contacting him by phone.

It was a running joke throughout the congregation that the Pastor only carried a cell so he'd look as cool as the other kids. He rarely answered and, as usual, the call went straight to voicemail. She hoped he had gone home to bed. He was facing a really hard day.

Daisy talked non-stop, all the way home from O' Hare International Airport. After kissing his wife, Carl fastened his seatbelt and sat back to listen. He knew that she'd missed him and she would remember to tell him that, once she ran out of steam.

"Suddenly, the girl has turned into Martha Stewart. Everything has to be like something she's seen on that woman's show. She's been reading books on wedding etiquette, so she's always going on about what is and isn't done—like she's some Gold Coast debutante. She's driving everyone crazy!"

Daisy fell on the horn for a long, angry blast at a driver who'd swerved into her lane. "She's acting like she's the first person to get married in the history of the world. You know me; I'm the very soul of patience..."

She gave her husband a quick glance, to make sure he agreed with her. Carl nodded and smiled.

"...but Miss Keisha would try the patience of Job, the way she's acting. And everything I say is so old-fashioned. 'Oh, Aunt Daisy, nobody does that anymore!'" Daisy finished in a whiny voice that didn't sound anything like Keisha's. None of Daisy's imitations ever did.

Daisy lowered her window so she could yell at the car in the next lane. "Those lines painted on the street are for more than decoration! Jackasses!" she bellowed, mashing the window button so hard she hurt her finger.

"Pull over," Carl told her.

"What?"

"Pull over and let me drive, before you kill us both."

She stared at him and saw that he was serious. Slapping on the turn signal, she moved onto the shoulder. Carl got behind the wheel as Daisy slid into the passenger's seat. Before starting the car, he leaned over and pulled his wife to him, kissing her again.

Rubbing her back he said, "Okay, what I heard is that Keisha is being her usual headstrong self and she doesn't want to listen to any of your ideas for the wedding."

"I think Miss Keisha lost her mind the very moment that Steve got down on one knee!" Daisy snapped. She folded her arms and sulked the rest of the way home.

4

Lee's Unleaded Blues was typically dead so early in the evening and that's why Darnell decided to stop in for dinner. He could be miserable in peace. Slide guitar music played softly on the jukebox and there were only two couples sitting at tables.

Couples. Just the word made his head pound. He didn't want to see them, so he stationed himself at the bar with his back to the room.

"Iced tea and a menu, please," the pastor said to the bartender's back.

"Long Island?" she asked, slapping down a napkin and menu in front of him.

"No, just plain iced tea, Wanda." Even if her name hadn't been embroidered on her shirt, he would have remembered her. The flamboyant blonde bouffant hairdo and her cannon-shot gum popping were hard to forget. Wanda had been the server the first time he'd gone to Lee's. He'd been with Chess Allen, the accountant who helped with the church finances. Chess had been called Jess until a baby brother came along — a brother who couldn't pronounce the sound of "J," but said "ch" instead.

Darnell had been having a great time with Chess that night—until he'd thought of how much he loved Georgia and then all the fun stopped. Thinking of Georgia now gave him a sharp ache.

He slammed his hand on the bar, saying, "I've changed my mind. Go on and put a little Long Island in that tea."

Darnell couldn't remember that last time he'd been drunk. Right now, drunk seemed to be as good a destination as any. He pushed his car keys toward Wanda.

"You'll probably want to call me a cab later."

As he sipped, he got busy with the menu. Lee's served mouthwatering soul food Thursdays through Sundays, but the rest of the week the kitchen provided only daily specials. Tuesday was burger day and the pastor chose a Bleu cheese burger with bacon and steak fries—he decided to really let himself go. "I don't want to see anything healthy and green on that plate!"

"Hey, young lady, I'll have what he's having." Detective Langston Hughes settled on the barstool next to Darnell. "Pastor, what *are* we having?"

"Long Islands, and I'm one up on you."

The door blew open suddenly and a few more men tumbled in, laughing.

"...snatched it right out of my hand!" Steve was saying. "Did any body hear about rain? Sure looks like a big storm's coming."

They were so involved in discussing the weather and how it might affect the night's ball game; it took a minute for them to notice Pastor Darnell. The younger men in the group were shocked to see their pastor holding down a barstool.

"Pastor Darnell! What are you doing here, uh, I mean, we didn't know you came here. Um, we don't come here that much..." Leon Long, the youngest of River Jordan's deacons finally stuttered to a stop. There was no help from Jerome Gray, another church member who was also at a loss for words.

Carl Franklin stepped forward to shake Darnell's and Langston's hands. "Gentlemen, what you see here is Steve's idea of a bachelor party. There's a baseball game coming on soon. We're going to shoot a little pool, eat some good greasy food and toast to the man's last days of freedom!"

Steve spoke hesitantly. "I would have invited you, but I didn't think you'd come to a bar, Pastor."

Wanda set the pastor's plate in front of him and said, "Last time I saw you, you looked like you just stepped off a wedding cake. Left your lady at home tonight, huh, Sugar? Ya'll was sure burnin' tha dance floor up that night!" She threw back her head and laughed as she placed more napkins on the bar.

The group of men looked everywhere but at the pastor. They all thought Wanda was referring to Georgia and felt bad for him. Darnell didn't want to be the wet blanket on Steve's party. And he didn't want anyone pitying him, so he chuckled.

"Yes, Chess and I had to work off some of that great food." After all, it wasn't a secret that he'd escorted Chess to the opera one night.

This was too much of a surprise for Leon. "You dance?" he asked, wide-eyed.

Carl smiled. "Boy, what do you think—the man wasn't born wearing a preacher's robe."

Everyone laughed and Langston teased, "Steve, who has a bachelor party on a Tuesday? And, it's supposed to be the night before the wedding, so you can show up at the ceremony all hung-over and remorseful. Well, if you don't mind, I'm inviting myself!"

Steve winked at him. "I thought you'd still have your hands full of wrenches and pipes! Besides, we didn't plan this; it just happened."

"Well, the first round is on me," Langston said, and the party kicked off in earnest.

Surprised, Darnell realized that he was having a good time. A relaxing night out with the boys was something he hadn't done in years. The White Sox were winning, the food and the company were good, and he hadn't thought about Georgia in nearly two hours. He did need to slow down on the drinking, though. He wasn't totally sure, but he thought he had a full day tomorrow.

Carl and Steve were head-to-head, talking over a game of pool. On his way back from the restroom, Darnell heard Steve say, "I love Keisha and those kids with all my heart. I'll take good care of them; you have my word on that."

"Steve, I never had a single doubt about you," Carl said.

I never had a single doubt about Georgia either, but she wound up stomping all over me, Darnell thought. He was feeling very sorry for himself until someone ordered a plate of nachos. What better to do than eat, drink and be merry? He shoveled a couple of cheese-soaked tortilla chips into his mouth and looked around calling, "Wanda, we need some help here! I can almost see the bottom of my glass!"

Langston raised his eyebrows, but didn't say anything. He knew what the pastor was doing. He'd spent a few nights bellied up to a bar himself, dulling the pain after a relationship crashed and burned. Or celebrating that he'd avoided a disaster when something bad was finally ended. The man had his sympathy.

Darnell had lost track of how much he'd had to drink, but he was certain that he didn't need anything more. It was time for that cab. Everyone was cheering a White Sox home run and the accompanying fireworks looked fuzzy in Darnell's sight.

The game was in the top of the sixth inning when the rain began to fall. It was the kind of windblown drizzle that made umbrellas useless. The pastor put his head down on the bar, planning to rest his eyes for a moment.

He woke up because Langston was shaking his arm. "Come on Darnell, it's time to go home." The lights were bright and the staff bustled around, stacking chairs on tables, wiping down the bar and mopping the floor.

"Keys," Wanda yelled and tossed the pastor's keys to Langston. "But Sugar, you don't look like you oughtta be drivin' nothin' either." She'd noticed the detective's slight sway when he began to walk.

"We've got a ride," Langston called over his shoulder.

Darnell concentrated as hard as he could on appearing sober. The floor was slanting away every time he took a step, so he overcompensated by slapping his feet down hard. Someone had once told him that if you hummed marching music when you were drunk, it would force you to walk like a soldier, tall and straight. Darnell began to hum the *Stars and Stripes Forever*, the John Phillip Sousa march. Now he walked like a zombie—stiff as a board, humming and stomping. Langston thought it was funny and began to imitate him, which Darnell thought was hilarious.

Chess Allen stepped out of her car and opened the passenger doors for them. "You two look ridiculous," she said. "And nobody gets sick in my car!"

They were finally settled in the car when the anticipated storm broke with a vengeance. Chess drove carefully, not only because visibility was so limited, but also because she didn't want to bounce two drunken men around in her Baby, as she referred to her red Camaro. She dropped Langston at his loft which was a quick trip, right off of the Stevenson expressway. Darnell was sprawled across the tiny backseat, snoring softly.

Chess sang along to a Temptations song on the radio and every few minutes, the pastor woke up enough to sing a word or two.

"...my 'magination," he sang before dropping off again. And a while later, "...away with meeee!"

Very soon, Chess shook him. "Let's go Pastor; karaoke night is over." She braced herself as Darnell grabbed her arms and she tried to haul him out of the car. "Up, up, up! I am not letting you sleep in my car!"

After much stumbling, bumping and tugging, they made it to the door. She was lining up the key with the lock when Darnell snatched the key ring from her.

He dangled the keys in front of her face. "Say pretty please with sugar on top," he giggled. He held the keys over his head. He lowered them just out of her reach and snatched them back.

At the end of her rope, Chess jumped up and grabbed the keys. She had thought the cool rain would help the pastor sober up, but it seemed to be having the opposite effect. Chess was drenched, her hair plastered to her head.

"Darnell, stop playing around," she snapped. "You can't be so drunk that you've forgotten that sisters don't like to get their hair wet!"

They stumbled through the door and Chess pushed Darnell toward the couch. That was it! She'd done her duty as a friend and look at what she got for all her trouble: she would have to pay to get her hair done! She couldn't go to a wedding looking like she did now.

She whipped the door open and looked over her shoulder at her friend. He sat there, soaked and shivering, reminding Chess of a wet kitten she'd found when she was a child. She blew out a deep breath and went back to help.

"Come on, you've got to change out of those wet clothes." She pulled his shoes and socks off and then helped him to his feet. He listed to one side and nearly fell back to the couch. She snagged his arm just in time.

"Pastor Davis, you've got to work with me here. I am not undressing you!"

Darnell tried to stare at her, his eyes halfway open. "Chess? What? I'm not undressing you!"

"Well that's fine, Darnell. Nobody is undressing anybody. So you go in the bathroom and I'll go upstairs and get you something to wear."

She put both hands in the center of his back and pushed-steered him into the bathroom. As she closed the door, he stood there looking befuddled. "Just wait right there," she said.

She raced up the stairs and rifled wildly through a dresser. Wonder of wonders—she found a full set of pajamas. She didn't think men even bought those anymore. Rushing back to the bathroom, she knocked on the door, opened it just enough to shove the pajamas in and closed it quickly.

"Darnell, put those on!" she yelled through the door. "I'm making you some tea."

She could hear the pastor moving around as she made tea strong enough to stand on its own without the cup. To see for herself that Darnell was functioning, she waited for him to come back to the couch. By the time he sat down, she'd run out of charity towards her fellow man.

Pointing out items on the cocktail table she said, "Darnell, here's your phone; here's the tea. Be careful; it's really hot. If you do manage to burn yourself, remember to use ice on the burn, not butter. Here's a blanket. Good luck with everything. I'll give you a call in the morning."

5

Keisha woke up long before everyone else in the apartment. She was too excited to sleep, but still she felt wonderful. Tonight she was having a wedding rehearsal and rehearsal dinner, just like some rich girl from a movie! She had been a bridesmaid twice in friends' weddings, but there had never been a ceremony as perfect as hers was turning out to be. She was getting it all—the handsome prince and the fairy-tale wedding—something she had never even allowed herself to dream of.

Even the proposal had been magical, although not quite according to Steve's plan. The entire family lounged around the table after Mother's Day dinner, too stuffed to move. Remnants of an apricot jam-glazed ham, string beans and macaroni and cheese had yet to be removed. Wisdom and Knowledge were arguing over the last buttered roll. Deanna was ready for them, because it happened every time she baked the bread.

"Come out to the kitchen," she told the boys. "I brought extra, just for you."

"Me, too!" Five year old Kiana cried, scrambling from her seat to join her cousins. Soon, Steve was left alone in the dining room with Kendrick and Carl.

"I need to talk to you both," Steve began. "Those rolls saved me the trouble of trying to come up with a reason to get you outside. I was about to ask you to come outside and take a look at my car."

He cleared his throat. "I know how important Keisha is to you and how much your approval means to her, even though she likes to pretend that it doesn't. I'd like to ask you both for Keisha's hand in marriage."

Carl was choked up. He thought of Keisha and Kendrick as his children, even though he and Daisy had always been more like godparents or guardians. Still, the old-fashioned display of good manners touched his heart.

"I'd like to give her this tonight." Steve showed them the half-carat solitaire in a red velvet box.

"Man, you can have her hand and all the rest of her, too!" Kendrick jumped up and clapped Steve on the shoulder.

The ring box fell from his hand and bounced under the table. All three men were on their knees when everyone else came back into the room.

"What in the world..." Daisy began, but Carl "ssshhh-ed" her.

Steve held the box behind his back. As Keisha walked to him, laughing and chattering about how silly they all looked, he took her hand and kissed it.

"I love you. I want to be with you and care for you. I want your children to be our children. Keisha Peak, will you marry me?" He popped the box open.

"Oh!" was all Keisha said. "Oh, oh, oh!"

Confusion painted Steve's face. Still on his knees, his glance zipped from one person to another. "What does that mean?"

Keisha began a jiggling little dance and held her left wrist, shaking her left hand in Steve's face. "Oh, oh, oh!"

"Mama!" Wisdom yelled, "You have to say 'yes!'"

"Yes!" she screamed. Steve stood and slid the ring on her finger, laughing as she leaped into his arms.

■

Tiffany got Tremain squared away in River Jordan's preschool and rushed to the church office, right on time to begin her shift as church secretary. She found a present waiting for her: a sparkling white lab coat was draped across the chair. Aunt Daisy had gotten her name embroidered on the pocket—*Tiffany Steele* flowed in red satin script.

The lab coat was part of the uniform for her part-time job at the Tinley Park Veterinary School. She was only a lab aide now, but once she'd completed prerequisite courses at college, Tiffany would be admitted to the veterinary technician program. After touring the facility during her interview, Tiffany had decided that she'd found her true calling.

The phone began to ring as soon as she'd lovingly hung her lab coat on the rack. It wasn't even eight o'clock yet! Who would be calling so early? She snatched the phone up, fearing bad news.

"River Jordan Full Gospel Church, how may I help you? No, Pastor Davis isn't here. Well, I'm sure he's on his way. When I hear from him, I'll have him call you."

Tiffany frowned at the phone as she hung up the receiver. She wasn't sure what to do. The caller said that Pastor Darnell was supposed to be at Roberts' Funeral Home, right now.

She checked the message pad while waiting for the computer to boot up. There'd been several calls the previous day, two from Roberts'. When she was able to see the pastor's schedule, she couldn't believe it. He had several overlapping appointments! He should be at the funeral home now and he'd need a time machine to handle the rest of his day. Who had planned this?

His tool belt clanking as he walked past the office, Steve heard Tiffany say, "Oh, Lord, what do I do now?" He poked his head in.

Tiffany was happy to see anyone. She quickly told him about the schedule and after glancing at it, he said, "This is bad. I'll call the pastor; you call Sister Dee."

He listened to his cell phone for a few minutes and then said, "Pastor, this is Steve. Roberts' Funeral Home is trying to contact you. If you're not on your way there, you should give them a call." He closed the phone. "Voicemail. Maybe he's there already and he's turned off his phone."

Tiffany had just begun speaking. "Auntie Dee, I'm sorry to bother you, but Roberts' called, looking for the pastor. He's supposed to be doing a funeral there this morning."

"Don't worry about it, honey, I'm just pulling up to his door and I don't see his car. He's may be on his way, but I'll knock just to make sure. The day is still a mess; everything's piled on top of something else. There's no other way to handle it—call Rev. Beem and I'll be there to help you as soon as I can."

"Yes, ma'am," Tiffany hung up the phone and took a deep breath. She understood about Christian forgiveness and all, but she didn't want to call the reverend. She didn't like him or trust him and had planned never to speak to him again. Her first visit to the church began horribly, with the deacon making unwanted advances on her in Rev. Beem's own office! When the story came out, Beem had sided with Deacon Uttley, blaming everything on Tiffany.

She hid a fleeting smile behind her hand when Kendrick came in looking a bit frayed around the edges after enjoying Steve's bachelor party. He scowled at Steve. "You don't look hung over at all. You drank as much as everyone else!"

"Nope, after a couple of beers, Carl and I switched to Pepsi. We figured we would need some designated drivers the way ya'll were bending your elbows," Steve teased his future brother-in-law.

Kendrick noticed the look of distress on Tiffany's face and jerked his head in her direction. Then he winced. The sudden movement hadn't been kind to his dully aching head. "What's wrong with my girl?" he whispered.

"She's got to call the reverend. You know how she feels about him." Steve filled Kendrick in on the scheduling disaster and then headed for the door. "So, Pastor Darnell might be on his way, but nobody knows for sure and I couldn't get him on the phone."

He turned to Tiffany and smiled. "Tiff, I've got to get busy. I'll be around if you need me."

"Thanks, but I'll be fine; Auntie Dee is on her way. And we'll see you at the rehearsal. I'm really excited; I've never been part of a wedding before!"

Steve clanked down the hall and Kendrick noticed that Tiffany kept gazing at her new lab coat. "Hey, that name looks good up there."

For a moment, Tiffany forgot all about the hectic day that loomed ahead and smiled at Kendrick. "Aunt Daisy had it done for me. And thank you for including me in the wedding. I don't know if it was your idea or Keisha's…"

"It was all Keisha's idea. You know she's been talking about how everything has to be 'perfect.' It couldn't be perfect without you."

The distressed look reappeared on Tiffany's face. Taking the phone from her, Kendrick dialed a number he'd known for years. "Rev. Beem, this is Kendrick. I'm at the church and there's a problem. We can't get in touch with the pastor and people are waiting at Roberts'. Someone scheduled a funeral for this morning."

He listened for a moment. Tiffany could hear the reverend's outraged rumbling even though she couldn't understand the words.

"Yes sir, it is ungodly early, but Auntie Dee says *you're needed.*" Kendrick placed extra emphasis on the magic words. He hung up the phone and grinned. "Mission accomplished."

■

Everyone in the family noticed that Kendrick had begun referring to Tiffany as "my girl." He made an extra effort to spend time with her and Tremain. It began with him gently teasing her, trying to bring her out of her shell and make her feel welcome. Now things seemed to be moving in a different direction.

The family considered it a miracle. Tiffany was the first woman—other than fellow church musician, Terri Blue—that Kendrick had noticed since his marriage ended nearly two years earlier.

His obsession with Terri had fuelled non-stop church gossip. Terri was the "unreachable star" where Kendrick was concerned. Not only was she several years older, but she was an out-and-proud lesbian. She thought of Kendrick as a younger brother, even though he had tried everything he could think of to be thought of as more.

The general consensus was that Kendrick's infatuation was the result of his marriage having ended so badly and so suddenly. Only his twin knew the truth—Kendrick's attention to Terri *was* one of the reasons that his marriage had failed. He was 19 when he married his 18 year old girlfriend—a pretty, big-boned girl with sandy brown hair. She was pregnant and Reverend Beem had encouraged him to "step up and take responsibility."

Daisy and Carl tried to assure him that they could help him be responsible *while* he and the girl finished school, but Kendrick had made up his mind. Once he made a decision, he was unshakeable, just ask Terri Blue. He dropped out of college and got a low-paying job. He worked most days, putting in long hours in order to make ends come close to meeting.

Crossing River Jordan

For a short time, everything looked good for the young newly wed parents. Then Lynn got pregnant again. Saddled with the prospect of another child, she became depressed and moody. She was suspicious of every woman who even looked at Kendrick. She was especially jealous of the time he spent with his music. That problem grew exponentially soon after Terri Blue joined River Jordan Full Gospel Church.

That Terri was attractive didn't help and that she was gay didn't matter. As Lynn became more demanding, Kendrick spent more time at the church. Even though he would often take his daughters with him, there were many screaming arguments that always ended in Lynn accusing him of having an affair. She and Kendrick continued to drift farther apart.

Rev. Beem offered the young couple counseling to save their marriage. His own first marriage had been a disaster and he didn't want Kendrick to go through the same downward spiral. He feared that it would affect the young man's playing or even drive him out of the church. Beem convinced Lynn to begin counseling with Deacon Uttley, who had taken on the role with great gusto. The reverend thought that he should work directly with Kendrick; after all, Kendrick was "his boy."

Lynn and Kendrick spent more time together with the girls as a family. Lynn seemed happy and hopeful. Then she found out she was pregnant for a third time and it was as if she couldn't get enough air. She couldn't sleep, wouldn't eat and everyone feared for her and the unborn baby. Deanna would drop by every couple of days for health checks disguised as visits.

Carl told Kendrick, "This is where the rubber meets the road. Your wife is in trouble and your marriage is, too. This is where you become a grown man."

Despite Rev. Beem's cajoling, Kendrick cut back on his services to the church. He spent as much time with his family as he could. Between working and practicing and church, he was forced to stop taking college classes at night. The bright spots in his life became his time alone with his daughters and time spent with Terri. She understood him—musically, they spoke the same language. She knew how hard it was to deal with a difficult life and still praise the Lord with joy every Sunday. She listened and didn't judge.

The friendship that he needed just to get through his days became the dynamite that blew his life apart. Less than four months after the new baby was born—Kensha hadn't even cut her first tooth—Kendrick came home from rehearsal and Lynn exploded.

"I came to the church," she screamed. "I saw you with her. You were sitting so close on the piano bench, you might as well have been doing her right there in the sanctuary!"

Kendrick was tired of *everything*. Tired of long days and short nights, tired of trying to reassure his wife that he wasn't having an affair with his gay friend, tired of dreams deferred, tired of being tired. He exploded right back.

"So, now you're spying on me? I wish there had been something for you to see. I wish Terri would give me just one minute of the time that I spend trying to get something going with you. If you feel like everything is so bad, why don't you just leave?"

When he got home from work the following night, there was no one in his apartment. He ran across the hall and banged on Keisha's door. She was dressed for bed when she opened the door. Her hair was stuffed under a pink satin cap with ruffles all around. She growled, "Ken, if that baby wakes up, I'll kill you."

"What's happening? Where is everybody?"

"The kids are here. Lynn is gone."

"What do you mean, 'gone'?" Kendrick looked at Keisha like she was speaking Martian.

"She took all her stuff. She walked out of the building. She got in a car. It drove away."

Frantic, Kendrick asked, "Where are my kids?" He rushed back to his front door with Keisha on his heels.

"Kendrick, I told you, your girls are with me. Your wife walked out and left them. Kiera tried to take care of things, but came and got me because Kensha wouldn't stop crying. I don't even know if they realize that their mother is not coming back."

"What do you mean?" Kendrick moved toward the bedroom. "How do you know she's not coming ba..."

The room looked like it had been hit by a hurricane. Drawers were emptied and hangers and clothes were scattered everywhere. All of Lynn's things were gone. The only things she'd left her three children were a few photos and hair the color of sand.

The twins sat together on the bed. Keisha held her brother's hand.

"Don't worry about the kids," she said. "You know I got your back.

6

Darnell woke because a shaft of sunlight was pressing on his eyelids. Groaning, he slid from the couch to the floor and covered his head with the blanket. He was afraid to move again, certain that his head would explode if he did. The more he thought of it, the better that idea seemed. That would definitely make the unholy pounding stop. He crawled to the bathroom, searching for aspirin and needing to brush his teeth. His teeth and tongue felt like they'd grown fur.

A shower, he thought. A shower and aspirin and much more sleep would be the prescription he needed to live through the day. His stomach churned at the very thought of food. Every sound was magnified. The sound of the flushing toilet almost made him cry. He could hear each individual drop of water in the shower hitting his skin. They reminded him of the claps of thunder the night before.

Finally he made it back to the couch. No way could he tackle the stairs leading up to his bed. Maybe later. He couldn't even make it to the window to close the curtains completely. He would just put his head at the other end of the couch. Seconds after he gingerly eased himself down and pulled the blanket over his head, there was a fearsome banging on his door.

The pastor sprang up, bumping his shin sharply against the cocktail table. Holding both his aching leg and pounding head, he hobbled to the door. He didn't care who was out there or what they wanted. He just needed for that horrible noise to stop.

"Please," he whispered. "Please just go away." He opened the door just enough for one of his eyes to be visible to his unwelcome visitor.

"Pastor Darnell, are you all right? We've been trying to get in touch with you!" Deanna tried to open the door further, but the pastor was leaning against it.

"You were supposed to conduct a funeral service today—right now, no, nearly half an hour ago. Everyone was waiting for you at Roberts'!"

She brushed past and whirled to face him.

"Don't you have your cell phone on? We couldn't even get you on your home phone!" Dee finally took a good look at the pastor. "My precious Lord, you look awful! Pastor, you've been drinking. Don't try to deny it; I smell it on you!"

Now Darnell was embarrassed as well as ill. "Sister Ramsey, please lower your voice a bit. I stumbled onto Steve's bachelor party last night. I think I got a little carried away."

"Oh, Pastor, if the Mothers hear that you were too hung over to do your job, you will *need* to be carried away! Get dressed; we have to go!"

Dee pushed him toward the stairs saying, "Rev. Beem is taking the morning funeral, but you've still got two weddings and a funeral to get through before you do Keisha's and Steve's rehearsal tonight."

"Why? Why is this all happening today?" Darnell was moving on his own, finally heading up the stairs to dress.

"Pastor Darnell, you've got too many cooks in your kitchen. You have to hire one secretary, but you can't worry about that today. I'll fix you some tea and dry toast, while you get dressed. Your stomach may give you a little trouble today."

The aspirin he'd taken was kicking in and the earlier shower had helped, but Darnell was still moving slowly. It took more than 30 minutes for him to get back downstairs to face Deanna and the day ahead. Dee had the tea and toast waiting in the kitchen. "Even if you're not hungry, you need something on your stomach. You'll thank me later."

They stepped out into sunshine so bright that Darnell's eyes burned behind his sunglasses. He abruptly stopped walking. He looked quickly to the left and then to the right, his head shooting tiny spikes of pain with each movement. "My car's not here." The pain he was enduring made calmness a necessity.

"Langston told me that Chess drove you both home," Dee said. "Your car and his are both outside of Lee's. I hope you both still have your tires and radios, but if you don't it'll be all your own faults."

Half to himself, Darnell said, "Chess *was* here. I thought I dreamed that."

"We don't have time to pick up your car. I guess I'm your official driver for the first part of the day. You do have everything you need, don't you."

"I do if there's a Bible at the—where is the wedding? I don't remember anyone decorating the sanctuary or either of the chapels. Is it in the dining hall?"

Someone had parked so closely to the front of Deanna's newly painted Sonata that she had a difficult time maneuvering out of the parking space. She loved the pearl bronze finish and she was determined not to get a ding or scratch. It took a few minutes before she answered the pastor.

"You can use my Bible if you need it and if you want to get in a little nap, there's time. We're going to Indiana Dunes State Park."

■

Even though she used a hands-free device, Deanna spent so much time on her cell phone during the drive to the Dunes that it made Darnell nervous. Her attention was definitely divided. She spoke to Tiffany first.

"How's everything? He got there on time? Thank the Lord. Sorry sweetheart, I know you didn't want to talk to him. Oh, Kendrick called? Well, I'll call and tell him about the other ceremony. There's no way we will get there in time."

She checked her rearview mirror before changing lanes. "Yes, we do have to talk to Pastor Davis about getting a full-time secretary." Dee gave the pastor a pointed look. "You're doing fine sweetheart, don't worry. I'll call you right after this wedding."

The phone rang before she could make another call. "Mama? Is everything all right? I know you went to the cabin. I called you there yesterday, remember? You're going to take a little trip to where? No Mama, I'm not trying to get in your business. You're going with your friend Jesse? Mama, I don't know Jesse, do I?

"Well, could I meet Jesse before you go to Indianapolis together? Mama, may I talk to Jesse? No, I'm not trying to get in your business. How about bringing Jesse to Keisha's wedding? You will be here in time tomorrow? Okay, call me when you get to Three Oaks. Bye."

Dee sighed heavily and asked, "Pastor, would you pray for my mother? She's more than a little crazy and she may or may not be driving here tomorrow with an imaginary person."

Not long after a call to Daisy to check on the wedding preparations, Deanna drove through to the guardhouse at the Indiana Dunes park entrance. She explained that they were members of the wedding party. The guard told them that their entrance fee had already been paid and directed them to a parking lot near the beach.

"There's the Visitor's Center, "she pointed. "I guess we can freshen up there and you have a few minutes to get whatever information you need."

"I've never been comfortable performing sacred rites for people I haven't counseled. I've never even met this couple. Who scheduled this?"

"Pastor, we're not exactly sure how this day was planned. Let's just get through it and we'll make a better plan at the first opportunity."

The Visitors Center was an imposing structure made of limestone and oak. The winds off of Lake Michigan weathered the building, giving it a noble antique façade. They entered and a woman with pencils stuck in her curly brown hair rushed to them. Wire rimmed glasses on a gold chain bounced on her ample bosom. The pastor knew her well; he'd officiated at many of her weddings. Dee considered her a friend, in spite of Lori having coordinated two of Dee's disastrous marriages.

"Mrs. Caswell, I should have known this would be one of yours." Darnell said, shaking her hand.

"Lori's Luxury Events is one of the busiest wedding planning services in the city," she said proudly. "Pastor, thank you for agreeing to conduct the ceremony. Dee, you look fine, but you might want to see if any of the boots fit you. Pastor, you can change in there." She pointed to a closed door across the room.

Both Dee and Darnell were confused. Dee hadn't planned on attending a wedding—she was certainly not dressed for the occasion. She had on jeans and an old blue and white rugby jersey that had belonged to one of her former husbands. She was dressed for cleaning out filing cabinets, which was what she'd planned to do at the church until it was time to go home and change for Keisha's and Steve's wedding rehearsal.

The pastor was appropriately attired in a black suit with a jaunty red and black tie. Unexpectedly, his clothing actually matched Lori's black pantsuit and red ruffled blouse. Why did he need to change?

"Oh, I'll be changing too," she assured them. "There's no way I could make it to the bluff in these heels," she laughed. "Come on, Dee, I'll show you where the boots are."

The wedding was like nothing Deanna had ever seen. Instead of the traditional processional, the bride and groom led the entire wedding party and their guests on a hike across the sandy beach to the first dune. Dee looked around, surprised that the heavy rains in Chicago the night before hadn't left a drop in northwest Indiana. The sand was as dry as—well, sand.

Everyone wore hiking gear and many carried hiking poles. The bride and groom wore matching hiking shorts and boots. The groom wore a tuxedo jacket and the bride wore a short veil attached to a tiara of pearls and Swarovski crystal beads. Along with her hiking pole, which was festively draped with streamers of multicolored ribbon, the bride carried a bouquet of peace roses and baby's breath.

Dee was exhausted and breathing heavily even before she got to the foot of the dune. "There is no way I can climb that big sand hill. I'm practically dead from trying to make it across the beach!"

She glanced around at others who were struggling just as hard. The mother of the groom seemed to be enjoying herself, but her husband and the bride's parents looked grim as they tried and tried again to negotiate the deep sands of the dune. Every step was a trial.

Dee would sink, with one leg entrapped in the sand nearly up to her knee and then try to pull the other leg forward only to endure the same process to take another step. Younger, stronger members of the group were helping other guests along. Dee decided it would be easier to sit and slide back down to the beach; after all, she hadn't been invited. Why was she practically killing herself to attend the wedding of a couple she didn't even know?

The bride urged her parents, "Don't give up, Mom and Dad. You can make it. I know it's not easy, but in the end it'll be worth it!"

"Just like marriage!" someone from the wedding party yelled.

Dee noticed that Lori, solid and strong, had already crested the dune and was helping the pastor haul another guest to the top. Dee tried to turn around. She was ready to head back, but she couldn't pull her leg out of the sand. Then, to her extreme embarrassment, she felt hands pushing her from behind. When Deanna finally neared the end of her climb, a young man reached down to help her make the last few steps. She was so exhausted; she couldn't even puff out a thank you.

For a few moments she warred with herself. On one hand, she was furious—*what kind of thoughtless dolts would put their guests through this*? On the other hand, she was disgusted that she was so out of shape. The groom's mother wasn't that much younger and she didn't have help making it up the dune. Finally, good manners won out and she smiled at the young men who had helped her. He offered his arm and she gratefully took it.

They walked a few yards on blessedly level ground that opened onto a field of wildflowers. Just beyond that there were folding chairs arranged in a half circle. Dee sank down into a chair near the back. Even from her seat she could see out over the bluff to the lake below. A brisk, refreshing breeze blew in off the lake and the breakers were flinging up a lacy froth. The sky was a cloudless, robin's egg blue. The view was breathtaking.

Crossing River Jordan

Pastor Darnell, now clad in the standard hiking boots and jeans along with his white shirt and tie, actually looked better for the exercise. He'd had time to speak with the young couple on the trek to the bluff and Lori had made sure that he was comfortable with the names. He took his position at the front and center of the group of chairs. Before he began to speak, music filled the air.

Dee was surprised—she hadn't expected music. Then she remembered that some of the wedding party had carried backpacks. Obviously someone had a CD player and speakers. The young man who had helped her up the dune stepped forward and began to sing a haunting song from an old movie, *Affair to Remember*. His voice was a rich tenor and he sang the beautiful old song so sweetly, she almost cried.

At the song's end, the pastor began. "Dearly Beloved, we are gathered here today—and Lord, you know we worked hard to get here—to join this man and this woman in the bonds of holy matrimony."

■

The walk back to the Visitors Center was much longer, but was far easier. On the other side of the wildflower field, there was a path that led down from the bluff back to the beach. The trip back across the beach was still a challenge, but they arrived at a transformed Visitors Center. Tables had been set up all around the large main room. Each table was set for fine dining and held a centerpiece made of gleaming polished driftwood and a candle in a shell.

Though dressed for roughing it outside, they were served a sumptuous fare of surf and turf. Champagne flowed and many toasts were made, both raucous and heartfelt. Deanna noticed that the pastor drank only cranberry juice for the toast to the new bride and groom.

As soon as they could, Pastor Davis and Dee offered best wishes and blessings to the happy couple and made their way to the changing rooms.

Lori intercepted them and slipped an envelope to the pastor. "I know it was pretty unorthodox, but you made it very meaningful for them, Pastor Davis. They're delighted."

"If I ever get married again," Dee said, smiling, "I wouldn't have anyone else plan my wedding. You did a great job, Lori."

"And I'd be only too happy to officiate at your ceremony, Sister Ramsey," said the pastor. "If you promise not to make me climb a sand dune to do it!"

■

As the day moved along, Tiffany settled into a routine, answering phones and correspondence, entering appointments onto the pastor's computerized calendar and glancing at her textbook to get a little studying done. By noon, she was ravenously hungry and she decided to stop for lunch. She thought of going to the preschool to eat with Tremain, but remembered that he was going through a phase of not wanting her to leave him. She hated when he cried for her, but everyone had assured her that he would grow out of it.

As usual, River Jordan was teeming with activity, with meetings and activities all over the place. People trooped up and down stairs, doors were constantly opening and closing. A constant buzz of voices and laughter ebbed and flowed.

She grabbed her purse and the keys to the car. She smiled down at the keys in her hand, still finding it hard to believe that she had her own car! Uncle Carl had gotten it for her for Christmas. He'd told her not to be too excited—it was a ten year old Chevy Cavalier. He called it a "beater," but said he had checked it out. If she took care of it, it would run for another 20 years. No one had ever given her anything like it before and she'd embarrassed him by crying all over him.

She was amazed at the way the Lord had moved in her life, since the day Aunt Daisy and Auntie Dee had come to her rescue at the church.

Those women, along with Uncle Carl and the twins, had enfolded her and Tremain into their lives so seamlessly; it was as if they had been part of the family all along. Like she'd been stolen at birth by the wicked fairy and was finally back in her rightful home. She and Tremain had their own apartment in the basement of the Franklins' building. Aunt Daisy said it was called a garden apartment, but Tiffany didn't care what it was called—it was hers. Two small bedrooms and a sitting room with a galley kitchen and bath.

There was no tub in the bathroom, so Tremain got his baths upstairs and she hardly ever used the little kitchen. Most of the meals in the Franklin household were large, noisy family-style affairs, either with Aunt Daisy and Uncle Carl or in one of the twin's apartments.

Keisha and Kendrick— they were like her real sister and brother; she couldn't have asked for better. Actually, lately she'd been thinking of Kendrick differently, but she would never let anyone know. He thought of her as another sister and she would have to be happy with that. His feelings for Terri Blue were a running joke at the church.

Tiffany stepped out into the hall. As she turned to close the door, she saw a man come out of a room near the stairs. He stood for a moment talking quietly to someone just inside. His silhouette made her heart stop. It couldn't be! She took a step forward, trying to make sure. His hair was shorter but, yes, it was Frank Willis! The last time she'd seen him, he was raging down at her just before kicking her in the head.

She reached behind her, fumbling for the door and backing into the office. Leaning against the door, she locked it and slid to the floor.

Oh God, how did he find me? How did he know I was here? Does he know about the baby? What was she going to do?

"Lord, please help me," she whispered. "He can't find us here!"

She didn't feel the tears trickling from her eyes. She didn't hear the phone ringing; in fact, she didn't hear any sound at all. Suddenly, she was back in the kitchen of Frank's house, lying on the floor after he'd beaten and kicked her. She could feel the pain and taste the blood and tears.

Tiffany didn't know how long she'd sat there blocking the door, hugging her knees and sobbing softly. She came to herself with a start when someone called her name.

"Tiffany, are you in there? I came to take you to lunch."

Kendrick! He had to stop calling her name; Frank would hear!

She jumped up and unlocked the door, pulling a startled Kendrick into the room and into an embrace.

"Tiffany, what..."

She slammed and locked the door behind him. "Sssshhhh! He's here, I saw him. Please don't say my name again!"

A tiny part of Kendrick's brain registered pleasure at the unexpected chance to hold Tiffany. The rest of his mind was focused on the young woman's obvious terror.

"What's wrong? Who's here?" He held Tiffany's arms and looked into her eyes.

She was vibrating in his hands. The blood had rushed from her face leaving it an ashy gray. He was afraid she was going into shock. He moved her into the pastor's office and lowered her to the couch, covering her with Pastor Darnell's White Sox blanket.

Kendrick knelt beside her and took her hand. "Who's here, Tiffany?"

"I saw...I saw Frank. In the hall. He was standing in the hall!" Her teeth chattered so violently she could scarcely get the words out.

"You're sure it was Frank? There's not that much light out there. It could have been someone else."

Tiffany tightened her grip on Kendrick's hand. "I heard his voice. I know his voice!" She began to cry again and turned her face away from him.

"I'm going to check it out." He stood, but she wouldn't release his hand. He leaned down and kissed her forehead. "I'll be right back, baby, I promise. You'll be safe here; don't worry."

Kendrick closed the office door firmly when he left. Flipping his cell phone open, he first called Deanna. The call went to voicemail and he left a message asking her to call him back right away.

Then he called Daisy. "I know you're busy with Keisha, but there's an emergency at the church. Tiffany's in trouble. Can you come down here now? To Pastor Darnell's office."

As he talked, he moved down the hall checking each room in turn. The room directly opposite the pastor's office was a locked storage closet. From the next room, Kendrick heard the excited chatter of the teen leaders meeting as they planned a fundraiser. The last door on that side, nearest the stairs, was open. Looking in, he saw Eula Dempsey seated at a

Crossing River Jordan

table. She was flipping through a stack of papers and looked up as he entered.

"Sister Dempsey, was there a man in here a couple of minutes ago?"

"There's been a bunch of people in and out of here all morning," she sighed, blowing a lock of hair away from her face. "I'm helping with Rev. Beem's Forgiveness Festival and I've been taking down registrations for the workshops. You here to take over for me? Ottistean was supposed to come, but that girl just won't get nowhere on time. I got to get something to eat—I'm so hungry, I could eat where I been!"

Kendrick shifted his weight from foot to foot, waiting for a chance to speak. "Sister, was a man named Frank in here a little while ago?"

Eula shuffled the papers, reading the names aloud. "Sherman Penn, Sharon Richards, Larry Green, Lauren Aikens, Todd, Lynn, Ray Gunn—-that's a funny name—R.J. Colton..."

One of those names plucked at Kendrick's attention, but he was listening for *Frank Something* with such intensity, that he couldn't get a handle on anything else. Eula droned on. Kendrick wanted to yell and snatch the papers from her so he could look for himself.

"Oh, hey!" Eula looked up, smiling. "That R.J. Colton, he was a pro football player a few years ago!"

That's what it was, Kendrick thought. *That was the name I've heard before.*

She continued to read names aloud. Just when Kendrick thought he couldn't take anymore, she said, "Here's a Frank Willis," and she looked up at him expectantly.

He spun on his heels and fairly ran from the room, calling back over his shoulder, "Thanks. I hope your sister gets here soon."

He hurried back and into the secretary's office but jerked to a stop. The door was wide open! He was sure he'd closed it when he left. Aunt Daisy couldn't have gotten here so fast and she wouldn't have come down the back stairs—they led down from the choir loft.

Kendrick was not a fighter. He took care of his hands the way a surgeon would. Still, he wasn't going to let some thug hurt his girl either. He grabbed the coat rack that stood near the door, holding it across his body like a soldier presenting arms. He never noticed that Tiffany's treasured lab coat was gone. Slowly, he rounded the corner to the pastor's office.

It was empty and the blanket was in a ball on the floor. He checked the pastor's private restroom. Tiffany wasn't there. He checked closets and looked up and down the hall. No sign of her.

The baby! She went to see about Tremain. Taking the stairs two at a time, Kendrick raced out of the main building and ran across the parking lot to the Children's Church. When he got to the preschool, he stopped to take a deep breath. He didn't want to frighten any of the children or alarm the staff. He also didn't want Kensha to see him—she'd be confused, thinking it was time to go home for the day.

He peeked in the window, hoping to single out either of the kids amid the busy groups of children in the room. They were all so active, moving from one bunch to the next, he couldn't pick his out of the crowd. He tried to remember when he'd started to include Tremain with the other children in the family. They were all part of "his" kids or "our" children whenever he spoke or thought of them.

Finally, he was able to identify Kensha. She wore a bright red Curious George shirt and blue jean shorts with red trim. She was at the water table, happily pouring water from one cup into another. He didn't see Tremain anywhere. He couldn't remember what the baby had worn that morning.

Giving up, he tapped quietly on the window in the door. One of the teachers smiled and waved him in. He motioned for her to come out. He stood away from the door, hiding from his daughter.

"Hi, did you come for Kensha? We're getting a lot of parents picking up early today. Tiffany was just here. Usually, she'd take Kensha, too..."

"That's what I wanted. I, uh, was trying to catch Tiffany before she got out of here." He gave a forced laugh. "That girl is fast! Well, I'll be back for Kensha in a little while."

As Kendrick hustled to his car, the phone rang and he answered with a hopeful "Tiffany?"

"No, it's Aunt Daisy. I'm standing here in the office and there's no one here. Not Tiffany, not any one covering for her. What's going on?"

Kendrick was driving by the time he finished telling Daisy everything, although he wasn't even sure exactly what had happened. He was only sure that Tiffany was terrified and he had to find some way to help.

7

Rev. Beem was at an unusual loss for words. He had arrived at the funeral home just in time to see several coffins being wheeled from one room to another as the staff tried to organize the viewings and services for the day. Why in the world would the family insist on holding services so early in the morning? The staff could hardly be blamed for any complications: the arriving mourners were causing "traffic jams" by blocking corridors and wandering into the wrong rooms.

The reverend was disconcerted by the strong smell of food in the building. Perhaps one of the staff was heating up a snack. The fragrance of fried chicken was deeply disturbing coming from a funeral home with a crematorium. Maybe he was hallucinating, but the reverend now believed he smelled bacon! The food odors mixing with the scents of lilies and gladiolas made him feel a bit queasy. *The management should do something about the ventilation in this place*!

He finally found a harried funeral director who stopped placing signs by each of the idyllically named rooms to usher the reverend into the correct one. Rev. Beem would be officiating at the home-going service for Willa Parker, 92 years old, death due to complications from pneumonia. He had written the name when Kendrick called him this morning and he checked the name on his note against the name on the small marquee by the room's entrance, just to be sure.

At the door of the Heavenly Rest room, the smell of food was much, much stronger. He heard a mourner saying, "Girl, this is a hot mess! They're calling it a 'pre-past' instead of a repast. People are in there loading food on plates like they at a party! They havin' breakfast with the body!"

Her companion, a silver-haired woman with a pinched mouth replied, "I ain't never heard tell of nothin' like this! We better get in there if we want to get some of that bacon. I think the grits are going fast, too."

It was true! There was a buffet table set up just inside the doors. The bereaved waited dutifully in line to help themselves to an old-fashioned Southern breakfast, complete with fried chicken and biscuits. They carried their loaded plates to chairs, many of them sending youngsters back to fetch them coffee or iced tea.

Rev. Beem felt like he had stumbled into an episode of the *Twilight Zone* or that new series, *Punked*. He clutched his dignity in a firm fist, determined not to be disgraced as the hidden cameras rolled. He approached the front of the room, stopping at the casket to say a brief prayer for the deceased. Around him, he heard whispered conversations.

"Didn't they do a good job? Granny looks better than she did when she was alive!"

"I told them not to put that ugly silver lamé dress on her. She looks like a space alien!"

"I'm leaving here and going right to Granny's house. Nay Nay thinks she's getting that armoire, but Granny promised it to me."

"Willa wasn't no saint, no sir! She didn't start that holy rolling until she was too old to do anything else!"

"They say she had more money buried somewhere in her back yard. Me and Pookie's going over there soon as this is over. I got some shovels in my trunk!"

These are her loved ones? This is the respect she's due at the end of a long life? Rev. Beem squared his shoulders, vowing to give this poor woman as dignified a service as he could, under the circumstances. He also vowed to get even with that Darnell Davis for setting him up like this!

■

Deanna stopped at a legendary barbeque restaurant by the highway just past the Dunes' entrance. She told the pastor, "We can grab something to go if you want. You need some more to eat if you're going to get through the rest of this day. Something hot will do you good. You should be able to handle real food now."

While they waited to be served, she excused herself and walked toward the back of the restaurant to check her messages. She had a weird call from Kendrick and when she rang the pastor's office, the call was answered by voicemail. That was strange; someone should be in the office. Dee was simply too busy to worry. She had to get Pastor Darnell to his next appointment.

More than anything, Darnell wanted another shower. The sand and the sweat and the remnants of a hangover were taking a physical toll, but Sister Ramsey turned out to be right. The rib tips, potato salad and cole slaw made him feel much more prepared to meet the rest of his responsibilities. And, as much as he hated to admit it, having Beem for backup eased his mind somewhat.

They were back on the road before Dee mentioned the secretary situation. "Pastor, you've got to find one person to assist you with the administrative chores. Keisha has done an admirable job, but she's overwhelmed. Tiffany has stepped up and done the best she can, but she's new and she's busy, too. We can't even figure out who scheduled all these overlapping events. You've got to hire someone who can commit to the job."

Before he could reply, Dee's phone rang. "Daisy, what's wrong?"

She relayed Daisy's words to the pastor. "Tiffany was working in the office and she thought she saw the man who hurt her. Now she's missing and the office is empty!"

Darnell felt the concern first in his stomach. Suddenly, the good meal had gone sour. "We can't worry about an empty office. Ask Sister Franklin to please keep us posted and just concentrate on Tiffany. Have they called the police?"

"It's too soon," Dee said. Between her love of mystery novels and her badgering Langston for information, Dee had become well-versed in police procedures. "She hasn't been missing long enough." Then back to Daisy, "Where's the baby? Okay, just stay in touch."

To the pastor's questioning look she responded, "The baby is with Tiffany, wherever she is."

"Where are we going now?" Darnell had stopped trying to keep track. He trusted Dee to get him where he had to be when he needed to be there.

"Lawnvale Cemetery is next," Dee said. "The service is at the gravesite, wake and funeral. I'm glad we've been blessed with good weather today. A downpour like the one last night would make this twice as hard. I wonder what that wedding party would have done if it had stormed?"

"I think they would have gone on and slogged up that sand dune in the pouring rain. What's a torrential downpour and a little mudslide when you're with the ones you love?" The pastor replied and they both laughed.

Dee was pleased to see the pastor rallying from the overwhelming sadness that had enfolded him since Georgia left. He'd probably still have some bad days, but meeting the day's challenges seemed to be renewing him.

Darnell sensed the shift, too. Throughout the day, he had repeatedly promised the Lord that he would enjoy any subsequent bachelor parties with a heady mixture of ginger ale and cranberry juice. He realized that he hadn't given one thought to Georgia Beem. Even now, thinking of her didn't cause a pain in his chest as it had before. He didn't have time to allow living in the past to prevent him from functioning in the present.

Lord, thank you for always providing us with what we need, even if it's a hangover and a long, hard day, he prayed silently.

■

Kendrick ran straight to Tiffany's apartment, relieved to see her car in front of their home. The car was a couple of feet from the curb. It looked like she had merely stopped and gotten out, instead of taking the time to park.

He called her name as he clattered down the stairs. He didn't want to frighten her by suddenly appearing behind her. She was in Tremain's room, throwing his things into a huge black contractor trash bag—toys, clothes, books—everything he had been given by the people who'd grown to love them both. She didn't want to leave anything behind. Not because they were material things that she would have to replace, but because the love they represented could *never* be replaced.

She had stopped crying, but her face was streaked with tears. "I'm so sorry; tell everyone, I'm so sorry. I don't want to go, but I can't let him find me! I can't let him find Tremain!"

Kendrick had been afraid for her; now he realized that he was afraid *of* her. He didn't know what she would do if he tried to stop her. She was frantically scooping things up and stuffing them into the bag. Tremain stood in his crib, his eyes round with alarm.

That was how he could reach her. Kendrick knew that she would do anything for her child.

"Tiffany, slow down and I'll help you. Calm down, now, you're scaring the baby." He began to fold Tremain's clothing very slowly, arranging everything in neat piles. "I'll do anything you need; you know we all will. Could you tell me what happened? Did he threaten you?"

The prolonged adrenalin rush that followed her seeing Frank had subsided. Tiffany moved as if she were underwater, as if gravity had doubled its pull on her.

"I've called everyone and they're all on the way. You don't want to leave without saying goodbye to everyone, do you? The kids would be so upset. They'll miss you very much." Kendrick's voice broke and he coughed to clear his throat.

He put the little piles of clothing in the plastic bag. "We'll really miss Tremain, too. He looks pretty tired. How about putting him down for a nap until you finish packing? By the time you're done, the family will be here and you can see everyone before you go."

She was on auto-pilot, her motions sluggish. Kendrick settled the baby in his crib and took Tiffany's hand, leading her into her bedroom. "You could stretch out for a few minutes while I finish packing for you," he suggested.

She had no energy left. He sat on the bed with her curled beside him. Kendrick gently stroked her back and spoke softly.

"Do you think you could tell me what happened now? You saw Frank in the hall at the church..."

"He didn't see me." Her voice was so low that even the sound made by the motion of his hand rubbing her back seemed loud. "I ran into the office. I was so scared!"

He felt her shudder. "I couldn't think. How did he find us? Who would tell him we were here? I had to get the baby. I have to take the baby somewhere safe!"

Her voice rose and Kendrick slightly increased the pressure of his hand. "You know you're safe here, right? You know we would never let anything happen to you."

Kendrick had never hated anyone in his life, but in that moment, he would gladly have killed Frank Willis with whatever was handy. He understood that no matter what Tiffany had suffered at Frank's hands, her entire focus was on saving her child and keeping him out of harm's way.

She was drifting off to sleep. He studied the curve of her cheek and the softness of her skin. He gazed at the shape of her mouth and breathed in the scent of her hair.

He had cared for Lynn with a combination of youthful lust and dramatic passion. He'd idolized Terri because of her talent and compassion. Tiffany Steele was courage and gentleness. In spite of the hand she'd been dealt, she had an amazing sweetness in her spirit. She embraced life with a force of goodness that wouldn't be denied. Kendrick wasn't sure he understood love, but he was beginning to think that Tiffany was the one who could teach him.

■

Uncle Carl arrived home first. He came downstairs wearing a jacket, which struck Kendrick as odd because the temperature hadn't been out of the 80s for days. He kept his right hand in his jacket pocket.

"I'm going to look in on Lucky, but I'll be right upstairs if you need me," Carl whispered. He patted his pocket. "I've got a little something here for anyone who's fool enough to want it." All of the adults knew that Uncle Carl kept a gun in the house. It was always locked in a box on the top shelf of his closet.

A short time later, Kendrick heard the thumping and squealing that meant the children were home. He could hear his sister's tone and could separate it from Aunt Daisy's and Uncle Carl's. Some other voices he couldn't recognize, but he didn't want to leave Tiffany. He knew she'd be frightened if she woke up alone.

He quietly took off his shoes and settled down beside her. She sighed and burrowed into his arms. He would stay there as long as she needed him.

■

Crossing River Jordan

Langston was having a less than stellar day, beginning when he'd awakened to a throbbing headache—*just what you deserve after all those sweet drinks*, he thought. *Should have gone with straight whisky or beer.*

He'd had to take a cab to his car and when he got there, he was getting a parking ticket. Trying to talk the beat cop out of giving it to him had made him late for work. He arrived to find a mountain of paperwork and no partner to help him with it. Javier had been temporarily reassigned—loaned out to a special operation in the Little Village neighborhood.

Langston had tried to call Dee three times and gotten only voicemail. Was she ignoring him? Had he done something to make her angry? Had something gone wrong with the work he'd done on her sink? Those were the thoughts of the man.

Then came the thoughts of the cop. What kind of trouble had she gotten herself into this time? She had a talent for sticking her nose in where it didn't belong—what if something had happened to her?

He shook his head. After all, the woman was older than he was, as she so often reminded him. She'd been taking care of herself for a long time.

She's fine, he assured himself. She's just busy—as he should be. Langston rolled up his sleeves and got to work. Thank God his mother had insisted that he take a typing course in high school.

Before he could get more than one report done, there was a disturbance in the station. High out of his mind, some clown had actually walked in with a gun to his own head He yelled and babbled, threatening to blow his other personality's brains out. The bullpen emptied. Every officer drew his or her gun and raced downstairs.

It turned out to be nothing. The gun wasn't even loaded. The goof had sold his prescribed medication and spent the few bucks on a cheap high. Two beat cops took him down to the psych ward at Stroger Hospital for an evaluation. As they left the station, the desk sergeant said, "We know the diagnosis—he's nuts."

That was when Langston's day hit the high note. He was Walking back to the squad room, laughing and joking with the other detectives, he missed a step, tripped and tumbled back down the metal and cement stairs. As he lay at the bottom, the cops ordered an ambulance right away because, as that same comic sergeant said, "We know his diagnosis, too—broken leg."

■

Rev. Beem arrived at River Jordan to find Pastor Davis's office empty, but just down the hall Eula was still busily taking reservations for the Forgiveness Festival. He smiled, well pleased with his latest brainstorm. Surely, he'd found the full favor of the Lord this time. The Forgiveness Festival would be just the beginning. Soon, he'd be back in his home and back in charge of this church!

Even though he was supposed to be on equal footing with young Davis—and that was an insult—he saw that many members of the church, as well as staff, deferred to the young pastor in everything. It was "Pastor Darnell, could we?" and "Pastor Darnell, what do you think?" for everything from the Saturday School awards for the children to rubber stamping the budget for mission trips. No one had asked Rev. Beem his opinion on anything more important than if he wanted any flowers on the altar when he preached.

Well, things would change once everyone saw the crowds attending the Forgiveness Festival. They would soon remember what a powerful, motivating speaker he was and what a commanding presence he had in the pulpit. They would appreciate the money the attendees were bringing in and there was sure to be an increase in membership once the Festival ended. He would try to get Vanessa there to see him in action. The woman needed to see what she was missing!

Once in his office, he checked his only message. Sister Ramsey was reminding him that the wedding party would be at the church at 2 pm. Irritating woman, she'd left the same message on his cell phone. Did she think he was like Davis, a mewling pup who had to be led around by the collar?

He had just enough time to freshen up, change his shirt and tie. He would put on a more festive tie to officiate at a wedding. He checked the shine on his shoes and pinched the creases in his pants.

Crossing River Jordan

The first thing he'd do when he was back in charge would be to move into the senior minister's residence on the River Jordan property. He was shocked to hear that that foolish young dog had no intention of taking up residence in the proper place. Davis was happy with the little townhome he'd inherited from his parents.

The boy just didn't understand that in the business of influencing the thoughts of others, appearances mattered. Why did he think that the most successful ministers drove Cadillacs and Lincolns? A minister had to be an example of the blessings the Lord bestowed on a Godly man.

The best thing Georgia had ever done was to leave that fool down on his knees in front of the entire congregation. Davis was nowhere near good enough for his daughter and Beem was glad she had come to her senses. Still, he blamed the pastor for making his daughter run all the way to another state. She probably feared that Davis would become a stalker.

Climbing the back stairs to the sanctuary, he allowed himself to acknowledge a sense of loss. *Vanessa should be here for this*, he thought. She had always enjoyed the role of First Lady, playing hostess and being deferred to by the church members. He liked the adoring looks she gave him when he spoke or conducted a ceremony.

Although he would never admit it to anyone, he missed his wife. She may have never learned to cook a proper meal, but she had made a comfortable home. And she was a good girl—obedient, soft-spoken and very pretty. Vanessa's attentions made him feel that everyone was in their rightful place— him at the head, with her by his side. Besides, she always loved a beautiful...

What in the name of all that is holy has happened to this sanctuary? At first, Rev. Beem's mind refused to acknowledge what he was seeing. It looked like an overgrown jungle or an explosion in a greenhouse. Every square inch of the sanctuary—his sanctuary—seemed to be covered in leaves! The room looked like a Rose Bowl float!

Many of the wedding guests wore flowing robes in a rainbow of colors and they were draped in flowers, too. A man stood by the altar rail in an outfit that was even more outlandish than the others: a sky-blue robe with ivy encircling his neck and forming a crown on his head. The man was barefoot, standing at the altar of God!

The groom approached him, hand outstretched. "Pastor Davis, thank you for agreeing to marry us so quickly. Once we found out about the little bud waiting to bloom, we knew we wanted to be married right away."

The reverend wondered if he could be dreaming. Maybe nothing that had happened today was real. There had been no "pre-past" breakfast with a body. There was no rainforest sprouting up in his church. There was no man—dressed like something out of a book on Greek mythology—talking to him about buds blooming and waiting to shake his hand. Beem willed himself to wake up.

"That is not Pastor Davis!"

Rev. Beem knew that voice. Now, he was sure he must be dreaming. What would his wife be doing in the middle of this madness?

"Vanessa? Why are you here?"

"Why are *you* here? We specifically requested Pastor Darnell to perform this ceremony!" Vanessa spoke with the sharp clipped tones she had been using with him since she'd told him that he no longer lived in their house.

Rev. Beem looked at his wife. She too wore a robe that swept the floor. Beneath it, her toes peeked out, her nails the pearly pink of tiny seashells. Her robe clung to every curve of her body and was belted with a silver cord. Her hair was swept up and a wreath of cornflowers encircled it. She was stunning, but this was *so wrong*.

Beem feared that his wife had become unhinged by those images she had been exposed to, thanks to that idiot Uttley using hidden cameras to photograph the reverend in some very compromising encounters with other women.

He gaped and then he roared. "What is this, some kind of devil-worship? Vanessa, have you been brainwashed into joining a coven? I can bring you back to yourself. Come here and pray with me!"

"You go pray with one of the women in those pictures, Albert Beem. You are not wanted or needed here!" She turned and walked away.

The reverend was enraged. How dare she speak to him like that in public? He wanted to rush after her and make her apologize for humiliating him. Instead he chose to turn his anger on the situation.

"How dare you heathens..."

"Just one minute," the groom interrupted. "We are not heathens! For your information, we are Christian Pagans. There's no devil worship or covens or cults here."

Vanessa whirled to face him. "Albert Beem, you should be ashamed of yourself!" she blazed. "You, with your high-class education, you should be ashamed to display so much ignorance!"

The very pregnant bride came charging down the aisle, towing a man who must have been her father. He also wore a robe, but it was easy to see that he didn't feel comfortable and beneath the robe he wore a regular suit.

The bride was a vision in green taffeta that shimmered and played with the light. She held one arm protectively over her prominent belly. "What's wrong? Why haven't we gotten started?"

Vanessa hurried over, speaking quietly. "It's just a little delay, dear. Don't worry; I'll just make a quick call and find out what's holding up the pastor. You go back to the dressing room and wait. You've got to make a grand entrance!"

The bride nodded and gave Vanessa a wavering smile. He father took her arm and escorted her away.

The guests were understandably confused and the decibel level rose as they discussed the delay. Rev. Beem heard more than one "What's wrong?"

An elderly woman rose near the front row on the bride's side. Her diaphanous robe was much too big and kept dropping off of her shoulders to reveal a lavender jacket and a roped pearl necklace. Her voice pierced the air as she asked, "It's not the baby is it? She didn't go into labor, did she?"

Vanessa grabbed a fistful of the reverend's sleeve and tugged him toward the back stairs. Once they were out of sight of the wedding guests, she got right in his face.

"Go away!" She whispered fiercely. "You are ruining everything!"

"Vanessa," Beem began.

She interrupted saying, "Quiet!"

He tried again, quieter this time. "Vanessa, how did you get mixed up in this...this travesty? Christian Pagans! Who ever heard of such a thing? It's pure blasphemy!"

"You don't know anything," Vanessa stunned him with her vehemence. She'd never spoken to him this way before. "Pastor Darnell says we should try to respect the religious beliefs of others. He believes in the exchange of differing viewpoints. That's the only way we can learn to celebrate our similarities and acknowledge our differences!"

This was almost more that Rev. Beem could stand. His wife was quoting Darnell Davis, that no-account pretender. He could hear that idiot's voice in every word Vanessa had just said.

The reverend dropped his head and clenched both fists. How had he let this happen? While he had been thanking the Lord that Georgia had broken away from Davis, that...that serpent had gotten to Vanessa!

He clutched his wife's wrists and stared into her eyes, searching for signs of madness or possession.

"You are spoiling my first wedding!" Vanessa looked like she was going to cry.

The reverend was now sure that his wife had lost her mind. "Sweetheart, this isn't your first wedding," he soothed. "This isn't your wedding at all. You're already married—to me."

Vanessa jerked away from him, her anger flaring again. "You pompous ass!" she hissed. "I'm working. I have a career now. This is my first job as a wedding planner and you're making a mess of it!"

"Job? You're working? What happened to your bath salts business?"

She straightened her shoulders. "I have a *real* job now. I haven't used one dime of the money you've sent to me. It's in an account for Cory's education. Not long after you left, I got a job with Lori's Luxury Events. We're the hottest ticket in town; everybody wants Lori to do their weddings!"

"You planned this fiasco?" Beem still hadn't wrapped his head around the idea of Vanessa having a job. She'd only been a makeup consultant at a department store when he'd met her. At the time, she seemed glad to give it up for a life with him. Now she stood before him, yammering about her "career." *She* was responsible for the awful scene up stairs.

Vanessa actually stamped her foot at him. "It's exactly what they wanted. This 'fiasco,' as you call it, is a Fantasy Wedding. It's just one of the company's offerings. We can do Adventure weddings, Other World weddings—we even offer Time Travel weddings.

"Lori is incredibly creative and she hired me to work with her. She had faith in me, even though I didn't have any experience. This is my first time taking charge of a ceremony and you will not ruin it for me!"

He could hardly believe this was Vanessa speaking. His sweet little wife was raising her voice and publicly defying him. This was all Darnell Davis's fault!

They were both startled by a disembodied head floating in the gloom of the darkened stairwell. It was a young woman, barely out of her teens. "Excuse me Mrs. Beem, they're getting really nervous up here."

"Whoever you are, go away. We're busy!" Rev. Beem roared.

"That's my assistant," Vanessa said, coolly. "And we're done here, Albert."

The assistant's eyes widened as she started a sputtered apology. "Oh, I'm sorry; I see you're busy…"

"Get my cell and call Deanna Ramsey. Tell her this wedding cannot take place without Pastor Davis. He's the minister we requested and he is the one we expect. I will be right up to babysit the bride. Get some music going. We're not running that far behind and people are used to weddings starting late." The head floated away.

"That kind of ceremony does not belong in the house of God!" Rev. Beem thundered. He started up the stairs. "I'm going up there and throw them all out. You take off that ridiculous get-up and wait in my office. We need to pray!"

Vanessa spoke quietly. "If you take another step, I'll kill you."

The reverend refused to believe that he'd heard her at all. "What did you say?"

She repeated the threat. Speaking slowly, Vanessa made sure that he heard every word.

The reverend was rooted to the spot, staring down at his wife as if she had just turned blue and grown horns. Holding her head high and lifting the hem of her robe, Vanessa swept past him.

"I mean it, Albert. You were not invited to this wedding. You have no reason to be here. If you show your face up there again, you'd better hope the police get to you before I do!"

8

Dee reached up to run her hand through her tangled hair. One more thing to add to her to-do list: she'd have to somehow finagle an appointment with Mr. Bernard. The previous December, while following Deacon Batt, she'd had to get her shoulder-length hair cut very short. Though she liked the cut—it made her look years younger—it required more upkeep than she had time for so she had let it grow. This in-between stage wasn't working for her either.

More than anything else, Dee wanted to take a nap. Her day had started way too early and had been filled with too much excitement. Playing chauffeur to Pastor Darnell was proving to be more of a challenge than she had expected. Once this service was over, she would be happy to drive him to his own car.

Like the sand dunes wedding, this funeral was far out of Deanna's realm of experience. In all her life, she had never seen or heard of anything like it. Lawnvale Cemetery, in the southern suburb of Calumet Park, was a community landmark. Encompassing several city blocks, it included a sculpture garden and a walking trail. In winter, it was home to a herd of reindeer. With the addition of a Starbucks, it had actually been reviewed by a local newspaper as a "don't-miss destination."

Dee thought the grounds keepers must have used some kind of magic. There was no evidence of the storm anywhere she looked. No broken tree branches, no piles of litter blown up against the fences. Even the ground was dry.

Crossing River Jordan

As the pastor led the mourners in prayer, Dee smelled the enticing odor of grilled meat. Across the lane from the gravesite, the repast was being prepared, even as the goodbyes were being said. Beneath a blue canopy, several long tables were covered in red-and-white checked table cloths that flapped in the gentle breeze. The caterer and his busy crew placed covered silver serving dishes at one end of the row of tables and set up another table, forming a T at its head. This table held plates, plastic utensils, napkins, paper cups and large urns of coffee and other beverages.

It's a cookout, Dee marveled. Her grandmother, Miss Mattie, would have considered a funeral cookout the epitome of bad taste, but Dee reminded herself not to judge. She tried to view the event with an open mind.

First, it would save money—no need to rent a hall for the repast. Second, it would encourage young people to see death as more than a terrifying end to life. After all, this was like a party, with the deceased as guest of honor. It was just another way of celebrating a life. And it was a beautiful day to be outside. A funeral cookout—why not?

Pastor Darnell had just finished the benediction, when a teen-aged boy walked to the edge of the grave and turned to face the mourners. He cupped his hands around his mouth and began to "beat box" and rap.

"Yo Granddad, go Granddad. Cool OG, now you free. Followed yo' plan, now be with the Man. Never be another, word to the mother..."

Several of the family members, began to wave their hands in the air, clapping and calling out, "Go Ray-Ray, go Ray-Ray! Wooh, wooh! Wooh, wooh!" as the boy continued his tribute.

Finally, Ray-Ray did a few dance steps, spun around and went down on one knee, his arms crossed in front of his chest. "Peace!"

The faces of the mourners were a study in diversity. Some cheered, whistled and clapped. Others, especially the older members of the group, sat in stunned silence. Whatever had happened to the old-fashioned solemn occasion when, after the final prayer was said, a woman would scream and fall across the casket before being carried away, sobbing and calling for the dearly departed? So much more appropriate than funeral hip-hop!

After patting a few backs and shaking a few hands, the pastor and Dee walked in silence back to her car. They sat for a few minutes, each wrapped in thought. The pastor was the first to break the silence.

"Well, that was one of the most unusual ways of honoring a loved one that I've ever seen."

Dee took her cue from his thoughtful words. "Yes, I guess the child was honoring his grandfather in the best way he could. And the cookout—maybe that was something the man had enjoyed when he was alive."

Political correctness aside, Dee couldn't wait to sit down with Daisy and tell her about the "Barbeque Funeral with Floor Show!" Her phone rang before she had to struggle any more with controlling the laughter that threatened to bubble out of her.

Mentally, she congratulated herself—all day she had remembered to turn her phone off before the various ceremonies. More importantly, she also had remembered to turn it back on.

"Pastor, there's a problem at the church. They're holding up the wedding to wait for you. They refuse to let Rev. Beem perform the ceremony. I've got a bunch more messages, but I'll check them once we get to River Jordan."

"I guess getting my car will have to wait, too."

"On the bright side, you're in demand. People love you, Pastor Darnell." As Dee made her way down the winding driveway to exit the cemetery, she had to pause for a flock of geese waddling across the road toward a pond. She wondered if she could finish this day of driving without having to stop for gas.

"These people don't even know me," the pastor pointed out. "I'm not sure why they chose me or River Jordan. Maybe they live in the neighborhood."

He adjusted his seatbelt so that he could turn to face her. "You're right about one thing, Sister Ramsey. I can't continue trying to function without a full-time secretary. I'd better call whoever's in the office now and say we're on our way."

Crossing River Jordan

He listened quietly for a while as the phone in his office rang unanswered. Just as he was going to close his phone, he heard, "Hello, uh, I mean, River Jordan Church, Pastor D's office."

The pastor stared at the phone before putting it back to his ear. "Cory, is that you?"

Dee cried, "Cory who? Cory Beem?"

"Hey, Pastor D. What's up?"

"Cory, why are you answering my phone?"

"It was ringing."

"Why isn't Tiffany answering the phone?"

"She's not here."

"She's not in the office or she's not in the building?" Darnell was using up his entire quota of patience for the day trying to pull information out of Rev. Beem's youngest son.

"I don't know. I just came from my game—we won! I'm only here because my mom is having a wedding upstairs and I have to wait for her. I was walking past your office and the phone started ringing."

"Your mom is having a wedding? Your mom is getting married?" Darnell felt his head spinning.

"Hah, good one, Pastor! She's working, you know, running the wedding. It's her new job. I put her wedding on your computer—you know, on your schedule." He was very proud of himself.

Daylight was dawning. The pastor asked, "Cory, have you done this before? Answered my phone and put things on my schedule, I mean."

"Sure, all the time. I take good messages, too. Like a few weeks ago, I talked to a lot of people and I hooked you up, Pastor D. I got you a lot of jobs for today. Just because my stupid sister dumped you, doesn't mean you're not down with me."

"Thanks, Cory. Good looking out," Darnell said, drily.

"Hey, aren't you supposed to be here doing my mom's wedding?"

"That's why I called. Please let your mother know that I'll be there in a few minutes. We're just getting on the Dan Ryan. And Cory, don't worry about the phone anymore. Just let it go to voicemail."

Tiffany wasn't having the kind of dream that she could recognize as a dream—one in which she could tell herself something like, "You're not really the Queen of Cartoon Land and you're not married to Fred Flintstone."

She was enduring a sheet-drenching, throat-closing nightmare that was all too real. Flesh-eating vampire zombies were chasing her and Tremain, who was a fuzzy brown bunny. She fought fiercely, stabbing and hacking away at the hordes of hungry creatures, but every time she managed to break away, they always found her again. They always surrounded her and threatened to overwhelm her.

She was getting so tired. She didn't think she could run another step, when she found a train pulling out of a station. She ran to catch it. She could feel the hard concrete beneath her feet. She was chilled by the cold, iron railing as she latched on with one hand and pulled herself and bunny Tremain onto the safety of the train.

She was so exhausted she could hardly walk, but she stumbled into an empty compartment and closed the door. They'd made it! The train was moving them away from the terror and the monsters.

Breathing a sigh, she sank down onto a cushioned seat and closed her eyes, Then she felt it—the sense of being watched. She sprang to her feet, but it was too late. A hoard of vampire zombies clung to the window of the train! She whirled to face the compartment door and saw even more. The corridor outside was clogged with them, sharp-toothed and red eyed. They scratched at the window and came pouring through the door. It was a trap!

She screamed aloud, "It was a trap! It was a trap!" and struggled against the arms that were holding her.

Holding her, not binding her. "Ssshh, baby, it's a dream. Just a bad dream." Kendrick was right beside her. She turned to face him, laid her head on his chest and sobbed quietly for a time. And suddenly, she was done.

She pushed herself away from him and sat up. "This was a trap." She seemed to be talking to herself.

Crossing River Jordan

Kendrick sat up too, crossing his legs on the bed. "What do you mean? You don't mean living here, do you? Everyone here loves you and the baby."

"That's the trap." Tiffany scrubbed her hands over her face as if wiping away the last vestiges of the dream. "Don't you see? Coming here and finding you—all of you—and being part of this family was too good to be true. It was a trap that I fell into and now he's found me. He'll try to take my baby. He'll try to hurt me again."

The little bedroom was filling with people. Carl held Tremain, who giggled and tried to imitate the faces Carl was making. Daisy came around and sat next to Tiffany on the bed, forcing Kendrick to stand. Keisha, Steve and all six children crowded in.

Holding both of her hands, Daisy looked into the young woman's eyes. "Nothing can take you or Tremain from us if you want to stay. You are part of us now. We can't guarantee that nothing bad will ever happen to you again, only the Lord could take care of that. But God does send us angels. Remember, that was Pastor Darnell's sermon, just last week: 'For He shall give His angels charge over thee, to keep thee in all thy ways.'"

"Pastor said that they come looking like regular people," said Hope, Keisha's serious, quiet daughter. "He said that we should stop under, under..."

"Underestimating," Keisha prompted, proud of her little girl for paying such good attention to a sermon.

"Under-es-ti-mating God 'cause we don't know how the Lord does His work," Hope continued. "Anyone of us might be someone's angel."

"You're all my angels. Is that what you're telling me?" Tiffany allowed herself a tiny smile.

"I don't see any angels in here," Daisy laughed. "But people who love you are the next best thing."

They began to plan, as they helped put clothes, toys and keepsakes back in their proper places.

The preschool already had a list of people who could pick the baby up. Tiffany would make sure to stress that no one else could even visit Tremain at lunch times. Tiffany should never be alone at the church or anywhere else, as far as Kendrick was concerned. Daisy and Steve would make discrete inquiries around River Jordan to find out why Frank suddenly showed up.

"Tiffany, you never told Frank you were pregnant. Did you tell anyone else?" Keisha wondered just how he could know that he had a son.

"I never told anyone. And after that nurse told me, I never saw her again."

"So he may have been looking for you, not necessarily the baby," said Daisy. "I could keep him at home a few days, until we find out what's going on." Tiffany gave her a grateful smile.

Carl said. "We have to learn more about this Frank. Maybe I'll show up at his garage Monday for an oil change.

Daisy looked surprised. "You just changed your oil."

"Yeah, but I didn't change yours."

9

The decorating that Vanessa had done for the wedding was breathtaking. Dee had always thought that Vanessa's taste was a bit extreme, but in this case, extreme was required and it worked well. To his credit, Pastor Darnell didn't bat an eye when he was informed that he was performing a ceremony for Christian Pagans. He had never heard of the term and promised himself that he'd do some online research when he had time.

Aside from the extremely pregnant bride, the ceremony was quite similar to any other that he'd done. One exception was that the entire wedding party formed a circle around the pastor and the happy couple as they said their vows. Blessings were also offered by each parent and each member of the wedding party, before the vows were said.

The ceremony included many references to the elements and nature, but in the end, the pastor still pronounced the couple husband and wife and invited the new husband to kiss the bride. His favorite part of the ceremony was announcing the newly married couple to the guests. They moved down the aisle to the musical accompaniment of pan pipes, drums and tambourines.

The pastor went to his office, hoping that Deanna would be there and ready to give him a ride to his car. He planned to stop at home for a shower and a short nap before the Peak/Kent rehearsal. Instead of his "driver," he found a scrawled note. Detective Langston Hughes had been injured and Dee had gone to the hospital.

Darnell was about to call a cab, when the phone rang on another line. It was Chess.

"We really have to teach you to use your cell phone," she said in response to his greeting. "I've been trying to call you all afternoon."

"It's been a very strange day. And I wanted to thank you for helping with what turned out to be a very strange night."

"Maybe we can talk about last night later," she said. "I was calling because I've got to take you to your car."

"I appreciate the rescue last night but I don't want you to go out of your way..." Darnell was very embarrassed that she had seen him so drunk. He wasn't thinking only of his job and his faith, but he didn't want to lose her respect.

Plus, you were not cool, hummin' and marchin'—not cool at all. The voice of Darnell the Cool was faint, as if the pastor's alter ego didn't want to associate himself with such a loser.

Chess was still talking. "Did you even notice how light your keychain is? I have your car keys. I left in such a hurry that I forgot to leave them last night."

He hadn't noticed. Between his rude awakening, his pounding head and the insanity of the day, he hadn't had time to notice anything.

"I'll be there in about 20 minutes. See you then."

Thinking he would enjoy a few more minutes of the great weather, Pastor Darnell decided to wait outside until Chess arrived. He stood and stretched, yawning widely. Rev. Beem chose that moment to burst into the office. He stood in the doorway, holding a fistful of leafy decorations from the Fantasy wedding. The reverend vibrated with fury. He extended his arm, pointing a finger at the pastor.

"You are the spawn of Satan! You have torn apart my family and corrupted my wife and child. You are ruining this church with your insipid tolerance. We have to keep ourselves separate and apart from the world. You invite the world to come in and take over! Tolerance is not a mandate of the Lord!"

Pastor Darnell was too tired to react. He walked straight toward Rev. Beem, who stood blocking the door.

"I can take you," Beem yelled. "I faced down demons from hell itself when I performed Sister Ogilvie's exorcism. I wasn't afraid then"—he'd forgotten scrambling crab-like across the floor to get away from the tiny woman—"and I'm not afraid now!"

Beem's stentorian tone echoed around the room, doing nothing for the pastor's headache. Darnell stopped about a foot from Rev. Beem and said, "I have to leave now."

"What?"

"I have to leave. Now."

"You can't just...we have to settle...what's wrong with you?"

The pastor stepped around Rev. Beem and left him standing just inside the empty office.

"Close the door when you leave," he said, heading for the stairs.

Beem's rant had cemented Darnell's decision to wait for Chess outside of the church. As he walked past the sanctuary, he noted that the cleanup was going well. Cory had joined his mother's team of helpers and the fantasy forest was disappearing quickly. The sanctuary would be back to normal in plenty of time for Beem's Forgiveness Festival.

Once outside, he sat on one of the broad concrete steps and turned his face to the sun. Eyes closed, he listened to the sounds of the wind and the birds singing. Even the sound of traffic was soothing compared to Rev. Beem's bellows.

Man, you better watch your back, Darnell the Cool cautioned. *That dude is losing it.*

The pastor had to admit that Beem seemed even more out of step with reality than ever before. "Tolerance is not mandated by God?" What did that even mean?

Chess's shiny red Camaro slowed and stopped in the ministers' reserved parking area. She had the top down. "I always wanted to park here," she called. "Makes me feel all special!"

Crossing River Jordan

Darnell laughed as he slid into the passenger's seat. Chess knew just how to ease him past his discomfort after she had seen him at his worst. "You *are* all special, Ms. Allen. I'll never be able to apologize enough for last night. And I can't thank you enough for helping me out again today."

"You *can* thank me enough. Food always works. Feed me tonight," she said.

Chess felt a twinge of guilt; she hadn't been a very good friend. After Darnell's failed proposal, she hadn't come around very often or done anything to help him through his pain and disappointment. One reason was because she had been keeping busy. After her relationship with Tommy Odom came to its long-overdue end, she had thrown herself into work, taking on extra clients to fill her time and her thoughts.

The other reason was because she was afraid of herself. Shortly before she'd ended it with Tommy, she had kissed Darnell, knowing full well that he was in love with her friend, Georgia. It was purely a stress reaction and had happened just that once, but she'd felt that kiss down to her toes. Since than, she had spent a lot of time—far too much—daydreaming about it and what might have come after.

Chess couldn't think of a better way to destroy a friendship—one person fantasizing about the other and that person longing for someone *waaaay* over there. She needed to wait until she got herself under control before she could simply hang out with Darnell again.

Her showing up at Lee's the night before had been pure coincidence. She'd been working late, so late that none of the restaurants near her office were delivering anymore. On her way home, she remembered that the only things in her refrigerator were a wilting head of lettuce, half a bottle of white wine and a jar of Miracle Whip Lite. Grocery shopping had been on her to-do list for a week. Besides, she was too tired to cook and Lee's Unleaded Blues was burger heaven on Tuesday nights.

Hoping to get home before the storm, she stopped at Lee's. Instead of the usual quiet Tuesday night diners, Chess found a loud, but well-mannered bachelor party. She was shocked to see that the party included Pastor Darnell Davis, who right then was being anything but pastoral.

Darnell drunk was something to see. In trying so hard to make it seem that he wasn't impaired, he simply made matters worse. He spoke very s-l-o-w-l-y, but LOUDLY, as if he thought that people couldn't understand or hear him. He peered owlishly at everything because he was trying to focus his wavering vision. And the marching and humming—Chess wished that she had been able to use her cell phone for video, but she'd needed both hands to help Darnell and Langston, who wasn't much better off.

Once she'd gotten the pastor home, she found herself making excuses to hang around. That storm was pretty bad; maybe she should wait it out. Darnell looked so pitiful; she had to resist the urge to stay and take care of him. All excuses and all designed to create a big mess between her, Darnell and the absent Georgia Beem. As soon as she was sure that he was safe—not trying to cook, not drowning in the bath tub—she braved the wind and rain and took her untrustworthy heart home.

The bright light of day gave her a new perspective. The man was a good friend. Why should she go out of her way to avoid seeing him? Why couldn't two good friends just enjoy each other's company? It didn't have to mean anything more than that. After all, she wasn't trying to be anyone's sloppy seconds. The man was trying to heal and a true friend would be supportive of his efforts.

Chess was well aware that the pastor was ashamed of the spectacle he'd made of himself the night before. She knew from experience just how he felt because she'd certainly made a fool of herself with that kiss. She'd been so mortified that she had run all the way to Cabo San Lucas for nearly a month. She just wanted everything to go back the way it was between them—fun and free and easy. Helping him last night was the opening she needed.

"How about tonight?" Darnell was saying. "I know you're invited to Keisha and Steve's wedding and the rehearsal is tonight. Of course, there's a dinner afterwards. Come with me; be my "plus one.""

Chess laughed. "There's no "plus one" for a rehearsal dinner, Pastor, and you know it. Besides, that's a pretty sneaky way to have a date on the cheap!"

As the words rolled from her lips, Chess cringed. *Date*, she thought, horrified. *I said, "Date!"*

Darnell was laughing and didn't seem to notice. "I'll make it worth your while. We can leave before dessert and I'll take you to Zephyr's for ice cream."

Pastor Darnell surely knew how to seal a deal. Ice cream from Zephyr's was a great treat. The décor of the north side restaurant and ice cream parlor was awash in neon lights. Hip, young servers delivered generous portions of delicious food and ice cream-centric desserts. Chess would walk across hot coals for a pineapple sundae from Zephyr's.

She only had one question. "Do I have time to change?"

10

Dee's head was spinning. How could Langston be hurt? He was like an oak tree—massive, strong. His voice was so weak when he'd left the message. He hadn't even been alert enough to tell her what was wrong. Had he been shot, stabbed? His work with the fraud unit wasn't supposed to expose him to as much danger as say, narcotics or gang crimes. She had spent so much time telling him how wrong they were for each other, but he kept coming around. She'd never thought that he might suddenly not be there.

The hospital parking lot was jammed. She drove round and round, mentally ranting about the handicapped parking spaces—thinking of people who jumped out of vehicles and practically danced to their destinations, despite the special disabled parking permits dangling from their rear-view mirrors. Many of those folks didn't look disabled at all!

Deanna realized that she was being unfair—that many disabilities couldn't be identified just by looking. As a retired nurse, she knew better. She was merely reacting badly to the fact that something had happened to someone she thought of as indestructible. She couldn't find a place to park—it seemed that something was conspiring to prevent her from getting to him.

Finally! A young woman with several small children was loading them into a minivan. Dee sat, turn signal blinking, drumming her fingers on the steering wheel as she waited for the space. When they were finally loaded, the woman backed slowly out and pulled away. As Dee began to turn, a small sports car sped toward the spot. Dee accelerated and whipped her older, larger Impala in. The other driver sat right behind her, laying on the horn and shooting up her middle finger. She was much younger, maybe early 20s, Dee thought. She was wearing too much makeup and had a nest of weaved hair piled spectacularly high on her head.

Dee walked up and gestured for the driver to lower the window. Rap music poured from the window along with fumes of cigarettes and less legal substances. She was greeted with, "You got something to say, old woman? You betta come correct."

"I was just going to say that I hope you find a parking space soon. It's obvious you need to be in the hospital."

"Wha' choo trynta say, you old bi...?"

Dee couldn't let her finish; she had never suffered that particular insult lightly and she didn't have time punch this girl in the mouth. "I'm saying, you insipid little sow, that you're demented and could probably benefit from 28 days in the rehabilitation ward. I'm sorry if you didn't understand that, but I don't have time to give you a proper English lesson right now!"

Dee hurried away between the cars, leaving the girl sputtering and cursing in her wake. Ordinarily, she would never have confronted the driver of another car. These days something as insignificant as a glance could end in bloodshed or worse. But she'd had a tiring day and now she was afraid.

On one hand, she was afraid of what her reaction might be when she saw Langston. Even though she'd been a nurse for nearly two-thirds of her life and had seen some truly horrific injuries, everything was different when it involved someone you lo-...um, cared about. On the other hand, she was terrified that there would be nothing to see when she got upstairs, except perhaps a shrouded body being wheeled to the morgue.

She took a deep breath and moved slowly along with the revolving door.

Crossing River Jordan

■

She found him in an examining room. The doctor had just put the finishing touches on a cast on his left leg, a cast that went from his toes to just over his knee. Langston gave her a loopy smile. "Doctor, here she is. This is my girlfriend! The one I've been telling you about. Isn't she beautiful?"

Dee introduced herself adding, "We're just friends" and then realized that nobody cared. The hospital staff hustled, taking care of business. Dee tried to move out of the way, but Langston had a firm grip on her hand and refused to let go.

She was relieved to find out that all he had was a broken leg and some powerful painkillers. The adrenalin left her with trembling knees and she had no choice but to sit down on the bed with the detective. She planned to file all this unexpected emotion under "think about it later" but as soon as they were alone, she exploded. "You inconsiderate cretin, you scared me half to death! What were you doing, hurting yourself that way?"

Startled by her outburst, Langston tried to pat her on the back, but she wasn't in a mood to be soothed. She jumped up and began to pace. "Where was your partner? How could Javier let this happen to you? And another thing..." She didn't have another thing; all the panic-triggered energy suddenly left her. She sat next to Langston again, put her head in her hands and began to bawl like a baby.

Langston let her cry herself out, timidly touching her back from time to time. Finally, she looked at him and snapped, "What are you smiling at?"

"You're not acting like a girlfriend; you're acting like a *wife*." He gave a goofy giggle and drifted off to sleep.

■

Rev. Beem breathed a huge sigh of relief. Contrary to his assumptions, Vanessa and her crew had done a thorough job of restoring the sanctuary. There wasn't a stray vine or leaf in sight as the Forgiveness Festival attendees began to arrive.

Playing to a packed house, Beem's Forgiveness Festival began promptly at four o'clock with a literal bang. Rev. Beem projected footage of a prolonged WWII battle on a large screen. Explosions, gunshots and men's cries filled the sanctuary. Before the lights came up at the film's end, his ethereal voice quoted a tragic statistic.

"The estimated death toll in World War II was 62 to 78 million, making it the deadliest war in human history. How many of those people died with an unfulfilled desire to forgive and be forgiven? How many of those people would have made forgiveness a priority if they'd been given a second chance?"

A follow-spotlight framed the reverend's face as he stepped in front of the lectern. "I have sinned against so many in my life—against my God, my wife, my children, my church. And what have I done to deserve forgiveness? Nothing I do could ever be enough! Even if I got down on my knees and begged, even if I donated every dime to charity, even if I lived on an island and devoted the rest of my life to caring for the sick and outcast, it would never be enough!"

Suddenly the room filled with light. Wearing a pure white robe, trimmed with silver, Rev. Beem stood before the crowd and raised his arms. "Look for yourself in John 5:30. Even Christ Jesus said: 'I can of mine own self do nothing...I seek not mine own will, but the will of the Father which hath sent me.'

"It is the will of God that you forgive each other and that you be forgiven. The cross is the greatest symbol for the Lord's forgiveness. The Bible is the story of God's love and repeated forgiveness!"

He patted a perspiring brow. "My actions and intentions won't earn the Lord's forgiveness. Jesus stayed on that cross to ensure that every one of us already has the Father's forgiveness. The Bible tells us to repent and live! What our actions and intentions *will* do is open a door and make a path. Your actions will open a door that allows others to forgive you. Your intentions will lead you on the path to forgive others!"

Strains of Handel's *Messiah* played softly in the background. Rev. Beem moved down the stairs to the center aisle. "For the next four hours, in our workshops and lectures we will learn to use the tools of forgiveness. We will learn how to repent, how to make amends and how to accept forgiveness. We will explore ways to apologize and to accept apologies. We will examine forgiving others and forgiving ourselves."

Crossing River Jordan

The *Hallelujah Chorus* poured out of the speakers. The reverend roared, "Are you ready to be forgiven? Are you ready to open your hearts and forgive?"

"I want to be forgiven!" Ray Batt yelled from the back of the room. He ran down the aisle and fell on his knees before Rev. Beem.

Right on cue, Deacon Uttley shrieked, "Me too, Lord. I want to be forgiven too!" He collapsed halfway down the aisle and had to crawl the rest of the way.

Suddenly shouts came from every corner of the crowded sanctuary.

"Lord, forgive me!"

A young man with close-cropped hair threw himself to the carpeted floor. "Oh, Jesus, help me! Forgive me!"

"Oh, me too!"

"Lord, forgive me too!"

Soon, there wasn't a dry eye in the room. Everyone who was able to kneel was on his or her knees, hands to the heavens, calling on the Lord. Rev. Beem looked around, wishing that he'd thought to televise the event. How many other poor, tortured souls could he have reached? How many more would come to hear him speak after this?

I wish that Davis punk could see me in action! He smiled broadly, thinking, *I might just come out on top, after all.*

Things settled down in the Franklin household, moving from negative chaos to positive chaos. Tiffany decided to give it all to the Lord. She wouldn't run away from the first real home she'd ever had. She would trust and believe, though the thought of going back to the church was making her a nervous wreck. Frank could be at River Jordan right now.

Keisha's nerves hummed like a tuning fork; overtaking her completely. A part of her didn't believe in "happily ever after." She was on the edge of panic, waiting for something else to go wrong.

Keisha believed in "burning bushes," omens and signs. She had never quite gotten past the magical thinking stage—*if I count to five and blink twice, the traffic signal will change.*

Intellectually she knew better, but her heart always hoped. Tiffany's fear at seeing Frank had affected Keisha more than she was willing to acknowledge.

She also worried about having the rehearsal so late at night. Because of the Forgiveness Festival, they couldn't get into the sanctuary until 6:30 pm, a half hour after the Festival attendees left the sanctuary to break into small group activities. The children wouldn't get to bed for hours past their bedtimes.

She nearly jumped out of her skin when the doorbell rang. Keisha shook herself thinking, *snap out of it, girl! That Frank chump wouldn't dare show his face around here. That's probably just Auntie Dee at the door. She's the only member of the family who's not already here.*

She squinted through the peep hole and her voice came out as a squeak. "Miss Grandma!"

11

In her prime, Birdie Lee Streeter had been a butter-colored version of a 1940's bombshell. Her favorite picture showed her with long brown hair swept over one deep brown eye. She was posed to imitate one of her Hollywood idols, movie star Veronica Lake. Birdie had the "look, but don't touch" beauty that reeled men in before they could save themselves. Most men raced away just as fast. The truth was: Birdie Lee was as mean as a snake and as nutty as a fruitcake.

Now, the brown hair was completely silver and was worn in a twist fastened at the nape of her neck. She was still lean, with wiry muscles and ropy veins standing out on her arms and legs. The buttery skin had spent a lot of time outdoors and the sun had wrinkled and weathered it. The eyes were a little cloudy, but still sharp, as was the tongue.

Keisha threw open the door, watching as the woman turned to wave at the driver of an enormous eighteen wheeler. He blew her a salute on his horn, tipped his cap and drove away. Keisha wrapped the old woman in a hug. "Hey, Miss

Grandma, what are you doing here? We weren't expecting you until tomorrow!"

Birdie shrugged her off and ordered, "Girl, go get your mama!"

Long ago, Keisha and Kendrick had realized that Birdie Lee was special. They learned not to mind being called by the wrong names and being snapped at whether they had done anything wrong or not. Although it had been hard at first—it eventually stopped bothering them that Birdie insisted that Aunt Daisy was their mother. After all, she had also decreed that Uncle Carl was her younger brother, Walter, who had been dead for more than 30 years. Birdie called Carl, "Watty," her brother's childhood nickname.

Before Keisha could make a move, the hallway filled with children, peeking shyly or staring boldly at the older woman. She was a sight to behold in a red and white jogging suit and plaid platform shoes that were at least four inches high. The ropes of turquoise and silver chains draped around her scrawny neck must have weighed ten pounds. It was a wonder that she could stand upright.

Daisy pushed through the crowd. "Miss Mama! Where's Dee?" She peered over the smaller woman's head, searching for Dee's car. Not only wasn't Dee's car anywhere in sight, Daisy didn't see *any* unfamiliar cars. How had Birdie Lee gotten there?

"Well, that's what I want to know. Where is Deanna and when are you going to do something about those clothes you sold me?"

"We'll talk about those clothes later, I promise. Come on in; you must be tired after such a long drive." Daisy ushered Birdie Lee into the living room. "Miss Mama, where did you park your car?"

Keisha was making all kinds of faces, trying to let Daisy know that Birdie hadn't driven herself and that they should talk about that later too.

Birdie settled into a chair and rounded on Keisha. "Girl, when are you going to stop having babies? Daisy, didn't you teach her to keep her girdle on and both feet on the floor? Sweet Jesus, I counted nine or ten kids when I came in."

"Miss Grandma, you count better than that," Keisha said, airily. "There are seven children and only three of them are mine. Did you forget about Kendrick?"

"I don't forget nothin', missy! That's why I'm here about those clothes your mama sold me! They're all too long and I can't wear none of them."

Carl, Kendrick and Steve came upstairs from Tiffany's apartment. Kendrick carried Tremain in one arm and leaned over to hug Birdie with the other. "Miss Grandma! How's the prettiest grandma in the world?"

Birdie beamed. "Butterbean! Look at how tall you are! And who's that, another one of that girl's babies?"

"He's mine." Tiffany had come silently into the room and took her son from Kendrick. "I'm Tiffany Steele and this is my son, Tremain. We're both happy to meet you, Mrs. Streeter."

Tiffany would have known Deanna's mother anywhere. During many family gatherings, Birdie Lee's exploits were the highlights of conversation—a source of wonder and amusement. One of Tiffany's favorite "Birdie stories" told how, at 75 years of age, Birdie walked five miles to and from a job where, six days a week, she stood shucking bushels of corn by hand. She kept the job so she could hang out with her friends, a group of migrant workers who hardly spoke a word of English. Tiffany was happy to finally meet Birdie Lee in person. Plus, the visit distracted her from thoughts of Frank.

No one was sure why Birdie had christened Kendrick "Butterbean," but at least she always called him the same name. Keisha, when she wasn't "girl," could be anything that began with the letter 'K'—Kita, Kicker, Keeper, Kizzy. With the passing years, Keisha had become accustomed to gritting her teeth and responding appropriately.

Birdie Lee had long ago had given up trying to match the twins' offspring to names. They were referred to as "the babies" or "the kids." All except Wisdom. She had a soft spot in her heart for most males of all ages, but something about Wisdom touched her. Wisdom was her "Little Man," and she reached out to him now, showing a fist full of silver foil-wrapped chocolates.

"Little Man, I got more candy for you in my bag. You can share it with the other babies if you want to. You been a good boy?"

"Yes, ma'am. Thank you, Miss Grandma." Aware of his lofty status, Wisdom was always on his best behavior when Birdie was near.

Even though Birdie Lee probably wouldn't remember new names, Daisy went through the ritual of introductions anyway. She felt that it was important to model the behaviors she wanted the children to practice. They should definitely learn to respect their elders, even if those elders were a few bananas shy of a split.

Steve had met Dee's mom before at a church function some years earlier. "Ms. Streeter, you remember me, don't you? I'm Steve Kent."

Birdie looked him up and down. "I see stone in you. You're a strong man, just like my Watty," she pronounced and beamed at Carl. "I remember, you were supposed to come build me a wall to keep that river from flooding me out!"

"Yes, ma'am, you did ask me to do that. I told you I couldn't do such a big project." The adults were a bit surprised that she remembered Steve at all. "I called some friends in Michigan and they said they would take good care of you."

"Never did a gol-dang thing!" Birdie snapped. "My whole dang house liked to floated away!"

Steve looked alarmed and Daisy put a hand on his arm, shaking her head. "They did a very good job and charged Dee a reasonable price. Miss Mama lost about three feet of land along the river bank, but the wall stopped the erosion and everything is fine," she whispered.

The phone rang and Birdie called out, "It's probably for me!"

Daisy checked the caller ID. After "Dee, where in the world are you?" everyone surmised what they could from her comments:

"What?"

"Oh, my God!"

"Praise Jesus!"

"I understand."

Then Daisy dropped *her* bombshell. "Your mama is here. No, right here in my living room. We don't know how she got here. You're still going to come? Okay, we'll see you at the church." She placed the phone back on its base and took a deep breath.

"Langston got hurt at work..." She was interrupted by the family's gasps of shock and disbelief.

"He was just with us at Steve's party last night!" Carl said. "What happened?"

Daisy fanned the air, as if waving away their concerns. "It's not what you think—he fell down the stairs at the station and broke his leg."

"Oh, thank goodness!" Keisha was weak with relief. Then she realized what she'd said. "I mean thank goodness it wasn't something worse, like a shooting or something!"

Steve excused himself with a loud kiss to Keisha's cheek. "My folks are waiting at Midway Airport. I'll pick them up and meet you all at the church."

Carl looked at his watch and then at the children. "Time to go. Line up for inspection!"

Giggling and pushing, the kids formed a line and stood, with their hands held out, palms up. Carl made a great show of checking faces, ears and the backs and fronts of hands. Even Tremain had learned the routine and squirmed until Tiffany put him down so that he could line up with the others.

Hope was, as usual, a perfect little lady and he kissed her forehead. "You and Kiana will be the prettiest flower girls in the world," he said.

He looked in one of Knowledge's ears saying, "There's a bushel of potatoes growing in there," sending the children into fits of laughter. They all loved Uncle Carl's inspections and right after, he "forward, marched" them into cars.

Keisha's only thought was that she was one step closer to a future she had never known she wanted. Now, it was *all* that she wanted. Still, she couldn't shake the feeling that something bad was waiting just around the corner.

■

The Forgiveness Festival offered five workshops, each conducted by a different expert. Rev. Beem was the facilitator of "Forgiveness—What's in It for You?" which was quite well attended. Just down the hall, a psychiatric social worker led

"Forgiving, not Forgetting" which was almost as full. The large crowd had Rev. Beem's brain full of the possibilities of taking this show on the road. There might even be a chance for a book deal and a reality TV show!

He took his place in a chair and looked over the people seated in a circle. He knew a few from the church, but most were people he'd never seen before. This could be a gold mine. Talk about turning lemons into lemonade—his indiscretion was letting him turn sour grapes into champagne!

He was briefly distracted by an attractive young woman, who apologized for being late before taking her seat. Even with so much on his mind, Rev. Beem noticed how striking she was: curvy and statuesque with a creamy, copper complexion and short auburn hair. There was something about her—he just couldn't put his finger on it. Perhaps she had been a friend of Georgia's. She was about the right age.

He cleared his throat and began. "What's in it for you? Quite simply, everything. Forgiveness is not something you do for the other guy; it's something you do for yourself. Believe me; forgiveness is all about you!

"Letting go of the mistakes of the past brings you peace. Letting go of the anger and resentment can actually improve your physical health. Don't you deserve that? Don't you all deserve to be contented and healthy? Of course you do. Say it with me: I deserve to be happy and healthy!"

The reverend continued with his workshop, leading the participants through a series of writing exercises. "First, we're going to write to those we have wronged. Don't write about the offense you allegedly committed against this person. I want you to focus on how sorry you are and what you wish for that person's future."

He felt the auburn-haired woman staring at him. Her eyes had hardly left him. He was pleased to see that he was really reaching her. Perhaps she needed in-depth assistance. Maybe he'd ask her out for coffee after the workshop. She was a fine-looking woman and technically, he was a bachelor for a while, at least.

Toward the end of the class, the reverend led the group in a guided meditation designed to relax them. He closed his eyes, after instructing them to do the same. It had been a long, hectic day and he was glad to see it winding down.

He felt her before he opened his eyes. She was watching him with an intensity that made him rethink the coffee invitation. Now he was certain that he did not want to be alone with the woman.

The reverend was very relieved when she left the room as soon as he'd finished saying a prayer to close the session. He still had one more group to go, but his earlier good mood had faded. He couldn't put his finger on it, but there was something about that woman that just wasn't right.

■

No one had to go to the bathroom before they left the house, but as soon as they entered the church, the urge hit.

"Mama, I gotta go!" Wisdom began dancing in the aisle, just inside the sanctuary doors.

"I gotta go, too," Kiana chirped.

"Okay, everybody's going right now, because when we start rehearsing, we won't be stopping until we're done," Keisha warned. "We'll be right back!" she called, waving to Pastor Darnell who stood with Steve and his parents at the front of the room.

She and Kendrick led the children to the restrooms in the basement. Shooing the kids in, she pulled her twin to the side and leaned into his arms.

"Kendrick, I think I'm going to have a stroke! I've never met Steve's parents before; what if they hate me? Steve would never marry someone his folks hate."

Kendrick hugged his sister hard. "Nobody could hate you, Keisha Peak. You're my little sister and I'll beat them up for you."

She laughed at his repeating something he had said to her many times as they were growing up—it had become a kind of code phrase. A family joke for years was Kendrick's insistence that his 11-minute head-start made him Keisha's "older" brother.

Hope screeched, "Kiana!" and Keisha rushed to make peace. Kendrick, noting that the boys were too quiet, turned to push the door open when he heard his name. Later, he wouldn't be able to say for sure if he'd really heard anything or just imagined it. He looked down the hall and straight into the eyes of his ex-wife.

"Lynn?"

The woman at the end of the hall froze and then she was caught up in a mass exodus of people pouring out of the workshops.

The boys came tumbling out of the restroom and latched onto their mother, who headed up the back stairs to avoid the surging Forgiveness Festival crowd.

Kiana was tugging one hand. "Daddy! Daddy, Hope is being mean. She hollered at me!"

Kiera had the other. "Daddy, let's go. They'll start the wedding without us!"

"They can't start without the bride," he assured his eldest daughter. "And she won't start without her flower girls." Hand-in-hand-in-hand, they headed for the stairs.

Kendrick felt foolish. Lynn would never cut her hair that short and that woman's hair was the wrong color. No way would he mention his ex to Keisha now. She was already as nervous as a cat in a leaky row boat.

12

Dee couldn't believe the day she was having. If it had been a movie, it would have been called "One of The Longest, Most Tiring, Scariest Days in the History of the World." She could only remember one other time that she'd been as afraid as she'd been when she gotten the call about Langston.

Many years before, when her children were young and she was between husbands, she'd gotten a call at work. It was her 14-year old daughter, Elise, crying so hard that Dee could hardly understand her.

Elise and Paul, her ten year old brother, had taken a forbidden short-cut on the way to the park. Crossing the railroad tracks and moving through the tall grass that grew on either side, they'd disturbed a bee hive. Both of Dee's children and the friend with them had been stung several times.

As a nurse, Dee had been required to handle many frightening situations calmly, but none had involved her own children. Her children had never been stung by bees before and all she thought of was anaphylactic shock and immediate death! She went to pieces before managing to call Daisy, who rushed right over and made sure that other than a few painful bumps and bruises, everyone was fine.

Dee arrived at River Jordan for what should have been an enjoyable event. Though she wasn't an official member of the wedding party, Keisha wouldn't have dreamed of excluding Auntie Dee from any facet of her one and only wedding. Dee regretted that the scary portion of the day had extended into the night—she still had to deal with her mother.

Forgetting that her mother's untimely early arrival meant that Dee wouldn't have been home anyway, she wondered why Birdie Lee had gone to Daisy's house instead of coming straight to Dee's? How had Birdie Lee gotten to the city without her car?

Dee stood aside to let some of the Festival goers pass through the doors. Then swallowing the fear of what havoc her mother might be wreaking on the rehearsal, she straightened her back, squared her shoulders and went inside.

Keisha was trembling so hard her teeth chattered. She couldn't figure out who this person was. Keisha Peak wasn't afraid of anybody! She didn't bite her tongue or bow her head or walk two steps behind anyone on this earth. Keisha Peak talked to Jesus every morning, every night and a lot of time in between. If she could talk to the Lord, she could talk to anyone! But her words and her confidence failed her as she approached Steve's mother and father.

Steve was a perfect blend of both of his parents. He had his father's muscular build, though Steve stood several inches taller. His face, eyes and hair were his mother's—a round face with high cheek bones, soft brown eyes and thick black hair. Mr. Kent's shining bald head made her wonder if Steve would lose his hair when they were older. She wouldn't mind a bit; Mr. Kent was a fine old dude!

She shouldn't have worried about a thing. In the Kent family, the apple didn't fall far from the tree. The apple rolled right under it. Mr. and Mrs. Kent were as warm and welcoming as any in-laws Keisha could have wished.

"M-mister Kent?" She held a shaking hand out to him. He pulled her into a bear hug.

"Finally, I get a chance to meet you in person! Steve sent us pictures of you and the kids, but they don't do you justice—any of you! You're getting yourself a beautiful family, boy!"

Keisha was so pleased by Mr. Kent's words and actions that she wanted to cry, but it wasn't over yet. She turned to Steve's mother, who moved to her and took Keisha's face in her cool hands. They were about the same height; Keisha was looking straight into Mrs. Kent's eyes. What she saw there caused her own eyes to fill.

"We've been waiting for you for a long time." Mrs. Kent's voice was much softer than her husband's. Keisha got the feeling that she was intentionally speaking so only Keisha could hear. "Steven is as much in love with you as Martin was with me when we married. It's the most amazing gift that I can imagine."

"Yes, ma'am, I know," Keisha spoke very softly, too.

"Well, don't you forget that you're a gift as well—to him and to us. Steven is happier than we've ever seen him and we've always wanted a bunch of grandchildren!" She kissed Keisha on both cheeks.

Keisha couldn't help herself; the tears leaked from her eyes. "Please come and meet them." She escorted the grandparents-to-be to meet the children, who sat with Tiffany and Kendrick on the front pew and were being deceptively quiet.

At last, all the introductions were made and in the following seconds of silence, Birdie Lee narrowed her eyes and asked Ruth Kent, "Where did you get that sweater? I got a sweater just like that at home."

Dee faked a coughing fit. To distract her mother, she asked, "Mama how did you get to Daisy's house? You were driving in from the cabin the last time I talked to you."

"That old car stopped dead at the gas station, so I gave it away." Dee began coughing again.

"What's the matter with you? You need some water or something?" Birdie asked. Dee shook her head.

"That's how I met Jesse. He gave me a ride in his truck. He was on his way to somewhere in Iowa to drop off some kind of equipment—I forget what. He wanted to date me, but I told him he could be your boyfriend 'cause he was too young for me. He said he'll be back through here in about three days."

Dee clapped her hands over her ears. She was afraid her brain might leak out.

"You'll like him," Birdie promised her daughter. "He was good looking and he didn't smoke and he had some real nice manners."

Silently asking for the Lord's help, Dee made a mental note to call Officer Pink in Three Rivers and have him find out what he could about the car Birdie may or may not have given away. Maybe he could find out something about an over-the-road trucker named Jesse, too.

Pastor Darnell positioned everyone for the processional. Keisha suddenly felt the absence of a wedding coordinator. She thought it would be a waste of money—after all, she knew exactly what she wanted and how she wanted it. Chess stepped in to help, coaching the flower girls (she told them to pretend they were setting butterflies free) and reminding ring-bearer Knowledge to slow down so he wouldn't race past them.

Keisha had never planned to get married. After Hope had been born, she figured two kids equaled no husband. Men didn't want ready-made families—who could blame them? A wedding hadn't been something she though much about; the big fairy tale ceremony was something for other people—rich people and characters in books and movies. That stuff didn't happen to practical, realistic Keisha Peak—*Holy cow, I'm getting married!*

Right after the proposal she got to work, pouring through magazines, reading books on wedding etiquette, watching televisions shows. Keisha studied, taking note of what she liked but also keeping track of what she didn't like. She thought that the demanding, shrieking brides on cable TV shows were ridiculous. What kind of pitiful man would want to marry one of those women?

Keisha had drawn up a list of what she needed to make her wedding special. Steve told her the plans were all up to her.

Crossing River Jordan

"We'll do this anyway you want. We can elope or have a big ceremony. We'll wear what you want and have it where you want. Even if we have to wait a while to save up for it, you decide what will make it special for us."

Steve was more than she had ever dreamed of and she didn't want anything else. Keisha wasn't going to wait one minute longer than she had to. It had taken her about two months to pull everything together.

Aunt Daisy had tried to help, but her suggestions were things she or Auntie Dee had done. Keisha loved both women, but with nine marriages between them, neither woman seemed qualified to give relationship advice—even though Aunt Daisy and Uncle Carl *had* found their way back to each other.

As soon as the church elders came back from their trip, Keisha planned to talk to the Taylors. Theirs was the marriage Keisha hoped for: 50 years of love and friendship. Mrs. Taylor told her that she and Henry had gotten married right after World War II. They'd had a simple ceremony in her parents' parlor with just the preacher, their families, and a few friends. At the time, Keisha wasn't certain what a parlor was, but it sounded perfect to her.

Aunt Daisy put her foot down at the idea of having the wedding in the Franklin home. "I know you don't want a large wedding, but it's just too small here. You don't have to invite a lot of people, but what about Steve's family and friends? Just get married at River Jordan. That *is* Steve's home."

Finally, Keisha could accept one of Daisy's ideas! The wedding was scheduled to take place as soon as the afternoon service ended. Keisha and Steve wanted the unconventional ceremony so that all of their River Jordan family could attend.

Daisy had even disagreed with Keisha's color choices until Dee pointed out, "Look at her colors: yellow, white and black. Yellow and white"—she waited for her sister to catch on. Daisy stood with her hands on her hips and a frown on her face.

"The colors of *daisies*," Dee continued. "She didn't shut you out. It's all about you!"

Daisy finally saw it: Keisha's dress, white with a yellow bodice and sash and the bridesmaid's dresses—yellow with white sashes—all referenced the daisy. Steve and the groomsmen would wear traditional tuxedos and white shirts, with yellow bow ties and cummerbunds.

Uncle Carl had surprised Keisha the most. Staying well out of the line of fire as Keisha and Daisy battled over every small detail, he had insisted on one thing, "You're my princess and I want to have a dance with you in a ballroom."

He had secretly rented the ballroom in the stone field house at Promontory Point just as soon as he'd found out the wedding date. The Point was a man-made peninsula that jutted out into Lake Michigan, near 53rd Street. It boasted a gorgeous view of the sky line

In addition to terraced stone steps leading down to the lake, there was a fountain and a stone council ring that was often used as a fire pit. Keisha had never considered the site, but she was delighted that her Uncle had chosen it for her. The reception at the Point was invitation only; they could only afford 60 guests, as the young couple insisted on paying for the catering themselves.

Steve kept his promise, agreeing to every one of Keisha's ideas, but he had one secret. He hired a horse-drawn carriage to convey Mr. and Mrs. Steven Kent from the church to the reception. The girl was going to get some fairy tale whether she wanted it or not!

■

They went through the rehearsal twice. The second time, everyone knew when to enter, where they were to stand and how Pastor Darnell would conduct the ceremony. There was no reciting their own vows. "The old ones are good enough for me," Keisha said.

Steve gave her an arched eyebrow. "Oh, so what are you going to say if the pastor tells you to obey me?"

"I'll say 'I will if he will'," she said and squealed when he grabbed her and twirled her around.

"That girl ain't never obeyed nobody, not even when we were little girls," Birdie told Dee.

"Mama, who is that?" Dee wondered who her mother thought Keisha was.

"Girl, what's wrong with you? You don't know your own auntie? That's my sister, Nancy!" Birdie glared at Dee.

Only Chess seemed to notice Darnell covering a yawn. He caught her looking, gave a sheepish grin and mouthed "Zephyr's."

She couldn't help but feel for the man. Even though he'd truly earned the hangover he'd started out with, he had admirably met all of his obligations and was still ready to keep a promise to her. Maybe she'd give him a break. She could make up an excuse for skipping dessert and let him get home to bed. But—well, it was *Zephyr's*. She'd think about it more over dinner.

As they left the sanctuary, everyone's mind seemed to be focused on food. Fuelled by the hyper-active energy that tired children use to keep themselves awake, the children chattered about what they planned to order. Darnell felt that he could finally see the end of the long tunnel that had been his day. *A nice meal with friends, ice cream with Chess and then home to bed.* He was being rewarded, though he didn't feel that he deserved to be.

They were climbing into cars when Tiffany suddenly remembered. "Oh, my phone! I left it in the office. I'll be right back!"

Steve caught up with her on the steps of the church. "You need these." He handed her the keys.

The church was her second home. Tiffany wasn't afraid to walk through the dimly-lit hall and down the stairway. She was pretty sure that she'd put her cell phone in the drawer where she and Keisha kept their personal belongings while they worked. She found it right where she thought it would be.

Tiffany hated drawing attention to herself. She preferred being in the background as much as possible. Having the entire family gathered around her today was at once comforting and embarrassing. She didn't like being the reason that everyone had to wait.

She headed back toward the stairs, stopping suddenly when she heard a noise coming from the dining hall. She wasn't sure what to do. Should she investigate or go for help?

She'd already made a hysterical scene once today. They would send her to a loony bin if she came screaming out of the church for little or no reason. So, she walked forward slowly, listening for the sound to repeat itself.

Maybe she had just imagined it. No, there it was again. It wasn't the small sound of a mouse scampering or even of a trapped bird fluttering. It was a metallic click—the sound of a door closing.

Tiffany tiptoed closer, realized she was holding her breath and let it out slowly. There was a light in the kitchen for just a moment and then it was gone.

"Hello!" she called. "Is someone th..." She reached into the room and flipped the light switch.

"What are you doing in here?" Rev. Beem bellowed.

Tiffany choked back a scream. "Reverend, you scared me half to death!"

Now she was angry. Not only had he frightened and then yelled at her, but she just plain didn't like the minister. "I heard noises in here and I came to see if everything was okay! What are *you* doing here?"

The bluster left Rev. Beem and he looked like a tired, older man. He was padding around without shoes. His shirt tail hung out, the tie was gone and his collar was undone. He had removed his cuff links and his shirt sleeves were rolled.

"I didn't want to go back to that apartment after the Festival. It was a big success and I wanted to celebrate it with my wife, but of course I couldn't do that. I decided to come in here for a snack."

Then she saw the saucer on the stainless steel counter. Crackers and cheese. Rev. Beem had been telling the truth. Tiffany didn't have time to respond before there was another noise.

"That's the sound I heard," she said. "Sounds like it's coming from one of the new storage rooms."

Steve had worked diligently to improve River Jordan's storage facilities. With the stalled economy, more and more people were seeking assistance at the church's food pantry. That assistance included meals made for the pre-school, the Golden Age senior's program and the after school and Saturday School kids. The Jesus in Action ministry offered nutrition and cooking classes. In short, food was central to River Jordan Church (and to Steve's fiancée) so he'd made a point of keeping the food preparation area up to commercial code.

Crossing River Jordan

The new pantries were climate-controlled and state of the art. Both had stainless steel doors with vacuum seals. The doors could be locked, but that wasn't the River Jordan way. The sound Tiffany had heard was of one of the pantry doors closing.

Holding his finger to his lips, Rev. Beem moved toward the pantries. They were set in the wall, side-by-side at the back of the kitchen. Tiffany moved to stand beside him in front of the door. They each grabbed a handle and the reverend whispered, "One, two, three!"

They pulled the doors open. The only light came from the kitchen behind them, so the pantries were shrouded in shadows. Tiffany reached inside, patting the wall to locate the light switch. Before she found it, she heard a muffled noise from the other pantry.

"What?" she asked, going to the other door. "Rev. Beem, what did you say?"

She felt something move to her left. Then her head was covered and she was couldn't breathe! Her eyes, nose and mouth were clogged immediately and she fell to her knees trying to reach her face, clawing at the bag that was covering her head.

Where was Rev. Beem? Why wasn't he helping her? Was *he* doing this to her? Tiffany couldn't scream. *Not this time*, she decided. *I'm not going down without a fight!*

Reaching past her head, she tried to claw at the hands that were tightening the bag around her neck. Her nails slid off; she couldn't dig into skin. Red and black dots danced behind her eyelids. She felt herself losing the fight to stay conscious. She couldn't tear the bag away from her face!

Falling onto her side, she thought about Tremain. She hoped someone would tell him that his mommy had loved him more than anything. She listened to the thuds of her heart beating slowly, slowly.

Suddenly the covering was tugged from her head and Tiffany was yanked up, shaken and pounded on the back. She coughed, sputtered—she could breathe! Oh, thank God, she could breathe!

She began to struggle, fighting to get away. What she heard was a kind of chanting, something repeated over and over, but she couldn't make out what was being said.

"You're all right." She could barely understand the words. Her ears were clogged "Tiffany, baby, it's me. It's Kendrick. I've got you and you're all right." He gently wiped her face and she could see once again.

She was covered in flour. It was everywhere. She tried to stand, but Kendrick held her fast. She tried a choking whisper, "The reverend!"

"He's over there. We got to him in time, too," Kendrick assured her.

So Rev. Beem hadn't tried to kill her. Someone else had attacked them both!

"I hear the ambulance; they're almost here," Kendrick said. "Just be still until someone can check you out." He had flour all over himself, too.

"Water, please," Tiffany rasped. Her throat was on fire. Though she'd tried not to swallow any of the substance covering her mouth, some had gone down her throat.

Very soon, there were people walking and talking all around her. She was strapped to a gurney and, as the EMTs rolled her out of the kitchen, she heard, "not one useful foot print. Probably 20 people stomping around down here."

Brushing flour from her own hair, Deanna leaned over Tiffany. "You'll be fine, Tiffany. You're a strong girl. At least no one had to give *you* mouth-to-mouth!" She made a "just sucked a lemon" face and then laughed.

It was a laugh of relief and release. They had come so close to losing Tiffany and Rev. Beem. Dee pressed her back against the wall to let the two gurneys move out into the hall.

This was nothing like the acts of vandalism or attacks on church property that they'd endured last year. The reverend and Tiffany had been lured into the pantry. Someone had knocked Beem out and covered his head with a bag of flour. Tiffany's head had been encased in a bag of flour, too, that was then secured around her neck with a long strip of plastic. Someone had just tried to commit murder at River Jordan Church!

13

Keisha, Daisy and Birdie Lee sat in one car with some of the children. Hope, Wisdom and Knowledge were in Steve's car with his parents. Mr. Kent had insisted, saying that he wanted to spend time with his new grandchildren. Keisha was grateful to her in-laws-to-be for providing a distraction for her frightened children. Birdie Lee had given chocolate to each child, prompting Daisy to wonder just how much candy the old woman kept hidden on her person.

Keisha was waiting for a quiet moment alone so that she could fall apart. She knew a crying jag was due, but now was not the time. It was wrong of her, she knew, but when Tiffany had taken such a long time in the church, the first thing Keisha thought was that there was a problem and it was going to spoil her wedding.

Now she had to feel guilty for that bit of selfishness. Then she wondered how her almost in-laws would feel about her if they knew and what Steve would think of her. No way would he marry anyone who was so petty and self-centered. Her mood sank lower still.

What kind of friend was she—and what kind of mother? She hadn't given one thought to how this was affecting the children! She looked at them now, their eyes round and wide, staring at the flashing lights of the police cars and emergency vehicles. The poor things were hungry and tired; Tremain and Kensha were frightened by the loud noises as well.

She still didn't know what exactly had happened. They all had their windows down, chatting and laughing as they waited for Tiffany to find her phone. Steve checked his watch a couple of times and told Kendrick, "Maybe you should call her. She'd find the phone if it rang."

Remembering how terrified his girl had been just this afternoon, Kendrick got worried. She'd been in there long enough to have found the phone or come out without it. "I'll be right back," he said as he got out of the car.

Steve also got out of his car. As the sense of foreboding spread, Carl said firmly, "Everybody else, stay here. We don't want you kids running around in there, making us have to come find you, too."

Seeing what was happening, the pastor turned off his engine. He and Chess were each driving their own cars; he'd had enough of being chauffeured for one day. Darnell promised Chess, "This will only take a minute," as he walked past her car.

Dee had already started toward the building, looking over her shoulder to say, "Mama, please help Daisy keep an eye on the boys." Birdie was halfway out of the car.

"I didn't come all this way to be nobody's babysitter. If I wanted more kids, I'd have some," Birdie Lee complained, but she settled back into the car with Daisy and took Tremain onto her lap.

By the time Dee got down the stairs, the four men had already found Tiffany and Rev. Beem. There hadn't been any attempt by their attacker to hide what had happened; it was as if they were supposed to be found. From the looks of things, they weren't supposed to have been found alive.

Kendrick held Tiffany across his knee, pounding her back with the heel of his hand. The remnants of the 20-pound flour sack lay on the floor by his knee. Rev. Beem's sack hadn't been tied on and Steve had simply pulled it off of his head, but the reverend wasn't moving and didn't seem to be breathing at all. The pastor and Steve had turned the reverend so that he was facing upward, but they weren't sure what else to do. Dee knelt beside them, already in nurse mode.

"Who else knows CPR?"

Carl said "I do!"

"I'll clear his airway," Dee instructed. She got right to work on the reverend, not thinking about anything but what had to be done to save the man's life. Carl was on his knees next to her, starting chest compressions and counting as she worked to breathe life into Beem.

The pastor was on the phone with an emergency dispatcher. He gave the address and said, "There are two injured people in the basement of River Jordan Church. One isn't breathing." As soon as he was told that help was on the way, he got to his feet.

"Whoever did this may still be around!" He ran from the room to begin the search.

Steve saw that he was only in the way. "I'm going to see if everyone's all right outside and let them know what's happening. Then I'll catch up with Pastor Darnell. I hope whoever did this *was* stupid enough to stick around to watch!"

■

Ever since Pastor Darnell had mentioned in a sermon the previous year that God was always working, Dee had gotten in the habit of thanking the Lord first, in all situations.

After forcing another breath into Rev. Beem's mouth, she gasped, "Thank God!"

Carl sat back on his heels and looked at the reverend's inert body with hope. Frustrated, Dee shook her head, blew again and then said, "Thank God!"

Carl resumed compressing Beem's chest, looking at Dee in confusion.

Kendrick caught on, murmuring "Thank you, Lord. Thank you, Lord" again and again as he wiped Tiffany's face.

Dee glanced at him and smiled before taking another deep breath. They heard the pounding of footsteps in the hall and the crackling static of two way radios. Help had finally arrived. Gratefully, Deanna and Carl scrambled to the side, so that the emergency medical technicians could take over. After they'd gotten the reverend connected to an oxygen mask and checked his vitals, Dee told them what she and Carl had done. She knew it had to go in both the EMT and police reports.

Now that Dee had a moment, she was able to put on her other hat—Deanna Ramsey, amateur detective. She took in every action of the first police officers on the scene. One was moving around the kitchen making notes, while the other was talking to Carl. Dee wanted to do her own examination of the room, but she knew she should be quiet and still, making herself as unobtrusive as possible. If she was being too curious, the police would haul her away from the crime scene before she had a chance to look around.

The strip that had tied the bag over Tiffany' head was torn from a black plastic garbage bag. It lay curled like a sleeping snake on the floor. Dee could see the reddened skin on Tiffany's neck where the plastic had been yanked tightly to hold the bag in place.

The officer was right—everyone had walked over and through every trail of flour. There'd been no way to avoid walking all over the prints. Steve and Kendrick saw Tiffany lying on the floor of the pantry and had charged right in. They hadn't even noticed that there was a trail of flour leading from the kitchen.

Dee looked around as best she could from her vantage point on the floor. Rev. Beem had been unconscious. Had he hit his head as he fell? Then there should have been a wound of some kind on his face or the front of his head. No, he had fallen forward, so there was probably a baseball sized lump on the back of his head that she hadn't noticed with everything else going on.

She spotted the weapon, just as one of the officers said, "The reverend is a big guy. Whoever hit him was either pretty big or was strong enough to swing a mighty big stick."

"Officer, I think it was a mighty big frying pan. I see the handle sticking out from under that bottom shelf." As she pointed, a gloved police officer retrieved one of the cast iron skillets that the River Jordan cooks favored.

"I don't see any blood or hair, but the techs may find something. Maybe whoever did this didn't want to kill him, but wanted to take him down."

"I've got to get to the hospital," Kendrick insisted to the officer who was questioning him. "Can't we do this tomorrow or something?"

"There are probably detectives at the hospital already," Dee said. Even if she hadn't grilled Langston and Javi so thoroughly on police methods, she would have remembered the investigative process from watching hours of detective shows on television. "They'll probably want to talk to us, too."

The officers agreed to follow them to the hospital for more questions and they were separated from the crime scene investigation techs, who had closed off the kitchen with yellow crime scene tape. The church was alive with officers searching through every corner and cupboard. Steve and Pastor Darnell were enlisted to escort the officers, making sure they didn't miss any possible hiding places, especially the series of secret rooms that had been discovered the year before.

■

Crossing River Jordan

The night had taken a 180-degree turn—from a family celebrating new beginnings to the investigation of how and why two people nearly had their lives ended. Keisha was holding on by a slender thread. Even Birdie Lee noticed that her eyes glistened with unshed tears and she was speaking with a weirdly cheery tone.

"Kipper, everything is gonna be just fine; you wait and see," Birdie said, patting Keisha's shoulder.

It was now well after 11 o'clock. The youngest children had fallen asleep amid paper cups and little red-and-white cardboard containers. Chess had ordered from the neighborhood Chuck's Clucks Chicken Shack and had food delivered to the church parking lot. It had taken a lot of talking to convince the officers who were first on the scene that they didn't know anything and hadn't seen anything.

Daisy had gotten so incensed that she'd invoked the name of Sean DeLuna, the police lieutenant over Langston's unit. She was furious at being detained in the parking lot with seven exhausted children and a crazy old lady, none of whom knew anything that could help. It didn't do any good; Lt. DeLuna wasn't in charge of the Violent Crimes division.

Finally, rescue arrived in the forms of Myron Calvin and Volanda Merrill, two police officers who were also members of the church. They had just come on shift and had rolled out as soon as they heard chatter about the church on the scanner in their squad car.

Volanda waved at the little cluster of cars as she went inside to see what was happening. Myron exchanged a few words with Daisy. Very few.

"What's up, Sister Franklin?"

"We've told them a thousand times: We never left the cars. We didn't see anything. We need to get these children home to bed!"

"Got it," he said and walked up to a group of officers clustered on the church steps. Moments later, he was back. "Got your plates. Go home."

Their hero walked back to join the river of blue moving into and out of River Jordan.

Chess volunteered to drive the Kents to their hotel, leaving Steve's car in the lot. She told herself she'd go home to bed after that. She would *not* go to St. Benedict Hospital. She

97

would *not* concern herself with Pastor Darnell or anything else at River Jordan, other than its finances. She would *not* wait up for a phone call from a man who had so many responsibilities in his life and so much love in his heart for another woman.

■

Daisy and Keisha were both too busy tending to others to think of anything else. Daisy first made sure that Birdie Lee was comfortable in the guest room. Then she went upstairs to help Keisha with the children.

Tremain couldn't sleep alone in the garden apartment, so Keisha made a barricade of pillows on her bed and put him in the center. He slept right through being carried into the house, having chocolate and chicken grease wiped from his hands and face and being undressed for bed.

As tired as they were, Wisdom and Hope did their best to see that the younger kids got to bed. Daisy noticed and smiled, thinking, *They're such good kids, but I'd like to see them have a little more 'child' in their childhoods*. The drama in the twins' lives was causing their children to grow up faster than Daisy liked.

Daisy insisted that Keisha lie down with the children.

"You know the little ones will be up before day in the morning, in spite of being awake half the night. You sleep now"—she held up her hand to stop Keisha from protesting. "As soon as I hear something, anything, I'll come up and tell you."

At long last, the house was quiet. Daisy turned Miles Davis' *Sketches in Spain* CD down low and leaned back in her favorite chair with half a glass of pinot noir. She knew that someone would call when they could. She would just have to wait.

14

St. Benedict was as busy at midnight as it was at high noon. In a city like Chicago, someone was always trying to harm someone else and the parade of injured never stopped. Dee was tempted to jump in and help—she'd kept her nursing license current—but she knew she'd just be in the way. The hospital staff functioned smoothly, like a clockwork machine, and an extra cog would make everything come to a grinding stop.

The detectives had the five of them—Dee, Steve, Pastor Darnell, Kendrick, and Carl—sequestered in a small waiting room on the floor where Tiffany and the reverend were being tended to by various medical personnel. They sat in hard wooden chairs around a small wooden table at the far end of the room. Dee looked longingly at the comfortable cushioned chairs and the sofa lining the walls on each side of the room.

Every so often someone would come in to ask a health-related question or give them an update. A few of the staff members knew Dee or remembered the pastor from time spent visiting Deacon Thompson when he was recovering from his heart attack.

A Detective Lucas, whom Deanna vaguely remembered from her undesired visit to Lieutenant DeLuna's office, began asking questions. What made him memorable to Dee was his resemblance to the old television detective, Kojack. The main difference was that Kojack sucked lollipops. This detective chewed pencils. Dee watched him with concern; she couldn't remember if graphite poisoning was like lead poisoning.

"So what about enemies?" he asked. "Who would want to hurt a minister and a member of his church?"

The five of them all looked at each other. No one wanted to speak ill of the nearly dead.

The silence hung in the air for a full minute before Dee couldn't stand it any longer.

"This is ridiculous. Everybody knows about Rev. Beem and those pictures. We're not telling tales out of school."

"Pictures?" the detective prompted.

"There's probably a case file as long as your arm," Dee said. "It was that building inspector scandal last year. Detective Langston Hughes was the lead."

"I know Hughes," Detective Lucas said. "He's a good cop."

He turned away, checking to make sure that someone was following up on the information he'd just gotten. His partner, a leggy blond with a face like a fox, made a note and left the room.

Lucas called to her before she could close the door. "Hines, do we have to do the notification or did someone else go talk to the families?"

"We're all the family Tiffany has," Carl assured them.

Hines spoke to someone else in the hall and reported, "A squad was sent to get the reverend's wife."

The patrol officer she'd asked stuck his head in the room. "Calvin and Merrill are bringing her here," the officer said. "Should be any minute now."

Deanna clapped her hand to her head. "Nobody called Vanessa? How could we have forgotten to call his wife?"

Getting back on track, Lucas said, "So these pictures could have made someone's husband or boyfriend angry..."

"Or father or brother, or even mother," Dee interrupted. "Most of the women in the pictures were furious. So were their families and friends."

To the detectives' questioning look Carl responded, "They didn't know they were being photographed."

"Oh, so the reverend is into a kinky scene," Hines said as she came back into the room and took her seat, notepad in hand. "What was the deal, porn or blackmail?"

"The reverend is into adultery," Dee said. "He didn't know he was being photographed, either."

Hines leaned forward and put her elbows on the table, clearly fascinated. "So someone else was doing the blackmail?"

The male members of River Jordan looked decidedly uncomfortable. The two women faced each other, ignoring the men around them. It was like two friends having girl talk over lunch. Dee, in particular, seemed to be having a good time sharing embarrassing secrets about the men of River Jordan.

Crossing River Jordan

In spite of the reason she was there, Dee *was* enjoying herself. Talking to Detective Hines made her feel like she was involved in the investigation, like she was part of the team. Deanna was living her dream.

"*One* of the deacons was secretly taking those pictures of everyone," Carl said defensively. "He had cameras in almost every room of the church. He's crazy!"

"It wasn't a blackmail scheme," Dee continued. "It was more of a voyeurism kind of thing."

"So we've got an entire church full of suspects—any number of people who could have been angry with the reverend for not keeping his pants on." Detective Lucas gnawed on his pencil. "What about the wife? She had to be ticked off about the sex thing."

"Vanessa was very angry and hurt, but she didn't do this. Vanessa is the 'sleep with your best friend for revenge' type," Dee said. "But it's a settled fact that Vanessa wouldn't break a nail over any man. This took someone who didn't mind getting dirty."

Hines nodded. She understood exactly what Dee meant. "Well, what about Ms. Steele? She have any enemies?"

Kendrick, Carl and Steve all sat straight up in their seats.

"Frank!" Kendrick shouted, slamming his fist down on the table. "Frank was at the church today. She saw him and she was terrified!"

It was the first Dee and heard of the incident and she was livid.

"Frank Willis was at River Jordan today? What did he do to that poor child? How come nobody told me?"

Everyone began to speak at once—Pastor Darnell and Dee were trying to find out what had happened to Tiffany that morning. Carl, Kendrick and Steve were all telling what they knew. The two detectives alternately took down information and yelled for everyone else to be quiet. One fierce roar from Detective Lucas's finally ruled and calm was restored.

"Okay, this Willis was knocking Ms. Steele around and she left him. Is that right?" he asked.

"That was more than a year ago," Dee told them. "Why would he wait so long?"

The detective looked up from her notes. "Maybe he just found out where she was. So that still leaves us with a church full of possible…"

Lucas broke in. "And one Frank Willis who deserves a real hard look."

Detective Hines watched Kendrick's face as Dee gave them the location of Frank's garage.

"You go anywhere near Willis or his business, Mr. Peak, and we'll haul you in so fast your feet won't touch the ground," she warned.

■

As they walked toward their cars, Dee pulled Kendrick's arm, causing them to drop behind the others.

She whispered, "Are we going now?"

Kendrick jerked to a stop. "What? Going where?"

"Boy, don't play with me! I watched every move you made during that interview. You might have fooled the cops, but you didn't fool me for a minute. You're on your way to that garage and I'm going with you."

"Auntie Dee, I have to do this for Tiffany, but you don't need to go with me. You've got enough to do with Miss Grandma and all."

Dee waited patiently for him to finish. "Your car or mine?"

They decided to drive to the closest all-night grocery store and leave Kendrick's car in the parking lot.

"If the police are watching you, they'll think you're in the store. Just duck in one door and come out another. I'll be waiting on the corner," Dee said.

She felt confident that she knew how to handle things. After all she had experience, having tailed Ray Batt and staked out Rev. Beem's office last year. She'd practically handed the criminals over to the police! In spite of her excitement, she gave a huge yawn—she'd been going non-stop for nearly 24 hours. She was definitely too old for these marathon days.

The store on 95th and Ashland was always busy; the crowded lot made a great place to conceal almost any kind of vehicle. Kendrick was only gone a few minutes, rushing to

Crossing River Jordan

Dee's car in such a hurry that he banged his head on the door and yelled, "Ow!"

"Shhh! We're not supposed to attract any attention. That's why I'm pulling out so carefully and taking my time driving." She checked her side- and rear-view mirrors, signaled and eased into traffic. Dee drove at exactly 30 miles an hour, causing other cars to speed past.

Rubbing his head, Kendrick asked, "What's your plan? I was going to just check the place out and then go by in the morning. Uncle Carl mentioned getting Aunt Daisy's oil changed..."

"It's nearly dawn now; there's no point in going home. We can give the place a good once over and just wait until he opens. He can change my oil and we can check him out." Hot on the trail of another mystery, Dee decided that she never needed to sleep. "I'll stop at a donut shop and we can grab some stake-out fuel!"

After stocking up on coffee and donuts, they cruised past Frank's Auto Repair a couple of times.

"This place looks different," Kendrick noted.

The question was in Dee's glance.

"I drove past here a couple, well, a few times when Tiffany told us what he'd done to her."

"Kendrick..." Dee began.

"I never stopped or anything," Kendrick assured her. "I just wanted to...I don't know what I wanted. I never even saw the guy."

"Okay, I'll come clean. I drove around here, too" Dee's confession made them both laugh. "And you're right; this place *has* changed—a lot! Just a few months ago, it looked like it was going to close. Even the front windows were boarded up."

The outside was surprisingly neat; Frank's sign was a cheerful blue and white with a picture of a truck towing a car. Aside from a large flat-bed tow truck, there were only three cars parked in the lot, waiting to be serviced. Beneath a blue metal awning, there were four gas pumps and a coin-operated air pump. A long, wooden planter had been built near the sidewalk. It had been newly painted to match the sign and was filled with geraniums and petunias.

"Wow," Kendrick said. "*Something* big must have happened. I expected it to look like the same old dump."

There was a large padlock on the front door. They tried to look in the front windows, peering around the posters and signs, but it was far too dark to see anything inside. Deanna insisted on investigating the back of the shop.

Surrounded by a high chain link fence, a small junkyard occupied the rear of the property. Hunks and chunks of cars were piled everywhere—transmissions, engines, bumpers, fenders, doors. As they approached the fence, Dee and Kendrick discovered that Frank also had the ubiquitous junkyard dogs. Two large hounds of the mongrel variety jumped against the fence, barking and snarling. Startled, Dee spun on her heel and stumbled into Kendrick. He caught her before she could fall.

Back in the car, they each polished off two donuts and large cups of coffee. Too late, Dee realized that stake-outs didn't provide ideal conditions for ladies of a "certain age." That time of the morning, there were no businesses open that offered public washrooms. In spite of that concern and the caffeine, Dee's long day caught up with her and her chin dropped to her chest. She'd just begun to snore softly when Kendrick sighed; he felt like an idiot for having his no-longer-young aunt sleeping in a parking lot. He leaned over and kissed her on the forehead.

"Just resting my eyes," Dee mumbled.

"Auntie Dee, there's no point in staying here. There's nothing we can do now and I need to check on my girl."

Grateful that she hadn't been the one to give up first, Dee was quick to agree. "We can still come by later today. That oil change story is good."

She drove much faster, taking Kendrick back to his car. With a little luck, she could make it home and find relief in her very own bathroom.

■

The pastor's first stop was Rev. Beem's room. Vanessa had just arrived and, to Darnell's surprise, was speaking quietly with a nurse and the officer guarding the room. The pastor had dreaded Vanessa's arrival and the drama that he expected to go with it. Aside from wringing the handkerchief in her hand, she was dry-eyed and calm.

"Pastor Darnell, I'm glad you're here. I haven't gone in yet; the nurse was giving me an update on Albert." She took Darnell's arm. "I need a word with you, please."

They walked together down the hall, away from the reverend's room. "Pastor, I think this is my fault," she whispered, clinging to his arm. "Today, I threated to kill him...I wished that he was dead!"

"When was this? Did anyone hear you?"

Vanessa explained the circumstances of her earlier outburst. "I'm pretty sure my assistant heard me, but I'm not worried about that. Is this my fault?" Her voice rose at the end of the question.

"Sister Beem, I think you should definitely tell the police what you've told me. You don't want them to hear it from someone else. As far as this being your fault: the Lord may or may not answer our prayers, depending on what is best for us and what is in His plans. But rest assured, Sister Beem, God is not your hit man."

She was merely reacting to her shock and fear with guilt. She knew that the attack wasn't her fault. "Please come in with me. I'm sure Albert would appreciate a prayer, even from you." She almost smiled.

The separation from her husband had revealed a steel magnolia and the pastor mentally whispered a prayer that Beem would be around to see it. And that the reverend would have sense enough to appreciate it. The only other signs of distress Vanessa gave were a sharp intake of breath when she actually saw her husband and the way her hands continued to worry the handkerchief.

"Lord, Jesus" she whispered. "He looks awful!"

The reverend's face and head were swollen and there was a purplish bruise on his shoulder, as if he'd fallen on it when he hit the floor. Along with the bandages around his head, his torso was encased in brilliant white bandages too.

"The nurse said he got a couple of cracked ribs from the CPR, but it saved his life," Vanessa murmured to Pastor Darnell. "She said that he had regained consciousness and that the doctors were 'cautiously optimistic.' That was the phrase she used, 'cautiously optimistic.' I'm not sure how to explain that to Cory so that he believes that it's a good thing."

Almost as an afterthought, she added, "Oh, I have to call Georgia, too. She can call that brother of hers. You know, I've never even met him in person."

Darnell held his breath, waiting for the familiar sharp pain to begin in his stomach, but it didn't happen. There was only a dull, distant ache—a memory of pain. *So, that's what it takes to get over a heartache—a few months and a couple of attempted murders*, he thought.

Yeah, tough guy, but, what if she comes to see her old man? Darnell the Cool asked. *How over it would you be if you had to see her?*

The pastor had other things to think about. Rev. Beem was breathing on his own, with supplemental oxygen supplied by a tube in his nose. He was getting medication from an IV hanging next to the bed.

Pastor Darnell thought of how precious life was and wondered at the complexity of humanity—how fragile, yet how strong God had made His children. A lost love could break us, but "sticks and stones" made us grab life with both hands and hold on as tightly as we could.

A nurse came in to check the reverend's IV drip. She looked at Darnell as if she could tell what he was thinking.

"It's amazing, isn't it, how we manage to live through such horrible physical trauma. Out on the streets, youngsters keep coming up with more and more ways to kill each other and we keep coming up with more and more ways to keep them alive. What must God think of us?" she asked from the door.

"God must love us a great deal," Pastor Darnell replied. "We keep getting chances to get it right."

He moved to stand at the bedside next to Vanessa. Holding her hand, he bowed his head and began to pray for Rev. Beem.

■

After all the medical care was given, Pastor Darnell was allowed to visit and pray for Tiffany. She was on the same floor as the reverend, a few doors down and on the opposite side of the hall. From the window, he could see the first streaks of daylight and thought, *thank You, Lord for letting us all see another day.*

He stood at Tiffany's bedside and offered a silent prayer of gratitude for her life, requesting that the Lord protect and heal her. He put his hand on her forehead as he spoke the benediction and her eyelids fluttered. Tiffany was awake, but very drowsy. Whatever sedatives they'd given her were powerful and fast-acting.

"Hi Pastor," she grinned and waved her hand. She couldn't speak above a whisper. "How's my baby?"

"He's perfect. Daisy and Keisha took him home. He's sleeping like you ought to be."

"How's Rev. Beem? Nobody would tell me ...." Her voice faded.

"I just left him. I think he's going to be fine."

The pastor noticed Kendrick standing by Tiffany's door, chatting with a cop stationed there. "Tiffany, if you can stay awake for one more minute, there's someone who very much wants to say goodnight to you." He smiled at Kendrick as they exchanged places by the bed.

Kendrick kissed Tiffany's cheeks and the hand that wasn't attached to the IV. Her eyes were puffy and red-veined. The red, raw strip of skin around her neck made him furious. He wanted to kill the person who had dared to hurt her. *Lord, how much pain does she have to deal with?* He was angry with God. At the same time, he whispered his thanks for her life. He was pleased that he'd given up on the pointless stakeout so he could be with her.

Tiffany reached out to him and he took her hand. "Can you stay with me?" she whispered.

He nodded and pulled a chair close enough to sit on it and still put his head next to hers on the pillow.

Outside of the room, the officer assigned to stand watch was about to tell Kendrick to leave. Pastor Darnell shook his head and put out a hand to stop him.

"Officer, unless you want to have to arrest him, just let him stay."

15

As exhausted as she was when she finally got home, Dee couldn't fall asleep right away. Step by step, she mentally examined everything she'd seen from the time she'd entered the church doors until the time the reverend and Tiffany were wheeled away. She had to have missed something and so had the police. No one could have made the mess that the attacker had and walked away without leaving a trail of some kind. She wished she could have had some time to search the church on her own.

She could hardly wait to talk to Langston about this! Even though he didn't work Violent Crimes, she knew he would be able to give her solid insights on what the police were doing. Why, the two of them might just figure everything out by themselves!

Daisy had been a real trooper, dealing with Birdie Lee along with everything else that was going on. Dee knew that Daisy would agree; it was important to find out as much as they could about Frank Willis. As soon as she had a couple hours of sleep, she and Kendrick could pick up their surveillance. Then she could collect her mother from Daisy's and go to see Langston.

Ideally, Daisy would be focused on Keisha's wedding—but the situation was anything but ideal. Murder by flour! What kind of maniac were they dealing with? Tiffany had been looking forward to taking part in the wedding. Now she would be stuck in the hospital while the doctors made sure there was no residual damage to her lungs.

Dee knew that the best way to help with the wedding preparations would be to get Birdie Lee out of the way. After she helped Kendrick with Frank, she and Birdie Lee could spend the rest of the morning visiting Langston. That was win-win: she could make sure he had everything he needed and they could discuss the case. At the same time, she'd be able to keep an eye on her mother.

Dee was happy with her plan. Once she had her mom with her, she'd make a stop at Langston's favorite bakery.

Crossing River Jordan

Baked treats would provide the energy for a long session of crime solving. Cupcakes, donuts or muffins? She wasn't sure which Langston would prefer.

■

About three hours later, a fuzzy-brained Dee rolled out of bed and stumbled to the bathroom, depending on a quick shower to help clear her thinking. It didn't. She spent too much time trying to figure out if her socks were green or gray before deciding that real surveillance called for an all-black outfit anyway. She'd put water in the teapot, but forgot to turn on the stove. Grabbing an apple, she made it out of the door, only to have to go back in for her purse.

Kendrick was waiting when she pulled up to Frank's shop. The doors to two repair bays were up and there were cars being serviced in both.

"I've already been in," Kendrick said. "Nobody in there looked like Tiffany described, so I asked to see the owner. He's out on a tow job. I'm fourth in line for an oil change."

Mentally, Dee kicked herself. *Deanna Ramsey, get it together!* She hadn't even noticed that the truck wasn't there.

Employees leaned against cars and walls, chatting and laughing, in no hurry. That atmosphere changed when the boss showed up. Frank had hardly lowered the bed on the truck when one young man raced to get instructions from him. All the others began moving like their batteries had suddenly been recharged.

They're all scared of him, Dee thought. *He must really be a monster.*

Tiffany's description didn't quite fit. The man who climbed down from the tow truck stood not quite six feet tall and his upper body was that of a television wrestler. A noticeable difference was his hair—Tiffany had described a huge, unruly Afro. This man's hair was close-cropped and well-shaped, even down to his sideburns. There was no mistaking who he was, though. Aside from the workers' attitude change, he wore navy blue coveralls with a big, white FRANK embroidered on the front.

Dee expected him to snarl and yell, but as he walked around checking the work being done, he smiled and joked.

The workers seemed to like their boss. The scramble to get busy had been the result of respect, not fear.

Frank approached Kendrick with his hand outstretched. "Always happy to meet a new customer," he said. "I've got another quick run to make, but my guys will do a good job. You let me know if you have any problems." He handed Kendrick a business card.

Dee made a point of huddling in her car, keeping her head turned as she pretended to search for something in her bag. No point in him seeing both of their faces.

Kendrick wore a puzzled scowl, as he looked from the card to Frank's back. "He actually seems like a good guy. I'd been planning to punch him in the face as soon as I saw him. He didn't seem like a punk who would hit a woman."

"Get in; we've got to tail him!" This was one of Deanna's favorite daydreams—pursuing a criminal in a tire-squealing car chase down a busy highway, weaving in and out. She hoped Frank would peel out of the lot like a fleeing felon and take the corner on two wheels.

Kendrick was caught up in her excitement. "Don't lose him!"

There was no cause to worry. Frank drove at a truly respectable pace, down 83rd street. Dee earned some honks by angry drivers when she blew through a changing yellow light to turn left on Cottage Grove. She almost sideswiped a parked car.

"I thought we weren't supposed to attract attention," Kendrick said. His voice was calm, but his eyes widened and the tendons of his hands stood out as he clutched the dashboard.

Through clenched teeth, she said, "Just keep your eyes on him."

Another left and Frank pulled into a lot behind a brick building on 76th street. He checked his watch and hurried to the front door. Dee stopped in a bus stop zone. Leaving her car running, she jumped out to follow.

"Auntie Dee!"

"Kendrick, find somewhere to park and then come back, but you can't come in. He'd be suspicious if he saw you."

A triangle inside of a circle. She knew what the symbol on the window meant, but Dee was so focused on the chase

Crossing River Jordan

that she'd burst through the door and into the smoke-filled room without a thought.

Frank stood at a podium before a group of about 30 people. They were seated in folding chairs arranged in a semicircle. Many were smoking cigarettes; most had paper cups filled with coffee. They all seemed to know each other. Dee slid into a seat at the back of the room, just as Frank began to speak.

"Hello, I'm Frank and I'm an alcoholic."

A chorus of voices replied, "Hi, Frank!"

■

Kendrick wasn't nervous, not at all. The fact that he was sitting alone in a greenish-gray room on a hard chair that was bolted to the floor was nothing to be concerned about. That the two police officers who'd escorted him into the room had not explained anything to him and then disappeared was no big deal. He would just sit and look innocent, that's what he would do. He concentrated on music, actually tapping on the table as if it were a keyboard. He fingered a complicated piece that he'd been practicing recently.

When the door opened, he nearly passed out. He was so happy to see friendly faces—Auntie Dee, along with Officers Volanda Merrill and Myron Calvin—that he forgot to breathe for a moment. Now someone would tell him what this was all about!

A second look and his hopes dimmed. No one seemed particularly happy. Detective Lucas gnawed a pencil furiously and Auntie Dee looked...scared? He couldn't ever remember seeing fear on that woman's face.

"Did you not hear Detective Hines tell you not to interfere with this investigation?" Flecks of yellow paint clung to the detective's chin. "Do you not remember her promise to arrest you for obstruction?"

This was not at all what Kendrick expected. He appealed to Volanda and Myron. "I didn't do anything wrong. I just went and got my oil changed at Frank Willis' shop..."

"They know, Kendrick." Dee was unnaturally quiet.

"Tailed Willis," Officer Calvin spoke first and then yawned.

"Kept seeing you." Officer Merrill took off her hat and one of her long braids came uncoiled. "Busy night...and a very busy morning."

"These officers were assigned to Willis, but it turned out they were following you." The detective glared and pushed his face to within inches of Kendrick's. "Mr. Peak, believe it or not, my officers are perfectly competent."

"Yes, sir," was all Kendrick could think of to say.

"They don't need any help from you. Or you." His glare now included Dee.

He fished a fresh pencil from his pocket and waved it at them. "You are both very lucky. Apparently, Mrs. Ramsey has good friends in the department and I don't have time for this nonsense, but let me make one thing crystal clear."

Crunching down on the pencil, Lucas stomped to the door. "If you get in my way again, I will make time and I promise you won't like that at all. And another thing: Willis is not the guy. When your friends were attacked, he was here."

■

Birdie Lee had settled the idea of refreshments. Muffins and donuts were her choice and she chose two of every flavor that the bakery offered. They were buying enough food to feed an army, but she was having so much fun choosing that Dee didn't try to stop her.

Birdie's curiosity was piqued at the thought of meeting Dee's gentleman friend. When they arrived, she didn't want to listen to Dee talk about attacks and criminals. Birdie wanted to talk about Langston.

He was swinging around his loft on crutches. Lang leaned down to kiss Dee when she entered the room, but she moved her head quickly so he could see that her mother was right behind her. The kiss landed in her hair, just over her left ear.

"Woo wee, you're a tall drink of water!" was how Birdie Lee greeted the man after looking him over, head to toe.

Dee bustled around the galley kitchen, making coffee and setting the pastries on a large plate—*I guess a single man wouldn't have a platter*, she thought.

Crossing River Jordan

Birdie peppered Langston with questions. "What kind of cop are you? Where's your people from? What happened to your leg, somebody shoot you?"

"Mama, have some of these donuts; they're your favorites!" Dee practically shoved a glazed cake donut into her mother's mouth.

She tried to get in a few questions while Birdie busied herself with eating. She told Langston everything she knew about what had happened to Tiffany and the reverend. He knew almost as much as she did. After all, he had a direct pipeline.

"How can I help?" she asked.

"From what I heard, you already helped. You found some evidence in the kitchen…"

"I can do more," she insisted. "Just tell me how you would investigate a crime like this?"

"I'm in Fraud, remember? And you were in nursing. We don't do violent crime investigations."

He shook a couple of pain relievers into his hand and dry swallowed them, chasing them down with a sip of coffee.

"Langston Hughes, I'm sure that is not how your mother taught you to take medicine," Dee scolded. "You should drink a full eight ounces of water." She hurried to the refrigerator and poured a glass of water from the filtered pitcher she'd bought him. When she was first in the loft—held captive, she said; in protective custody, he said— she'd noticed that he drank either bottled water or unfiltered tap water and she didn't like either.

"You heard they were following up some leads, right?"

"Following leads?" Her voice came out nearly an octave higher. Dee would never tell Langston what she and Kendrick had done or how badly it almost turned out.

"Yeah, that Willis. The one Tiffany used to live with," Langston continued. "And you already know more than you should. Promise me you'll stay out of it or you might get yourself into real trouble this time. Keep away from the official investigation, Deanna Ramsey, or I might have to tell your mother on you."

Before her brain could send warning signals to her mouth, Dee blurted, "They already know that Frank's the wrong guy!"

"Dee, what did you do?" Langston couldn't believe that she'd already interfered.

Just then, Birdie rejoined the conversation. "Deanna was always the nosiest little girl you ever saw. Always asking a million questions. That's how she wound up hanging from a tree branch in the Millers' backyard up in Three Rivers. She kept seeing chipmunks go into the tree at the bottom and she wanted to know why they weren't up in the branches like the squirrels. So she climbed up there to see and the branch snapped. Left her swingin' by her britches!" Birdie threw back her head and cackled at what had been one of the most terrifying moments of her child's life.

Her reaction had been the same at the time. Dee vividly remembered staring through tears at her mother, who was far below her. Birdie pointed and laughed while the Millers raced around trying to get help.

"Yep, that sure was funny, Mama." Langston could tell from her tone that the moment had been everything *except* funny. Steering the conversation to safer ground, he said, "Miss Streeter, I'm sorry I won't be able to come to the wedding. I hear you're a great dancer and I was looking forward to dancing with you."

"Oh, that's all right," Birdie said graciously. "I got Deanna another boyfriend. He'll dance with me!"

Dee choked on her coffee, managing to cough out, "Say good-bye to Langston, Mama. I think we've visited long enough!"

Langston opened his phone the second the door closed behind them. Dee had been up to something and he needed some help if he was going to protect her from herself this time.

16

Before he'd even opened his eyes, Darnell had decided that it was going to be a perfectly beautiful Sunday. The first thing on his mind was Chess Allen. He hadn't seen or spoken to her at all after going into the church to look for Tiffany.

They'd been playing phone tag; he knew that she had visited Tiffany and Beem. Chess was invited to the reception and he hoped she would meet him there after the service.

Weddings were even more special when ministers performed them for friends. The formation of JAM had caused him to spend a great deal of time with those River Jordan members who were especially active. They met once a week and had several ongoing projects. Steve and Keisha were two of his closest friends. They spent a lot of time together.

He amused himself, thinking that he should celebrate making it through that fateful Wednesday—the longest day of his life. Then he realized that this was going to be a long one, too. There would be two church services, a wedding and the reception afterward. He checked the clock on his nightstand, amazed to see that he'd only slept for a few hours. Still he bounded out of bed, energized and looking forward to the day ahead.

During his time as a missionary for refugees in Sierra Leone, Darnell had seen enough death to last him a lifetime. What made the attacks at the church seem so horrific was that they were *out of place*—what could be safer than a church kitchen?

The events of that night could have turned out much differently. There could have been two funerals to plan instead of thanksgiving for two lives spared and the opportunity to celebrate the union of two more—well, the union of five lives, if he included the children.

He was anxious to get to River Jordan, but regretted that he wouldn't have time to check in at the hospital first. While showering, he sang *How Great Thou Art* at the top of his lungs. His God was truly good all the time!

■

Not even her swiftly approaching wedding could stop Keisha from checking on Tiffany. They had become so close in such a short time. She loved her twin with all her heart, but when Tiffany joined their family she filled a space that Keisha hadn't known was empty. She knocked softly on the door, went in and had to stifle a gasp.

You won't cry, Keisha told herself, sternly. *Don't you dare upset her after all she's been through.* She had tried to imagine what her friend would look like, but wasn't prepared for reality. Bandaged, bruised and swollen, Tiffany still managed a grin.

Kendrick went straight to the hospital after the police let him go. He didn't say a word about his adventure with Auntie Dee. He wouldn't mention Frank Willis's name until Tiffany was much stronger. Keisha looked at her twin and shook her head. He was sprawled in the chair beside the bed with his head thrown back, snoring softly.

"My hero," Tiffany whispered and then she smiled. "What are you doing here? You should be getting beautiful."

"You mean I'm not already beautiful?" Keisha had on old jeans and a green t-shirt with the words, "Ask me if I care." Her hair was done up in pink foam rollers and she had a blue and white bandana covering them.

"I wanted to let you know that Tremain is just fine and tell you not to worry about him. And I wanted to see for myself that you were all right." Keisha gestured at the chart hanging on the foot of the bed. "What are they saying?"

"Something about abrasions to my throat and lungs. I think I'll be fine, but they don't want to commit to anything. I'm so sorry about the wedding. I really wanted to be a part of it."

"I honestly thought about postponing it, but everything is in place. Steve's parents are here and Uncle Carl would lose the money he spent on the reception."

Tiffany looked horrified. "No way! You go and marry that man today," she whispered urgently. "He loves you and the kids. We don't want you apart any longer than absolutely necessary. Besides, I want to see pictures of everyone looking gorgeous!" Tiffany fell back against the pillows

"Speaking of gorgeous, guess who's coming all the way to the church to do my hair and makeup? Don't guess; you shouldn't be talking—the one and only Mr. Bernard of Chez Beautique!"

Tiffany fanned herself with her hand and pretended to faint.

Crossing River Jordan

Laughing, Keisha gave her a little salute. "Okay Captain, I've got my orders. You just follow the doctors' orders and get well as soon as you can. I love you, girl."

Tears spilled from Tiffany's eyes. "You're the closest thing to a sister I've ever had." Her raspy voice was losing sound; Keisha could hardly hear her.

Tiffany nodded at the napping Kendrick. "Wake him up and take him with you. He promised to bring me a piece of wedding cake."

***

"Mama, you're not going to cry are you?" Hope's eyes were beginning to fill at the mere thought. She'd been charged by Uncle Kendrick with giving her mother a tiny box—a gift from Tiffany. Inside was a shiny penny dated the year Keisha was born and a note:

It's from the old traditional English rhyme:
Something old, something new. Something
borrowed, something blue and a sixpence
in your shoe. I couldn't find a sixpence, but
I hope this works.
    Love, Tiffany

Keisha smiled down at her little maid of honor. "No, sweet girl, I'm just a little sad that Aunt Tiffany can't be here. But I sure am lucky that my big girl could help me out today."

Hope looked adorable in her dress and couldn't stop stealing admiring glances at the one-inch heels on her shoes. Suddenly a study in seriousness, she stood before her mother, holding the crown of daisies, yellow roses and baby's breath that Keisha would wear instead of a veil.

"Mama, we look beautiful, don't we?"

"Like something out of a dream," Daisy answered before Keisha could speak. She had quietly entered the room and stood near the door. As she watched mother and daughter, she silently thanked the Lord for providing her with a family to love. She walked over to plant kisses on cheeks.

"Hope, please go downstairs and see if Auntie Dee is here." Keisha needed a moment with Daisy. She watched Hope close the door behind her and then she whirled into her aunt's arms.

"Aunt Daisy, I'm scared! What if I mess everything up?"

Daisy was confused. "Mess everything up? Everything's perfect, just like you wanted it."

"Not the ceremony—the marriage. Almost nobody gets marriage right!"

"Keisha, people who go into it with their eyes open and their heads on straight have a great chance of getting it right. You and Steve were blessed to find each other—look where you met!"

"Steve is perfect for me..."

"And he believes you're perfect for him..."

"But, I'm not perfect and when he finds out, he'll leave, just like Lynn left Kendrick." Fat tears made slow tracks through Keisha's makeup.

Daisy dabbed Keisha's face and before she knew it, she was crying, too. "Steve has known you for a long time. You did it right; you started as friends and took things slowly." She looked into Keisha's eyes. "After all that nonsense your uncle and I went through, we've finally got it together. Remember this: on that day when you look at Steve and wonder why in the world you married this awful man..."

"No, Aunt Daisy..." Keisha interrupted, trying to pull away.

Daisy held her firmly and continued "All wives all go through it from time to time; so do husbands. On that day, take a moment to think of who he is to you—he's the friend that you're lucky enough to love. We tend to be more accepting, forgiving and tolerant of our friends than we are of our lovers. Always remember that Steve is your friend."

"My friend that I'm lucky enough to love," Keisha repeated.

Both women, smiling through tears, turned at a knock on the door.

Immaculate in another Armani suit, Mr. Bernard was talking as he swept into the room. "It's almost time...oh, Sweet Jesus, look at your face! What have you done?" His horrified glance took in Daisy, too. "You were perfection. You both were!"

He removed his jacket and rushed to his makeup kit. Through clenched teeth, he ordered, "Don't either of you dare drop another tear!"

Crossing River Jordan

■

Contrary to Bernard's instructions, Daisy began to cry again as soon as Kendrick began to play the wedding march. Keisha had chosen a perfect cream-colored raw silk dress with a matching jacket for the "mother" of the bride and Bernard had reapplied her makeup perfectly. She was elegant and Carl told her that if she hung around after the ceremony, he'd be happy to marry her a third time.

What set her off was remembering the twins when she'd first taken them in—tiny, quiet, both with the biggest, roundest eyes she'd ever seen. She loved them both, but Keisha was her secret favorite. She saw so much of herself in the girl.

She smiled across the aisle at Steve's parents. It seemed that Keisha was getting in-laws as wonderful as the husband she'd chosen. What a bonus! Carl's mother had hated Daisy, barely making an effort to tolerate her even after she and Carl had remarried. Loving in-laws might have helped them make a go of marriage the first time they'd tried it.

Dee sat on the row behind her, feeding her tissues in an almost continuous stream, while keeping one eye on Birdie Lee and the other on Tremain, who spent the first part of the ceremony trying to launch himself forward to get to Carl. Just before the pastor got to the vows, she gave up and Carl took over. Kensha who was seated between Daisy and Carl, took an interest in all of the activity for a while, before curling up in the pew for a nap.

Birdie Lee loved to dress up and any wedding, funeral or church event delighted her to no end. She had fought with Dee for the better part of the morning over what outfit she was going to wear. Dee had tried to buy her something new, but she insisted that nothing Dee could buy would be as good as what she already owned.

As her mother began pulling clothes out of a suitcase, Dee mentally repeated, *don't show fear; just don't show fear.*

The first outfit Birdie selected started with a rainbow-colored handkerchief skirt and bright red tights. They were to be paired with a yellow satin blouse and a white fringed shoulder wrap.

"No fear," Dee muttered. "Mama, Keisha's colors are yellow and white and black. So let's keep the blouse and the wrap; they're just right. Do you have another skirt?"

"Well, if you don't want to add some color to the party, I can just be dull like you. Is that what you're wearing?"

Dee wore black palazzo pants with a yellow linen blazer and a white silk shirt. At first she thought it was perfect, but now she a pang of doubt. She hated to admit it, but even after all these years, this crazy woman could shake her confidence. "Yes, Mama, Daisy and I picked this out together. We thought it was perfect. I think it's perfect," she corrected herself.

"I got some white pants in here somewhere," Birdie mumbled, pulling more clothes from the bag. She grunted and held up something that looked like Miss Muffet's pantaloons. There had to have been three yards of lace ruffled around each leg. "These are pretty enough," she pronounced.

Dee resorted to the coughing fit. She was afraid she would spend the rest of her life dreaming of her mother wearing those pants. With tears streaming down her face, she coughed out, "Yes Mama, those are pretty. That's the problem; you don't want to take all the attention away from the bride on her day, do you?"

"Yeah, I didn't think of that. You're right; it's Keister's day and she needs all the help she can get."

Dee started coughing again and excused herself to get some water. *Lord, help me to be strong*, she silently prayed. *Here's my mother looking like a rubber chicken and she's signifying about a girl as cute as Keisha. What does she see when she looks in a mirror?*

When she got back to the bedroom, Birdie was turning this way and that, looking at herself in one of Dee's skirts. It was too big and spun around her mother's skinny waist like a hula hoop, but Dee yelled, "Mama, that's great!"

She was prepared to do whatever it took to make that skirt fit—safety pins, duct tape, whatever it took. It was plain black with a slight flair and hit Birdie at mid-calf—the answer to a prayer.

When Birdie Lee was finally dressed, she slapped a large pink hat with a hot pink feather band on her head. Dee was too weak to fight.

17

The wedding service was nearly perfect. It had just the right touch of humorous flaws—it would be a delightful memory to share at family gatherings for years to come. The youngest flower girl got the giggles as she moved down the aisle. She tipped her basket, dumping a pile of petals at her feet. Looking at the packed church around her, she smiled as if it had been her plan all along, knelt down and grabbed a fistful of the flowers. She took them to one side of the aisle and threw them at the people in the pews and hurried back to the pile to do it again on the other side. She flung her arm forward each time with such force that the folks closest to her flinched and drew back before being showered with petals.

Kiana followed her sister with a more traditional distribution of flower petals, but Knowledge got bored halfway down the aisle and decided to balance the pillow on his head. The rings slid off and dangled on each side of his head by their tethering ribbons.

The three couples, bridesmaids and groomsmen were to have been four, but because of Tiffany's absence, one of the groomsmen wound up escorting the maid of honor. Hope performed her processional duty, preceding the entrance of the bride with a stately march that brought back the solemnity and tradition of the event. Uncle Carl beamed as he escorted the radiant bride toward the waiting groom, who was attended by best man, Wisdom.

In a moment of silence before Pastor Darnell began to speak, Birdie Lee could be clearly heard. "That Keeler cleans up real nice, don't you think?"

Embarrassed, Dee said, "Mama!" but Keisha doubled over with laughter.

She turned and said, "Thank you, Miss Grandma," dropping a tiny curtsey and after the resulting laughter, the pastor continued.

He began reading from 1 Corinthians, "Love is kind."

When he'd completed the passage, he said, "I have to ask this, in keeping with wishes expressed by the couple."

Keisha and Steve looked first at each other and then at the pastor. They didn't remember asking for any special vows.

"Keisha and Steve, do you promise to obey each other?" Pastor Darnell's tone was serious, but he had a broad smile on his face.

When they stopped giggling, both the bride and groom said "I do!"

"Well, then do you, Keisha Marie Peak take Steven Martin Kent to be your lawfully wedded husband?"

"Mama," Knowledge stage whispered from his seat with Carl on the front row, "you have to say 'I do' again!"

"I do," Keisha laughed.

"I do, too," Knowledge said, stepping between Keisha and Steve.

Me, too," Hope said.

Me, too!" Wisdom added, grinning.

When he could compose himself, Pastor Darnell said, "And do you, Steven Martin Kent, take Keisha Marie Peak to be your lawfully wedded wife?" He held up his hand to halt Steve's answer. "And do you take Wisdom Kendrick Peak, Hope Dana Peak, and Knowledge Carl Peak to be your children in the sight of God and this company?"

"I absolutely do!" There was spontaneous applause along with laughing.

"Well then, by the power vested in me by the Lord and the state of Illinois, I now pronounce you husband and wife and family! You may kiss your bride and everybody else!"

The first kiss went to Keisha as was befitting a normal ceremony. Then Steve gathered the children and placed a kiss on top of each head, which Wisdom stood still for even though he considered himself too old for such things.

"Ladies and gentlemen, family and guests, I give you Mr. and Mrs. Steven Kent and family!"

There was a standing ovation as the new family moved down the aisle and through the double doors at the sanctuary entrance.

■

The ballroom at the Point looked like a fairy palace with lights twinkling among the chandeliers, along banisters and around columns. The daisy motif was prominently featured on centerpieces on each table. Vanessa had worked very hard to make magic happen. Because of the flood of weddings in June, she and her team had only a few hours to work on the room. It was her gift, not just to the newlyweds, but to the entire Franklin family which had befriended her so readily after her family's disgrace.

The fall from her status as first lady of River Jordan hadn't been her fault, but there were many church members—"haters" her son Cory called them—who'd been delighted to see her knocked down a peg. Vanessa couldn't fault them; she had bought into her husband's attitudes and practices wholeheartedly. She hadn't tried to become friendly with a single person. She accepted that respect and admiration had been her right as the wife to the soon-to-be senior minister—the heir to Rev. Alden's throne.

As soon as the scandal broke, Vanessa learned not only who she was, but who she needed to be. Women who jostled to be seated next to her at church functions—who always made sure to compliment her on her hair or outfits—turned up their noses and hardly spoke to her. She could see pity in the eyes of some, but there was cold amusement in the eyes of others.

Men who had once followed her with their eyes full of admiration, still followed her with their eyes. But now, their looks cheapened her as if she was somehow second-hand goods, no longer worthy of respect. She must have done something to make her husband step out on her; she just wasn't enough to hold a man. Or worse, it was like some were watching and waiting for a sign that she was so desperate for a man that they could have a turn with her.

Fortunately, some women rallied around her. Dee and Daisy had experienced men in many flavors between their nine marriages to seven different men. They both knew the pain of having a cheating husband. They knew what Vanessa needed to get through a very tough time and they gave it to her—listening to her rant, holding her when she cried and being there with hot meals, rides for Cory and any other assistance they could give.

Vanessa found a resilience that even she didn't know was there. It didn't take her long to rise from the ashes, realizing that her son would suffer if she spent too much time being the wilting flower that Albert Beem was obviously waiting to see. He thought, no he knew, that she would soon be overwhelmed by life without him, unable to muddle through with-without his guidance.

Dee and Daisy got her involved in JAM, first helping with meal preparation for seniors (Daisy thought it would help the woman learn her way around a kitchen so she and her son wouldn't starve). Vanessa surprised herself by picking up basic cooking skills very quickly. She didn't like baking, it was too messy for her, but soon she was able to get a decent dinner on the table.

More importantly, she found that she enjoyed doing things for others. The time she spent with the seniors took her mind off of her own troubles. Vanessa learned that there were some people whose lives were more difficult than hers. She also realized that there were many whose lives were full and rich because that's the way they had lived.

She began performing extra services for the ladies, treating them to new hairdos, doing their makeup and gifting them with her special bath salts. The centerpieces she created for the lunch tables became very popular.

That led to her finding a career when Lori Caswell saw her work and asked her to do the flower designs for a wedding. Impressed by Vanessa's creative ability and organizational skills, Lori hired her as a full-time coordinator. Her talents were evident throughout the large ballroom and Keisha was delighted.

After she and Steve had entered and once more been announced to the guests, she swept Vanessa into a hug. "Thank you, so much! I can't believe what you did here!"

Vanessa basked in the praise, saying, "It does look nice, doesn't it? But it had to be special for you. Look at you; you're fabulous!"

"Yes, I must say I outdid myself." Mr. Bernard stepped up to kiss Keisha's hand.

"Thank you again, Mr. Bernard! I feel like a princess!"

Dee and Birdie Lee were next in line to greet the bride. Birdie took one look at Mr. Bernard and announced, "I think he's got a little sugar in him."

Dee held her breath, waiting for the floor to open up and swallow her or at least to swallow her mother.

Mr. Bernard cracked up. "More than a little, ma'am. I'm sweet all the way through!" He bent over her wrinkled, liver-spotted hand with a courtly bow.

Birdie Lee laughed, too, saying, "I like you. You remind me of my cousin, John. He changed his name to Juliette. Woo wee, we used to have us some fun."

She puckered her lips and frowned at Dee, before taking Bernard's arm to go to their table. "Juliette knew how to get dressed up for a party!"

The pastoring duties were done and Darnell settled down to enjoy himself. He and Chess were seated together.

Clever girl, that Keisha, he thought, as he pulled out Chess's chair. The catering staff was busily serving drinks and hors d'oeuvres. Chess raised an eyebrow when he reached for a glass of sparkling juice.

"Repenting?" she asked, clinking her flute of champagne against his juice.

"Enjoying," he replied, taking a long swallow. In truth, he did enjoy sparkling white grape juice more than champagne. "This is good and you look lovely."

She looks hot! Darnell the Cool was speaking to him once more.

He had noticed Chess at the church, but hadn't had time to speak with her. She wore a yellow sheath dress that followed her every swerve and a short white jacket. He liked that Chess always wore simple jewelry: a single gold chain and small hoops in her ears. She didn't smell like sugar cookies today. Her scent was citrusy and subtle; it drew him close.

It seemed to him that a dark cloud had lifted. Rev. Beem and Tiffany were going to be fine and the police were on the case. The wedding had gone smoothly and Keisha and Steve both looked radiantly happy. His personal joy came from a realization the night before when he realized that there was a noticeable lack of anguish when he thought of Georgia Beem. He no longer felt that fire.

Chess sighed and leaned back in her chair. "I'm officially on vacation as of tomorrow. I planned a whole week of doing nothing. My only intention is to get to a grocery store and have myself a home-cooked meal for a change."

"I could use one of those—I mean the vacation, not the meal." Not wanting Chess to think that he was fishing for an invitation, Darnell patted his stomach. "My church family makes sure I eat, well and often."

■

He scooted his chair closer to Chess, so they could hear each other over the noise in the ballroom. "I feel like dancing," he told her, his head almost touching hers.

"Well, I'm sure there are a lot of ladies here who would love to dance," she said.

"Let me rephrase: I feel like dancing with you."

She looked at him, unsure how to take what he'd said. She quickly made up her mind to go with face value. Her friend wanted to dance with her. Well, that was a good thing.

"I'll hold you to that when it's time to hit the dance floor," she said.

"You'll hold me, when it's time to hit the dance floor?" The pastor was in a teasing mood.

She smiled at him and shook her head, saved from having to answer by a musical flourish and an announcement—the bride and groom were done with the receiving line, the photos had been taken and dinner was about to be served.

■

All of the children, even Kendrick's, had joined Steve and Keisha in the receiving line. Tremain, because it *was* a line, kept holding up his hands for inspection. Wisdom's toast was a gem that made everyone in the room tear up.

"I'm the best man, so I have to make a toast and Steve said you're supposed to tell a joke first, so what's red and white and blue all over? A really cold peppermint stick!" He laughed heartily at his joke.

"Now, here's the toast part. Mama and Dad—I can call you that now, right Steve, uh, I mean Dad?"

Steve nodded; he didn't trust himself to speak. His eyes were full, even as his smile threatened to split his face in two.

"Okay," Wisdom held up his glass of punch. "Uncle Carl taught me this. Mama and Dad: 'May the sun always be at your back, may the road rise up to meet you, and may you be three days in heaven before the devil knows you're dead.'"

Laughing, the guests began to clink glasses. "Wait, I'm not through," the boy called. "Mama and Dad, we love you and we promise to be good until you get back. Now, I'm through!" Amid laughter and applause, he leaned over and clinked glasses with his parents.

Keisha's makeup was ruined. She had cried through Wisdom's entire speech. She was about to excuse herself to repair her face when Vanessa stood up and announced a special surprise. "We have a guest who wanted to sing for the newlyweds!"

Georgia Beem stepped up to the microphone. "Keisha and Steve, I wish you both the greatest happiness, health, prosperity. You deserve to have it all."

Kendrick and three of the River Jordan musicians had provided all of the live music for the day. He was as surprised to see Georgia as anyone, but when she began to sing, he and the others swung in behind her effortlessly. No one had ever heard her sing secular music, but she and Kendrick had played around with all kinds of music when they rehearsed.

"It's very clear; our love is here to stay." She started out slowly, giving them a beautiful ballad, but soon picked up the pace and had hands clapping and toes tapping all over the room.

Chess stole glance at Darnell, expecting to see him in the kind of pain she hoped never to know. She planned never to love someone so much that their absence would devastate her. Life was transient, everything changed and people were fickle. She had wasted enough time—years, in fact—thinking she was in love with Tommy Odom. Her father's business connections had been Tommy's real interest—she found that out the night she walked in on him spread out all over his young administrative assistant.

Chess felt her whole body tighten in on itself. She was waiting to see what kind of bad this would turn out to be. Would Darnell fall on his knees and beg Georgia to come back to him? Or would he sit there in shock before throwing up on her favorite white pumps? Maybe he'd make a big scene—accusing Georgia of humiliating him and lying to him. Or even worse, would he pretend to be with Chess now and make a big show of what a close couple they were?

No, Pastor Darnell Davis, you will not use me like that! She pulled her chair away, with the excuse of reaching for her water glass. Surreptitiously, she moved her feet to the other side of her chair. *He might think I knew that Georgia would be there and just didn't tell him.* Irrationally, she was making herself angry. *He should know that I would never betray him that way!*

Chess realized that her anger was a way to avoid being hurt when Darnell got up and walked away.

Darnell surprised her. After the initial shock made him look like he had turned to stone, he breathed out, lowered his shoulders and relaxed. He listened to Georgia with a smile that showed his appreciation of the irony. *"Our Love Is Here to Stay"*—well, maybe it was. He thought he might always love Georgia Beem, but even before seeing her, he had wondered about the quality of that love.

The music had him thinking in song titles. *Love Is Blue*—that title summed it up perfectly. Love had so many shades, just like the color blue—from the almost-white tint of blue in milk, to blue as dark as night. Now he considered that real love, lasting love, needed to be layered like music. Layering notes one on top of the other to make chords and songs and symphonies.

He was thinking in poetry. If he didn't know better, he would have thought he was drunk again. Sappy as his poetic thoughts were, he was thinking more clearly than he had in months. He still felt for Georgia, but he didn't feel *her* anymore.

After taking a bow, Georgia went over to speak to Steve and Keisha. Chess was at a loss. She didn't know what to do with her hands, what to think or where to look. She and Georgia had been friends for years. Would Georgia think that she had moved in to pick up the pieces? Once again, anger rose to shield her.

What do I care what Georgia thinks? She's not much of a friend if she thinks so little of me. And what if I had started seeing Darnell? Georgia was the fool for walking away from such a good man!

The pastor took her hand and said, "Let's go say hello to our friend."

Crossing River Jordan

Surprised again, Chess walked with him and they stood together, waiting for Georgia to finish chatting with other people.

When she looked up, Georgia had the good grace to look uncomfortable. "I had to come and see about my dad. I wasn't invited, although I certainly understood why, but we were friends—Keisha and Steve and I. I just wanted them to know I support them and wish them all the best."

Georgia seemed to be apologizing for showing up. She and Chess held each other briefly and air-kissed each other's cheeks.

"Georgia, how are you? I got your last e-mail, but that was more than a month ago," Chess said. "You look good."

"You look wonderful, too. I love that dress." They were still getting the niceties out of the way. "I got busy toward the end of the school year with all the testing and final projects this year." Georgia taught science at a high school in the Michigan town where she'd moved after not marrying Darnell.

He felt foolish for being surprised that Georgia and Chess had stayed in touch. Of course they would—they'd been friends since they were children. He took the time to look at her without interruption while she and Chess talked. She was still beautiful to him. She'd braided her long dark brown dreadlocks into a single braid down her back and wore a gold dragonfly accent in her hair. Her short, sleeveless dress showed off toned arms and shapely legs.

He held out his hand and shook hers firmly. No hug, no air-kisses. "I'm sorry about what happened to your father."

"Vanessa told me how you've been helping her and Cory deal with everything. I know that you've been going to see Dad and praying for him. Darnell, I really appreciate that."

Darnell the Cool scuffed his toe in the dirt. *Shucks, Ma'am, tweren't nothing.*

Pastor Darnell said, "We're all praying for him and for Tiffany. It was a terrible thing, their being attacked like that."

"I talked to the police about the investigation," said Georgia. "They promised to keep me updated, but I can't stay. I have summer school classes."

"You take care of yourself," Darnell said, giving her a small tight smile.

"Chess, you wouldn't mind if Darnell and I had a word in private, would you?" Georgia hadn't intended to ask for time with the pastor, but seeing Darnell with Chess had brought out that same illogical jealously that she'd felt every other time she'd seen them together. She wondered if they were "an item" now and why her "good friend" Chess hadn't mentioned that she was seeing the pastor.

"Of course not." Chess began moving away. "Georgia, I'll talk to you soon."

Darnell caught Chess's hand, saying to Georgia, "It was good seeing you, Georgia."

She smiled wistfully. She got the message. "Another time and another place?"

"We both know there'll never be one." He put his arm around Chess's waist and they went back to their seats.

As they settled into their chairs once more, Chess looked into Darnell's eyes. "I'm not sure what happened back there, but I hope I wasn't being used in any way." She took a sip of water and waited for a reply.

"I'm not sure what I did that would make you think that," said Darnell, truly perplexed.

"You took my hand when we walked toward her. You put your arm around me when we walked away. All that touching was sending messages, Darnell."

"Messages to you, Chess. Only to you. And I hope you don't mind getting them."

They never noticed Georgia leaving.

18

With a flourish, the master of ceremonies announced the happy couple, who swept onto the dance floor for their first dance as husband and wife. Carl finally got to have a dance with his Princess as Steve and his mother took a turn around the floor. There was much switching of partners so that even Dee danced with Steve, Carl and Martin Kent.

Dee missed Langston, but was having a wonderful time, thanks to Mr. Bernard who had become Birdie Lee's unofficial escort. They were in the middle of the dance floor, doing a cartoon version of the Lindy Hop. Wisps of feathers from Birdie's hat were floating all over the place and Dee couldn't remember ever seeing her mother enjoying herself more. Mr. Bernard was laughing up a storm, acting nothing at all like the drama-slinging, tortured *artiste* he was at his salon.

Their dancing had attracted a crowd and other couples were trying to follow their steps. Keisha and Steve, giggling together, were right in the thick of the dancing.

Daisy came over and plopped into a chair, waving for another glass of champagne as she landed.

"Girl, I'm already so tired, I don't know how I'm going to get through the next five days. Carl had me out on that dance floor, trying to keep up with Miss Mama!"

I saw you two jammin' out there. Carl is going to need a heating pad by the end of the day." Dee smiled at her brother-in-law, who was cutting in on Mr. Bernard.

Daisy took a long swallow of the wine. "I saw you out there trying to bop—wait, they call it stepping now, don't they? I've never understood how, as well as you dance, you could never learn how to step."

Dee shrugged. "That just wasn't my dance, I guess. "She looked around the room. "Vanessa did an incredible job in here. Keisha will never forget her beautiful wedding. I'm so sorry that the Thompsons and Mother Jessup couldn't be here for this."

"We totally forgot all about their mission trip when we were choosing a date, "Daisy said. "That's why there's more than one photographer. We'll be taking the photos and having a CD made for the people who couldn't be here. I don't know why none of us thought to have video."

"Speaking of people who couldn't be here, did you notice who *is* here? You've got a couple of crashers." She nodded toward a table near the back of the room.

Vanessa had set up a couple of tables for people like herself—invited guests who were also helping out with various tasks during the wedding. The tables were situated in front of a massive tapestry that hid a door leading to a corridor which ran along the perimeter of the ballroom. Servers and other staff used the corridor to move between the ballroom and the kitchen, bar and storage rooms. It also led to the rear entrance of the field house.

The photographers sat at the tables when they weren't moving through the room taking candid shots. A few of the teens from JAM who were interning with Vanessa at Lori's Luxury Events gathered there, when they weren't working.

A closet romantic, Keisha had planned for Rev. Beem to sit with his wife, even though they weren't on the best of terms. She had hoped to give him a chance to get back in Vanessa's good graces. The attack at the church had made that impossible. Instead, the former deacons, Ray Batt and Deacon Uttley were seated at the table, as if they were Rev. Beem's stand-ins.

Every time Dee saw Utley, her blood boiled. She understood the *idea* of forgiveness, but she was having trouble with the actual practice. His clumsy, unwanted attempt to seduce Tiffany Steele was always in a corner of her mind because she and Daisy had been unintentional witnesses. Uttley knew that the Franklins had taken Tiffany and her son into their family. The nerve of him showing up at this wedding!

Daisy put a restraining hand on Dee's arm. "There will be no kicking any one in their family jewels today, Deanna Ramsey. You stay on your best behavior so that Miss Mama will stay on hers."

Dee looked at the dance floor in time to see her mother pass by leading a conga line around the large ballroom. Mr. Bernard was now wearing Birdie Lee's hat. Steve's parents were proving to be kid magnets—all of the children had gathered at their table and were being highly entertained by Martin's sleight of hand and Ruth's grandmotherly attention.

The dancing was momentarily interrupted for a few traditional wedding practices. First, there was the cake cutting, tradition with a twist. Their cake was actually made of dozens of raspberry-lemonade cupcakes. His hand on hers, they slid the silver cake knife under one of the cupcakes, lifting it to feed each other small bites. This was accomplished with a lot of giggling and cameras flashing.

Then Keisha wanted to toss the bouquet. "Let's get all this over with so we can get back to the party," she said to general applause.

Crossing River Jordan

The single women gathered in a frothing bunch, jostling and giggling. "Chess, get in there!" Keisha ordered. "Come on, Auntie Dee!"

"Never in a million years!" Dee replied. "I'm retired!"

"Well, I'm not." Birdie Lee pushed her way to the front of the group.

Keisha turned her back and flipped the bouquet over her shoulder. There was some elbowing and foot shuffling among the women. The flowers soared into the air, hit a chandelier and ricocheted away from the waiting women, straight into Hope's hands.

She laughed delightedly, saying, "Thank you, Mama!"

The removal of Keisha's yellow garter was a G-rated event, quickly accomplished and Pastor Darnell tickled everyone, by standing right up in front and saying, "Maybe this will bring me some luck. Right here, Steve!" He clapped his hands and cupped them like a catcher.

Steve shot the garter into the air and it landed, dangling from the hand of a small statue that stood in an alcove near the men.

"Good luck, man!" Steve told the statue, amid the laughing and pointing.

■

Vanessa, her brow raised, called Steve away from the center of the dance floor, just as the DJ announced the Electric Slide.

Sister Louisa Carlton sang out, "That's my dance!" and bumped her way to the middle of the crowd. Looking like the sun, she hitched up her bright yellow dress and nimbly moved across the floor.

Finally, the live musicians were able to join the party. Kendrick grabbed his twin's hand and pulled her to the center of the floor. All around the room, chairs emptied as everyone, young and old, formed lines and joined the celebration. Pastor Darnell and Chess held hands and pulled off some fancy moves, dancing as a couple.

Kendrick glanced around as he danced, his gaze settling on the huge tapestry. What was that thing showing? He couldn't figure out if it was the last supper or a scene from the

Crusades. *Wait—is that Lynn?* He was sure he'd seen her standing right beside the wall-hanging, but when the dancers turned, he looked again and she was gone.

He leaned down to whisper in Keisha's ear. "Did you invite Lynn?"

"What?" The music was pumping and the bass was bumping; she wasn't sure she'd heard him correctly.

"I said, did you invite Lynn?" Kendrick was much louder this time. "I thought I saw her at the church yesterday and I just saw her again!"

"I wouldn't invite that witch to her own funeral," Keisha assured him. "Just how much have you had to drink?"

"Not enough, if I keep seeing my ex-wife," Kendrick said and they both laughed.

■

Steve and Vanessa spoke briefly. He waved to attract Keisha's attention and then held up one finger, letting her know he would only be away for a moment. Vanessa directed him through the hidden corridor, out the back door. His surprise for Keisha had arrived and he wanted to check it out and take care of the payment ahead of time.

On the way back into the ballroom, Steve stopped at the bar. All the dancing had made him thirsty and he craved a glass of ginger ale. The bar was unattended; Steve checked the ballroom and sure enough, even the caterers and staff were dancing.

Behind the bar, he tried to find ginger ale. Not seeing any bottles, he began to test the spigots, reasoning that some of them dispensed mixers. Any bar worth the name would have ginger ale as a mixer.

Only a few drops trickled weakly from the dispenser. Steve Kent, fixer of broken things, looked around for a tool box and, not finding one, went to the trunk of his car for the toolkit he kept there. Soon, he had removed his jacket and was happily engaged in unscrewing things. He wanted his wedding celebration to continue without a hitch.

■

After indulging in much more than he usually drank, Ray Batt had begun to relax. By the time the Electric Slide was called, Batt was well into a party mood. "C'mon, Deacon, let's get out there and shake it up with some pretty ladies."

Uttley wasn't as comfortable as his friend. He hadn't seen one welcoming smile the entire night and he knew they should never have come to the reception. He was just glad that crazy Deanna Ramsey was too busy to notice him and evil Louisa Carlton hadn't caused any trouble so far. *That* woman was always threatening somebody with bodily harm.

Ray Batt had started drinking as soon as he heard that Rev. Beem had been attacked. He hadn't been totally sober since that night and it had been his bright idea to go to the reception and represent the minister.

"Albert would have gone if he could, "Ray told Uttley. He's the true senior minister of that church and we can't let people forget that. Besides, he's always stood up for you, even after what you did."

"What I did!" Uttley squeaked. "I took discrete, artistic photographs. Heh, heh, you tried to destroy the church, throwing in with those mobsters the way you did!"

"I didn't molest any young girls!" Batt roared.

"Young women! They were young women and I was trying to teach them..."

"Pervert!" yelled Batt.

"Psychopath!" countered Uttley.

"I'm going to that wedding and the reception for Albert Beem, the only friend we've got. Are you in or out?"

■

Uttley sipped a glass of Jack Daniels thinking, *Jack, you're my one true friend.* He watched Batt slink around the edges of the dance floor, trying to pretend that he fit in, like he was just another guest having a good time.

Minutes later, Uttley jerked himself awake. *How much have I had to drink?* he wondered. Too much, if he could fall asleep in a crowded room filled with blaring music.

He leaned back in his chair, his head against the tapestry, with no regard for its value. His head dipped toward his chest as he drifted off again. When he jerked awake the next time, it was because something had startled him. He couldn't breathe! He couldn't see! *Oh, God, what's happening?*

He clawed weakly at his throat, his legs stretched straight out and his heels drumming the floor in front of him. He had awakened too late. He didn't have enough air left to fight for his life and he lost it.

19

Kendrick was sure that he wasn't drunk. He had the children to take care of and he had to get back to the hospital tonight. He'd only allowed himself a couple of glasses of champagne. So, why was he suddenly seeing Lynn everywhere he looked? Maybe she was on his mind so much because of Keisha's wedding. Or was it that he was somehow feeling guilty because of his growing affection for Tiffany? Either way, he might need to seek professional help if it kept happening.

There was a time when he would have gone straight to Rev. Beem for guidance, but those days were long gone. He still loved the reverend for helping him through some tough years after he and Keisha had lost their parents, but he no longer had much respect for the man.

When things settled down—after Steve and Keisha got back from their honeymoon, after Tiffany got out of the hospital—then he could sit down with Pastor Darnell or Uncle Carl and figure out why his ex was so much on his mind.

The dancers had done every kind of Slide imaginable, from Electric to Gospel to the Cha Cha. Then the music changed to a ballad. The party was winding down. Kendrick saw his twin talking to the children, who were still captivated by Steve's parents. Keisha had circled the room, thanking guests, acknowledging good wishes and saying goodbyes, but where was Steve?

He couldn't stop his eyes from returning to the tapestry where he thought he'd seen Lynn earlier. There she was again! The hair was different, but he knew the way she walked, how she held her head. He caught just a flash of her before she was gone again, suddenly swallowed up by the tapestry. She'd been dressed just like one of the wedding party— wearing a yellow dress with a white sash, but Kendrick didn't doubt his eyes or his sanity now; Lynn was in this ballroom!

Quietly, he hurried toward the tapestry, not wanting to disturb the happy couple. Just as he got to the spot where he'd seen Lynn, Ray Batt and Vanessa got there, too.

"Did anyone see a woman about this tall?" He held his hand up level with his chin. "She had bright red hair—short— and she was dressed like a bridesmaid."

"I think I saw her a little while ago," said Vanessa. She moved around the table, helping one of the teens stack dishware on a large rolling tray.

Batt kicked Utley's shoe. "Lesh, go, man," he slurred. "Party'sh over."

"You should never have been here in the first place!" Vanessa snapped. "Wake him up and get him out of here!"

Trying again, Batt pulled his friend's arm and Uttley fell, face first, out of the chair. Vanessa began to scream.

■

Deacon Uttley's lifeless form sprawled on the floor. When his head hit, there was a metallic clunk as a wrench dropped from someplace on the body. There was no blood, but it was obvious that a murder had been committed. Strands of his stringy hair had pulled loose and were caught in the yellow garter that encircled his neck. His eyes had rolled back so that only the whites showed and his purplish tongue poked out of his mouth.

Surprisingly, Vanessa stopped after the first long shriek. She seemed to come to herself immediately, remembering that she had a responsibility here; she was in charge. She sent someone to call the police and then pulled Ray Batt to a chair to keep him away from the body. Batt kept nudging his friend with his foot, telling Uttley to wake up. There was still enough of a party going on in the ballroom to distract most of the guests, keeping mass panic at bay.

Kendrick shook Vanessa's arm. "I'll stay with them," his gesture included both Uttley and Batt. "Get Pastor Darnell and my uncle. They can help us figure out the best way to handle things."

Dee had noticed the little group at the back of the room. "Mama, will you stay here until Mr. Bernard gets back from the restroom? Tell him I'm going to have a word with the pastor and then we can go home."

Birdie Lee had enjoyed a big day and it was taking its toll. Her eyelids were drooping and her head seemed too heavy for her neck. "I don't want to go home! The night is young!"

"Well, fine. We'll get Bernard to take us out somewhere else." Dee figured that her mother would be asleep before they even got out of the parking lot. "I'll be right back."

She went to Daisy, who stood by her table, watching the growing group in the corner with concern. "I don't know what's wrong, but I think we need to get the children home," Daisy said. "We need to get Steve and Keisha out of here, too. I don't want anything to spoil their plans. Whatever's happening, it doesn't have anything to do with them."

Keisha sat with her new in-laws and the children. Half of them were whiny and the other half were in a hyperactive melt down from too much sugar.

Daisy whispered, "You and Steve get going, now. We've got the kids."

She received a welcome and comforting nod from the Kents. "Go on, you've said enough goodbyes," Mrs. Kent agreed. "Just sneak out."

Daisy took Keisha's hand and led her through the arch to the bar just outside of the ballroom. That was where Daisy had last seen Steve—on his knees, shirt sleeves rolled to his elbows, contentedly repairing the soft drink dispenser.

Now, he was on his feet, speaking earnestly to a police officer.

■

As soon as she saw him, Dee knew there was nothing to be done for Deacon Uttley. She could only make sure that no one touched the body before the police arrived. Uttley was now evidence.

She tried to remember when she'd last seen the garter. Surely Keisha was still wearing one—the other should have been dangling from the statue's cold marble hand, but it wasn't there. She began to feel chills of fear—first, the savage attack on two people in the church. Now someone had murdered a man in a room filled with people.

The police were taking charge, giving orders and making calls. The first thing they did was to close off the exits. No one was leaving for the foreseeable future.

Daisy couldn't believe this was happening again. How was it that every time disaster struck, the children were caught in the net? Sleepy, crabby and confused, the two youngest burst into tears as soon as they saw blue uniforms. Wisdom and Knowledge were starry-eyed with admiration and curiosity, until they saw Steve being led away.

"Hey, where are you taking my dad?" Wisdom yelled, jumping out of his seat. His brand new grandfather put a large hand on his shoulder and told him not to worry.

A female officer came over to the table and spoke softly to the children. "Your father is going to help us. We need him to answer some questions, that's all."

The children were soon released, along with Martin and Ruth Kent. Carl and Daisy debated who would go along. The Kents were new grandparents to three children, not seven.

Keisha was in tears—a state Carl couldn't handle—leaving Daisy to attend to her.

"Aunt Daisy, I knew something was going to happen—it was too perfect! I thought what happened to Tiffany was the bad thing, but this—oh my God, they've arrested Steve!" She fell into Daisy's arms.

Ray Batt was taken to the station, until he sobered up enough to be considered a reliable witness. Kendrick and Dee were being questioned at a table just a few feet from where crime scene techs were taking pictures and collecting evidence in small plastic bags. They were soon joined by Vanessa and Pastor Darnell.

The pastor couldn't contribute very much, but he'd been among the first people to see the body. He'd been on the dance floor with Chess when the crime was committed, and it turned out that Chess provided the most important information of the night.

"Deacon Uttley was talking to a young woman for a while. I thought she was a bridesmaid," she told the cop taking notes.

Kendrick snapped to attention. "Kind of tall, with red hair?"

The officer looked up from is notes to ask, "Red, like the clown hair teens are wearing?"

Chess shook her head. "No, her hair was red, natural redhead color."

Kendrick jumped up and yelled, "My ex-wife *was* here. Her hair is different, but it was Lynn. Auntie Dee, I saw her at the church yesterday and I saw her here tonight. I thought I was going crazy!"

■

They asked several questions to determine if the crime scene had been compromised. Dee felt like she was on a course to meet every cop in the city. The police department was taking this very seriously, coming right after the attacks at the church. Several officers knew about the trouble River Jordan had faced the previous year. Dee prepared herself to answer their questions for as long as it would take. She wasn't getting the worst of it—poor Daisy would have to take Birdie Lee home with her again.

Hovering closely to the people working the scene, Deanna heard how the man had died. Someone had pulled the garter over his head, slipped the wrench under the garter at the back of his neck and twisted it to tighten the garter until Uttley was strangled to death. Dee longed for a chance to ask questions of someone—anyone. She wished that Langston had been there.

The police were making quick work of dividing the crowd into two groups: those who couldn't possibly have any information because they weren't anywhere near the crime and couldn't have seen what happened—like Ruth, Martin and the children—and those who not only could have had a ringside seat, but who might have had opportunity.

Fortunately for many, they all had dozens of witnesses. Most of the people who'd been on the dance floor were quick to list who they'd seen and who had seen them. The group dancing was a god-send for the investigators who wanted nothing more than to rule out as many people as possible. One man, a full-time member of the field house staff, took several officers on a tour of the building, showing them the basement and the service corridor.

"That's how he did it," Dee said, jerking the pastor's arm in her excitement. "That's how the killer got away! All he had to do was wait until everybody was looking at the dancing. Then he reached out from behind the tapestry, strangled Uttley and slipped away down the corridor. He was probably long gone before the police even got here!"

Dee had almost everything right. *Almost.*

The cops were letting people leave, a few at a time. The killer was still in the building, had spoken to the police and was trying to get on with the escape plan. "You know where to reach me, officers. And I'll contact you if I remember anything else. Thanks for letting me get back to work."

Uttley's murder had been the result of several fortunate accidents. Beem was still alive and would have to be dealt with later. Still, his being in the hospital was the reason that the other target could now be checked off the list. One down and one to go. Hospitals were busy places, lots of people moving in and out. Beem would be taken care of, but first things first.

■

The driver of the carriage Steve had hired to surprise his bride settled into the seat, flicked the reins and rolled away into the night. Lynn smiled and chatted happily with her horse. "It was easy, Topper. I wasn't sure how I'd get him, but I got him at last! He won't be ruining any more lives. He won't ever hurt another woman!"

She was on a street that paralleled Lake Shore Drive. She could see the lights of the city twinkling ahead. She might as well go downtown and see if she could pick up a couple of fares. Then the night would be perfect.

A rustling sound caused her to snap her head around. What was that old woman doing in her carriage?

Birdie Lee sat up and stretched. "I haven't been in one of these since I was a little girl," she said companionably. "My grandfather used to have a fine Brougham carriage and he'd take me to town for candy on Saturdays. Course it wasn't all prettified like this one. How'd you get all them lights on here?"

A carriage ride from the ballroom to Midway Airport had been Steve's romantic gift to Keisha. The frame of the carriage, along with the horse's bridle and reins, had been outlined in twinkling lights. It looked like something created by Cinderella's fairy godmother.

Jerking the carriage to a stop, Lynn turned and stared. Of course she knew Miss Grandma, but the old woman didn't seem to recognize her. Maybe it was because she had her hair tucked under the top-hat she wore as part of her uniform for the carriage company. The silk scarf she'd worn under the red wig peeked out of her jacket pocket. Dressed in trousers and suspenders with red shirt and black bow tie, the large framed woman could easily be mistaken for a man.

"What are you stopping for?" Birdie demanded. She waved her hat in the air and a couple of feathers drifted into the wind. "Get this thing moving! Yee haw!"

The well-trained horse looked around, shook its head and pawed the ground with one hoof. Otherwise, it didn't move one step. This horse was used to the blaring, screeching city sounds. Miss Birdie Lee Streeter didn't bother her one bit.

Lynn first thought of Birdie Lee as a complication and then she reconsidered. What if they knew what she'd done and were already looking for her? It might be good to have a hostage, especially one who didn't know she was a hostage. She could drag Birdie Lee around until she'd done everything she had to do. Who knew how handy a crazy old lady might be?

Lynn deepened her voice a little and asked, "Would you like to take a tour, ma'am?"

"I'm all ready to go. I took a little nap while I was waiting for you. Where are we going first?"

They head southeast away from Hyde Park into South Shore. The lights of the city are behind them now and Topper began to whinny and balk. These were not the familiar streets she was used to traveling and it wasn't the way to the stables for food and water and rest.

Lynn had been working her horse for more than a year and could sense when there was a problem. Topper was ready to go home. She also thought about what kind of attention a brightly lit carriage would bring as it traveled south on the Drive. As soon as they were within a couple of blocks of her

Crossing River Jordan

lake front destination, she turned the carriage and stopped by a short street that ended in a private driveway.

The South Shore neighborhood had seen better days. It seemed to be on the verge of gentrification many times, only to find itself continually stuck between boom and bust. Something always happened to keep it from attaining its former glory. Many mansions, in an array of conditions from the pitiful to the perfect, stood between tree-lined streets and beachfronts leading to the lake.

Lynn slapped Topper on her flank and sent the animal on her way, praying that she would make it safely back to the stable. She sadly watched Topper clop away, knowing that she probably would never see her horse again. It wouldn't take the police long to start searching for her. She couldn't believe that they hadn't captured her by now.

She'd always had buzzard luck. When she first attended River Jordan Church, she'd been about 14 years old. Rev. Alden was still the senior minister and Lynn loved her time there. She and Keisha became friends and she was astounded when Keisha's handsome twin brother began to pay attention to her. What she'd never told anyone was that Deacon Uttley had noticed her, too. Uttley kept telling her that she needed to pray with him—that she needed his counsel if she ever wanted to be worthy of a young man as special as Kendrick. After a while, she began to believe that she needed to so something to hold on to her young man and she turned to the deacon for help.

He'd helped, all right. Helped himself to her virginity and her dignity and her self-esteem. He used her for nearly three years. As she and Kendrick grew closer, she grew more depressed. She had to fight to seem happy when she was with the boy she loved. She struggled to show her happy face to the world.

She had to tell someone. Rev. Alden was cutting back on her duties around the church, so Lynn went to Rev. Beem. Mistake Number Two. He proceeded to tell her that what happened to her hadn't actually taken place. He insisted that she was "making a mountain out of a mole-hill" and she must have misunderstood.

When she threatened to go to her parents, Beem told her that she would be punished; if anything had happened, it must have been her fault. She must have enticed Deacon Uttley beyond his ability to resist. It was the curse of Eve. Women had a core of wickedness in them. He offered to pray for her to help her atone for her sins.

About a year later, she'd gotten pregnant and Kendrick was so wonderful, she thought that her problems were all solved. Lynn hadn't reckoned on the stress of marriage and parenthood, especially for someone so young. She fought as hard as she could to be a good wife and mother, but she was always just a blink away from the darkness inside of her.

It never went away and constantly threatened to swallow her whole. She had never felt any affection for the children—they were just gifts for Kendrick. By the time Kensha was born, Lynn had only one emotion left and that was anger. It was like a wild animal growing larger and more savage with every passing day. She knew that if she didn't leave, she would hurt someone that she should have loved.

"Why did you send the horse away? How long do we have to walk? Where are we going?" Birdie Lee's non-stop questions stepped all over Lynn's nerves.

She gestured toward a large building being rehabbed on the lakefront side of the street. Formerly an architect's mansion, it had been broken up into six apartments in the early 1950s. Now it was being turned into three condos. Lynn knew someone who was squatting there, until the repairs were done and the units were sold. She hoped he would help her get on with her plan and make her get away.

The condos were being remodeled from the top down, so one of the first things restored was the freight elevator. Under the guise of showing Birdie an apartment that she might want to rent, Lynn hustled her to the top floor.

The most stunning thing about the place was the view. Floor to ceiling windows looked out over the private beach below and far out across the lake to the towering buildings of Chicago's Loop. The rooms were massive and there was polished white oak everywhere they walked, except the entryway, which was tiled in marble. The bedroom door was closed, but when Lynn opened it, Birdie saw a filthy mattress on the floor surrounded by dirty clothes, crushed cans, wadded food wrappers and pizza boxes. Birdie could hear loud snoring.

"I'll be right back, ma'am, "Lynn said as she closed the door behind her. "Just one minute and we'll get back to our tour."

Birdie Lee sucked her teeth and walked over to peer out of the windows. That sure was a pretty beach down there. They had it lit up real nice with colored lanterns. Maybe somebody was going to have a barbeque! Birdie truly loved barbeque, even though sometimes it gave her partials a little trouble. She looked around for something to write on. She would leave that nice young man a note and tell him where she'd gone.

Before she found pen or paper, she'd forgotten what she was looking for and why she wanted it. She went out the door to wait for the elevator. She had to get downstairs before the food was all gone!

20

The empty ballroom was like an old prom queen whose glory had faded. The forensics people had completed their work and most of the police had moved on. Chess and Pastor Darnell sat at a table near the main entrance. They had searched the large room, the bar and the washrooms on the main floor. Dee and Bernard were with the remaining police officers, scouring the building for some sign of Birdie Lee.

To Dee's extreme disappointment, in what she thought of as the biggest case of her life, she was not the one to find the pivotal piece of evidence. Mr. Bernard had convinced the questioning officers that they should provide bathroom breaks for all the people still being detained.

"There's been a lot of drinking going on and things could get embarrassing, Officer, um, Hartman." Bernard squinted trying to read the young cop's brass name tag.

Officer Hartman apologized for not thinking of it himself. "We searched earlier. The restrooms are all clear, sir. Go right ahead."

Tossing the paper towel after drying his hands, Bernard saw the flash of yellow before the wastebasket door closed. Using another paper towel to cover his finger, he pushed the swinging door open again and stared at the yellow cloth, trying to understand what he was seeing. Then he opened the door and called, "Officers, there's something in here you should see!"

Hurrying down the hall towards the men's room, Hartman's partner, an older female cop said, "I hope he's not waving around anything that's gonna make us have to arrest him." She guffawed at her joke.

Hartman just glanced at her and shook his head. Many of her attitudes were from the Stone Age, but she was a good partner.

Bernard simply pointed when they walked into the room. Both cops gawked. And the young one announced, "That was not there the first time we searched. The techs bagged everything and took it to the lab!"

When Officer Hartman removed the clothes from the trash, a red wig dropped to the floor. "Bag that!" he yelled to his partner. "We'll get some hair off of that for sure!"

They checked the clothing for the size. It took just seconds for Kendrick to determine that the wig, dress, sash and shoes were what he'd seen Lynn wearing. The dress wasn't an exact copy of the bridesmaids' dresses, but it was close enough to fool everyone from a distance.

"None of the bridesmaids wore a size 14." Mr. Bernard gave an expert's opinion.

"There were only three and all of them had their dresses on when they left," Chess added.

"There's only one reason those clothes would be in the men's room," Bernard said to the young cop. "Either they were worn by a man who wanted to look like a woman or by a woman who needed to look like a man." Bernard spoke directly to the man, making sure the officer was taking him seriously.

"Lynn is not a small woman," Dee said. "If she wanted to look like a man, she could get away with it. Remember, Kendrick, when the two of you went to the Halloween party as 1920s gangsters? After Keisha got through with her makeup and mustache, Lynn looked enough like a guy to fool a lot of people. She sure fooled me."

"What about motive," Officer Hartman asked. "Did your ex have any reason to kill three people?"

Kendrick and Daisy told about Lynn's slide into depression, and told the officers how she just walked away from her family one day.

"But I can't see her killing anybody," Kendrick said. "She wasn't that kind of person. She never even raised her voice with the children."

"We need to find her," Hartman said. "She's the only one we're sure was lying to us about something."

The cops had their heads together, discussing Mr. Bernard's idea in low tones. They flipped through their notes and the young man grinned. "The detectives are gonna bust a seam," he told his partner. "While they're at the station questioning an innocent man, we can solve this thing!"

His partner looked like she'd heard these kinds of grand plans before.

"Let's at least try to figure it out," Hartman said. "You know we'll be blamed for letting her walk right out from under our noses, even though the detectives did the questioning."

Dee looked around the ballroom. "Are you done with us? Officers, have you questioned everyone?"

"Yes, ma'am. We've got all we need. You're free to go."

"No, there must be someone still talking to guests. Someone is still interviewing my mother."

"No ma'am, you're the last of the guests..."

No, no, no..." Dee began.

"Don't worry; we'll find her," the cop said and then spoke into his two-way.

■

Dee was running on anger, keeping her fear at bay. "She's always doing things like this; she thinks it's funny!"

"She's probably fallen asleep somewhere quiet," Bernard tried to reassure her. Even he looked wilted and his black Armani suit had dust on the knees from crawling around searching for Birdie beneath linen-draped tables.

"Deanna, I'm sorry. I shouldn't have left her alone for so long." Bernard couldn't help feeling guilty, even though he'd never been asked to watch over Birdie Lee. He'd stepped away to make a phone call that had stretched into several calls as he and his friends made plans for a Fourth of July getaway.

Bernard had never even had a pet, admitting to himself at a young age that he was too self-centered to look out for anyone else. His was glad he'd never wanted children; he'd always felt that his lifestyle completely ruled them out anyway. Today, even though things were different—Heather could have two mommies and Kyle could have two daddies—he knew that he'd made the right decisions for himself.

But he really did like Dee's mother; she reminded him of a dear aunt who had died long ago. He'd been having a good time with Birdie and had taken the task of being her escort upon himself without being asked.

Dee put her hand over his. "This is not your fault. Mama gets an idea in her head and she's off to the races. Psychologists would call it poor impulse control. I call it mean and spiteful. She knows it makes me crazy."

■

They were moving through the service corridor, checking each room once again, more to placate Deanna than because they expected to find anything. The police now knew that they'd been fooled by the carriage driver and an all-points bulletin was issued. The carriage driver was a person of interest in this homicide, but so was Steve, who was being interviewed at the station.

Dee, Bernard and the two officers with them stepped out into the cool air. Dee was surprised to hear birds singing—it was nearly dawn! She could see the sky lightening over the lake. The officers were checking the grounds one last time, before leaving the scene. They would have other cops continue searching for Birdie. Ordinarily, she wouldn't be considered missing for 24 hours, but because she was missing from the scene of a crime, the search would begin immediately.

Pastor Darnell, Chess and Kendrick joined them in the parking lot. The pastor asked Dee, "Where else do you think we should look? Can you think of anywhere she might try to go?"

"I hate to wake her up, but I was just about to call Daisy to see if she's there. It's where Mama went when she got here Saturday. I don't know why she went there instead of going to my house. I don't know how to think like a crazy woman."

Crossing River Jordan

She flipped her phone open. When she looked down to press Daisy's speed-dial number, she bent to retrieve a couple of silver wrapped chocolate candies from the ground. Dee looked around then, paying more attention to the area. A hot-pink feather clung to the branches of a small boxwood shrub.

"Mama was here," she said, with a perplexed frown on her face.

"The carriage was here," Kendrick told them. "I came out to see it because Steve was so excited about the surprise. Keisha would have pretended that it was too expensive or too flashy, but she would have loved it. Steve had them put those tiny lights all over it. Even the horse was glowing."

"My mother is like a magpie," Dee said slowly. "If there was something shiny and pretty around her, she'd be drawn right to it."

Dee's legs could no longer hold her up and she sank down on a low stone wall. Her voice quivered. "Oh, my sweet Lord, a murderer has my crazy mother!"

■

Lynn was losing her cool. She yelled and shook Spider, the nearly comatose man she had come to for help. He was her cousin, by way of a complicated series of marriages among people she didn't even know. They had never been close—Spider was bad news even as a child—but after walking out on her family there had been no one else for her to turn to.

Spider knew things, like how to get fake documents and how to go underground. As far as she knew, he'd never had a legitimate job or paid taxes in his life, but he still managed to drive nice cars and had never lived on the street. Looking at him, Lynn thought, *if he weren't such a dope fiend, he could be living large in this condo, rather than sleeping on a nasty mattress in one cruddy room.*

She checked the pulse in his neck. He wasn't dead, but he wasn't waking up either. She decided to see if he had any money. She needed to get out of the city as soon as Beem was taken care of. She wouldn't leave without ending his miserable life.

Lynn had a grim thought. *Will the Lord forgive me for the other one? I didn't want to hurt her; she was just in the way.*

Lynn hoped that Birdie wouldn't be freaked out by all the noise coming from the bedroom. As she rifled through Spider's pockets, she tried to come up with a plausible story to tell the old woman. She needed Birdie now more than ever. The police would be looking for a man in a carriage. They wouldn't be looking for a young woman who was taking care of her elderly aunt.

Finally, she found Spider's stash—a roll of bills as big as her fist, stuffed into the dirty pillowcase beneath his zoned-out head. Instead of a pillow, the case was stuffed with rancid clothes. The money was in the pocket of a shirt she'd found there.

"Sorry, Spider. I'll pay you back," she whispered, as she backed out of the room and closed the door. A rumbling snore was his only reply.

Birdie Lee was nowhere to be found. Frantically, Lynn checked every room in the condo. She wondered if the old coot had managed to fall from the balcony. When she stepped out and looked down, she saw Birdie Lee talking to teenagers on the beach. They were cooking breakfast—Lynn could smell bacon. It was a camp out.

There's nothing private about this beach, Lynn groused to herself as she clattered down the stairs. She was too anxious to wait for the elevator. She burst through the rear door and dashed out onto the sand.

Birdie waved a piece of bacon at her." Hey Lynn, where you been girl? I haven't seen you in years. Come and meet my new friends!"

Lynn realized that she had lost her hat while searching Spider. She was shocked that the crazy old broad remembered her. She hoped that Birdie Lee wouldn't understand that she was a hostage.

"Miss Grandma, everybody is looking for you. We've got to get home so they won't be worried," Lynn said brightly.

"I don't want to go home now," Birdie stuck out her chin. "I'm having fun with my friends."

Thinking fast, Lynn said, "Well, we weren't going straight home. First I wanted to stop at the store and pick up some new clothes. You like new clothes, don't you?"

There was a spark in Birdie's eyes and Lynn began to relax, but Birdie wasn't quite ready yet.

"I want to go junk shopping," she crowed.

"You want to do what?" Lynn was losing patience. She would have tried muscling the old lady, but she didn't want to involve the troop of Boy Scouts surrounding Birdie Lee.

Then Lynn recalled that "junk shops" were what Birdie called thrift stores. She gave Birdie a 100-watt smile. A thrift shop was just what they needed!

"That's just perfect, Miss Grandma! Say good bye to your friends and let's go!"

■

New Again was a thrift store just west of Hyde Park on 55th street. The store was a prime destination for thrift shoppers and even the occasional antique dealer. Buyers were often surprised by a lot of high-quality items—furniture, clothing and small appliances. Because it was close to an affluent neighborhood, its customers benefited from the cast offs of the wealthy. Some of the customers attended the University of Chicago and were the shabby-chic wearing children of those wealthy donors.

Along with Spider's money, Lynn had also discovered his car keys. The Ford Taurus was only a couple of years old, with valid plates and a city sticker. She never had figured out how someone as screwed up as Spider always managed to keep a reliable car and make sure it was legal, too. She pulled into the store's parking lot and as she turned off the engine, Birdie Lee woke up from a brief nap.

The store was cold; the air conditioning was more than was needed on an early Monday morning. Birdie insisted that she needed a coat and while Lynn collected the few items she wanted—pleated slacks and a pair of jeans, two blouses and a summer blazer—Birdie searched diligently for an item that was unlikely to be found in a Chicago store at the beginning of summer. She finally settled on a large red sweater.

"I need new clothes, too," she told anyone within hearing distance. "We've had on the same clothes for two days! You can buy almost everything you need in this store." Birdie thought she was whispering, "Except underwear and socks. You don't want nobody else's bloomers and socks!"

Lynn glanced around to see if anyone was paying attention. She rushed to help Birdie select the other pieces she wanted, black jogging pants and a green t-shirt with large picture of a parrot on it. Lynn tried, unsuccessfully, to get Birdie to give up the pink hat. The cops would surely be looking out for it.

They were headed for the check out line when Birdie saw the table. She topped dead in her tracks and stared. Then she began to tremble with fury. "That's my table!" she shouted, pointing to a drum table that was part of an arranged display.

Lynn grabbed her arm and said, "Miss Grandma, that can't be your table. Your table is at your house. That one must just look like yours."

Birdie shook her off and stalked to the furniture section. "The hell you say!" she bellowed. "That's my table and that's my chester drawers and my lamp. These thieves have my whole house in here!"

As she tried to move the old woman toward the doors, Lynn discovered that Birdie Lee was much stronger than she appeared. Store employees were moving their way and they'd certainly gotten the attention of most of the other shoppers, attention Lynn really didn't want. If Birdie didn't calm down, someone was sure to call the police! She had to do something fast.

She leaned down and whispered in Birdie's ear. "If we want to get your stuff back from these thieves, we've got to play it cool, Miss Grandma. We don't want to let them know that we've figured it out. They might take your things and hide them where we couldn't find them again."

She could see Birdie Lee drawing in a deep breath so she could start yelling again. She grasped a papery hand and began to move slowly toward the cash registers. "We've got to act like nothing's wrong; just go through the line and pay. Once we get outside, we can stop the first cops we find and they'll come running in here and arrest all these crooks!"

Birdie squinted at Lynn like she was examining something under a microscope, but she allowed herself to be led to check out. Then she gave Lynn co-conspirator's wink.

"Ya'll got some mighty fine things in here," she said loudly. "Some mighty fine furniture. Just the kind of things I would buy for my own house. I wish I had a nice drum table like the one you have here." She gave the cashier a big crocodile smile and winked at Lynn again.

Lynn was so nervous that she dropped half of the change. Birdie Lee went after a dime that was rolling away, lost her balance and tilted toward the floor. Lynn sprained every muscle in her body and bruised her knees as she slid across the floor as she sought to wedge herself between Birdie Lee and a grievous injury.

The cashier let out a shriek. "Oh, my God, is she all right? Somebody better call an ambulance!"

"No, no, she's fine!" Lynn hollered, heaving Birdie upright and springing to her feet. "Everything's fine; everyone's fine!"

She grabbed Birdie with one hand and their bag with the other, spun around and hip-bumped the door. Ignoring her aching knees, Lynn pulled the old woman out with her. Birdie grinned, triumphantly clutching the shiny dime.

21

Keisha had cried herself to a fitful sleep, but at seven in the morning, she padded into the kitchen to make coffee. Dee was snoring softly, her arms pillowing her head on the kitchen table. She held her cell phone in one hand, but even the bleat of the doorbell didn't wake her.

Keisha whipped the door open calling, "Steve?"

Her eyes welled when Detective Hughes hobbled in, followed by his partner, Detective Solis. She pointed to the kitchen, in response to Langston's unspoken question.

Suddenly, the household burst into action. The phone rang; Tremain began to cry. Kendrick's voice came quickly, soothing the baby.

Dee came from the kitchen, bleary-eyed. Some of her hair was mashed flat against one side of her face; on the other side it stuck up in a tuft. Ordinarily, she would have been mortified by her early morning appearance, but Langston dropped his crutches when he saw her and she marched straight into his open arms.

Daisy, swathed in a blue terry cloth robe with matching turban, came down the stairs, scolding Keisha. "Girl, did you get any sleep at all? You aren't going to be any good for anybody....." Seeing Dee with the two visitors, she shooed Keisha upstairs so they could both get dressed.

"Auntie Dee, I got coffee started," Keisha called over her shoulder.

"You've heard something?" Dee asked the detectives, her voice filled with hope.

"There are units on the street; they've been rolling all night. We'll hear something soon." Langston smoothed Dee's wayward hair. "I'm so sorry I wasn't there."

"Well, the Dynamic Duo is here now." Dee smiled at Javier, who began to hum the theme from the old Batman show.

"Actually," Langston said, "We're *not* here. I'm on sick leave and Javi has the day off. We're very unofficial."

"Yep, today we're Bruce Wayne and Dick Grayson. Wait a minute, I don't want to be *Dick* Grayson. I'll be *Ricardo* Grayson." He greatly exaggerated the rolling 'R' and then was interrupted by his cell phone.

Carl came down to greet the detectives and they all moved into the kitchen, settling around the table.

"Two lunches," Javier said, smiling as he accepted a steaming cup of coffee from Carl. "And if this turns out to be something, I'll go all the way to Chef Luciano's."

"That was my girl in Dispatch," Javier explained and then he turned to caution Dee. "Now don't get excited, but there was a report of a disturbance, something about a little old lady at a Hyde Park thrift store..."

Shrieking, Dee jumped up, sloshing hot coffee all over the table. "My mother is in Hyde Park? That's just west of the Point!"

Langston grabbed her hand. "Did you miss the part about not getting excited? We don't know that it's your mother."

"Did they arrest her? Where is she?" Dee was so desperate for news; it was as if Langston hadn't said a word. "Well, we've got to go! Oh, I need to change!"

She moved toward the door, but Javier barred the way. Langston struggled to get up from his chair while Carl wiped up coffee.

"I'll try to find out more," Javier told her. "I can follow you and Lang to your place and I'll make calls while you change."

Crossing River Jordan

"Carl, sorry about the mess. Someone please call me when you know what's happening with Steve," Dee called on her way down the front stairs.

A squad car double parked, blocking their cars. The officers who got out had a brief conversation with Langston and Javier, before ringing the Franklins' doorbell.

Langston began the task of lowering himself into the car as Dee demanded an explanation.

"Don't get crazy. They've come to take Kendrick in for questioning."

"Again?" Dee squawked and then she remembered that Langston didn't know about her adventure with Kendrick. "I mean, uh, what for? He didn't do anything."

Langston folded his arms and leaned back against the seat. "I'm sure you'll explain that reaction later. It's not about what he did; it's about what he might know. Seems like his ex looks good for the attacks *and* the murder."

■

"I'm not doing that!" Birdie Lee folded her arms and shook her head. "Hopping up and down on them bicycles like that—and they're not even going anywhere!"

Lynn pulled her away from the window; Birdie was watching a spinning class in action. They weren't at the YMCA to take classes.

"No, Miss Grandma, we came here to clean up and put on our new clothes!" Lynn spoke brightly, but with a brittle grin. She towed Birdie Lee toward the locker room.

Maybe it's time to ditch the old bird and get on with things. She still had to work out how to get to Beem in the hospital. He would have been dead, if she had just had a little more time with him. It was all that stupid girl's fault, getting in the way. What was she doing at the church that time of night? Lynn decided not to waste anymore energy on the "collateral damage." She hadn't meant the girl any harm; she was just in the wrong place at the wrong time.

Birdie Lee was happily putting on her "new" outfit and Lynn felt the fog lift from her brain; the hot showers had done them both a world of good. Lynn was ready to plan her next steps. If she could only have a moment to think!

Birdie was clawing through her purse. "I need some more candy!" She tossed a fistful of silver foil wrappers into the trash. "Did we have breakfast? I'm hungry and I don't think we had breakfast!"

"That's a real good idea, Miss Grandma!" Lynn couldn't remember the last time she'd eaten.

"I want a Burger Whopper!"

"Miss Grandma, there's no Burger King near here, but we're close to a McDonald's. It's right down the street!" Noting Birdie's frown, Lynn thought quickly to head off a tantrum. "We can stop and get more candy on the way."

Lynn had to take her time. There were people everywhere, enjoying the warm day and the small shops and restaurants. In her mind, she kept up a running talk with God, as she drove slowly down 53rd Street. *Lord, I know You said not to kill, but then why did you put so many people down here who need killing? You must be blessing me, because I haven't been caught yet. I think I must be Your instrument, sent to punish those sinners.*

Her thoughts hadn't been so clear in years. She was sure it was because she was finally doing what the Lord wanted her to do.

The cops had probably figured out who she was by now and having Birdie with her wasn't protection; it was more like having a bulls-eye painted on her forehead. The simplest thing to do was to put the old woman in a cab and send her to River Jordan—but walking around with a frail old lady in a hospital was like having an all-access pass. She needed Birdie Lee for a little while longer.

■

The pastor's head felt like it was full of cotton and he promised himself a week of sleeping late when things settled down. Sunday had flowed into Monday so quickly that only the changed hands on the clock told him that he'd slept at all. Pulling into his reserved parking space and running behind schedule, he barely registered that there were several dogs in the parked cars. What pulled him up short was the *number* of cars in the parking lot.

Crossing River Jordan

Did Cory schedule a pet-blessing service? His schedule had been—well, unconventional—since Cory Beem had been answering the church phones. Darnell knew he could easily have forgotten that a special service was supposed to take place today.

I hope they left the dogs some water. At least the owners left the windows open a little, he observed.

He rushed down to his office and was confused by what he saw—confused, but not surprised. Since coming to River Jordan, Pastor Darnell had become so used to the unexpected that he'd given up trying to identify "normal." He took it in stride when he found his desk and chair draped by a drop cloth. Perched on top of the cloth, Cory sat staring at the wall.

"Morning, Cory. What's going on?"

"Hey, Pastor D! I'm ready to be commissioned now." Cory hopped to his feet.

In the moment it took for the pastor to catch up. Just before Christmas, he and Cory had discussed a commission for the young artist—a mural for the pastor's office.

Man, the kid's had a major growth spurt since I first met him. Darnell smiled at the memory of the first time he'd met Georgia, wrestling with her little brother on the floor of the church art room. Now, Cory was almost looking at him eye-to-eye.

"You know what you want to do for the mural?"

"I read that book you gave me about being an artist and I was waiting for my Muse, you know, so I could be inspired. It came right in the middle of Sunday school. But, I can't tell you about it. It has to be a surprise."

Cory was still coping with his family splitting up and now he had to deal with his dad's injury. In light of the other worries the church family was facing: murder, attempted murder and a kidnapping—Cory's art project seemed a blessed return to a simpler time. As nervous as Darnell might be about Cory's idea, he didn't have the heart to stifle the boy's creativity. Art seemed to be the one thing that kept him out of trouble. He'd gotten the idea in Sunday school; how bad could it be?

"I can't lose this groove, Pastor D. I've got to get started now, but everyone's waiting for you upstairs."

"Everyone? Waiting? " The pastor got a sinking feeling in the pit of his stomach. "Cory, you better come with me."

Taking the stairs two at a time, Darnell made an undignified entrance through the choir loft. As soon as he faced the congregation, his eyes lit on Chess. She was sitting front and center, along with about 40 members of the River Jordan congregation. She gave him a tiny smile.

That made him more bewildered. She spent a great deal of time volunteering at River Jordan, but Chess rarely attended any services. Darnell momentarily wondered if he might be dreaming; maybe he'd gone too long on too little sleep.

Hiding his mouth behind his hand, Darnell leaned toward Deacon Long, who occupied the chair to his right. "Leon, what's going on?"

"Cory started a telephone tree this morning. Everyone is ready to search for Sister Ramsey's mother."

"Cory? Who would listen to Cory?"

"He's been answering your phone a lot lately," the young deacon explained. "We all thought *you* told him to call!"

Pastor Darnell searched for Cory among the members. When he locked glances with the boy, Cory grinned broadly and gave him a "thumbs up."

The pastor could feel the restlessness in the members. He didn't think they could do anything more than the police were already doing, but he understood the need. They wanted to get busy doing *something* to help. He sighed and stepped to the podium. As he always did, he bowed his head and silently prayed for the Lord to speak through him.

"Beloveds, once again we are faced with challenges to our courage and our faith. And once more, as a church family, we band together to face our fears and demonstrate our faith! In Isaiah 11:6, we find 'a little child shall lead them.' I guess that's true today, because young Brother Cory Beem started the telephone tree that has you here, ready to work.

"We're going to take a little time to put on our armor and seek the Lord first in prayer this morning. Then anyone who's willing is welcome to stay and help us bring Ms. Birdie Lee Streeter home."

■

After a stop at the drug store to stock up on candy, Lynn ran into an unexpected traffic jam. There was some kind of street fair going on and all cars were being re-routed. As she followed the long line heading north, Lynn glanced back to check on Birdie, who was unwrapping candies and popping them into her mouth, one after another.

Well, fine, Lynn thought. *At least she's quiet. Now I hope she doesn't go into some kind of sugar shock.*

Chicago in summer was one big party. The city and its neighborhoods observed every occasion, honored every hero and celebrated every ethnicity with a parade, fair or festival. Lynn could see a banner stretched over the boulevard: 25th Annual Alley Anniversary Celebration! How had she forgotten? She had planned to work with Topper and her carriage, giving rides at this event.

The Alley actually *was* a legendary alley on 50th street, behind the storefronts on St. Lawrence. Beginning in the 1950s, jazz records and live music were played every Sunday by DJs and musicians. As its reputation grew, the Alley stretched a couple of blocks north and south and food and drinks were served by various vendors, restaurants and bars along the route. For nearly thirty years, music lovers would bring their lawn chairs and settle in for DJ "battles" and great live jam sessions. When urban renewal finally brought an end to the Alley, supporters began a yearly festival of remembrance.

Lynn felt like she was going to explode. They were crawling down the street, with no way to peel off from the line of vehicles and she could see police cars and mounted cops every block or so. No wonder traffic was such a mess. This event was a big deal on Chicago's south side.

Suddenly, Birdie Lee lowered her window and stuck her head and shoulders out. "Sausage!" she yelled. "I smell Polish sausages and French fries. That's what I want to eat!"

Lynn was so startled that she nearly rear-ended the car in front of her. She swerved and slammed on the brakes. Birdie was thrown back inside the car and then she slid, face first into the front seat. Silver-wrapped candies flew into the air.

Birdie's first words were mumbled against the seat-back, but by the time she'd pushed herself upright, she was bellowing like a stuck bull. "...out of your dang mind, girl? You almost killed me and my hat just flew right out that window!"

Thank God, that stupid hat was gone! Caught by a gusty breeze, it was whipped beneath the wheels of the car. Two things occurred to Lynn. They were attracting way too much attention and—more importantly—Spider's car was *legal*. What if he'd reported it stolen?

"I'm so sorry, Miss Grandma! You scared me, leaning out of the car like that—I thought you were going to fall! Are you okay?"

"I'm fine, but my candy's not," Birdie huffed. "Look, it's rolling around all over the fl...oh, look, balloons!"

She'd forgotten about the hat that quickly, but before Lynn knew what was happening, Birdie Lee hopped out of the car.

"That's just great!" Lynn muttered as she slammed the gear shift into *Park* and turned the car off. It seemed that they hadn't moved in ages, anyway. Now was as good a time as any to ditch the car. She fumbled with her seatbelt, trying to keep an eye on Birdie, who was heading toward a table festooned with shiny Mylar balloons.

When Lynn caught up with her, Birdie was admiring her arm, which she'd draped with sparkly beaded bracelets.

"I like all of these," Birdie announced. "Lynn, girl, you need to get you some of these. Look how pretty they are."

Convincing her hostage to choose only two bracelets, Lynn wondered again just who was in charge. As Lynn fished in her pocket to pay for Birdie's treasures, the old woman took off again.

"See, right over there—there's the sausage man."

Near the corner, a vendor with a cart was doing a brisk business. Two lines of customers waited for hot dogs and polish sausages. Lynn snagged Birdie's arm.

"Miss Grandma, you hold a seat for us at one of those tables and I'll get the food. Look, there's a nice picnic table right under that tree."

Fearing that she might be distracted by another glittering object, Lynn walked Birdie to the table, got her seated and took her order. She had to trust that her hostage was hungry enough to sit for a few minutes, unattended.

Miracle of miracles, Birdie Lee did wait. While she ate, Lynn purchased two large straw hats. Birdie was delighted with the replacement—a red straw hat with a purple feather. She clapped it on and put her head down on her arms to take a nap.

Lynn took a deep breath. She felt that she'd been holding that breath since finding Birdie Lee in her carriage. *Finally, a*

Crossing River Jordan

quiet moment to think. The smart thing would be to walk away. Somebody would find the old lady and make sure she got home. She agreed with herself—*I don't really need her to get into the hospital. I'll find another way. Maybe I'll hide out until they send Beem home. Then I could get to him easy. He's too arrogant to stay out of sight.*

Gingerly, she rose, taking care not to bump her knees or shake the table. As soon as she turned to leave, there came the crash of cymbals and a drum roll. Birdie snapped up, wide awake.

"Let's go hear that music!"

22

Pastor Davis stared as the last of the cars left the parking lot. Everyone had their assignments, thanks to some quick computer work by Chess. Seeing him at a loss for a way to handle the impromptu rescue mission, she moved into action.

She had marched up to the podium and whispered, "Darnell, I'll print some maps of the city and you can give everyone an area to search."

Man, she is rockin' those jeans! Darnell the Cool quipped, and even in the midst of the disorder, the pastor had to admit that Chess in jeans was a pure pleasure. He'd never seen her casually dressed before and he took a minute to admire the view.

"Darnell?"

"Um, right!" He instructed the searchers to wait for their maps and reminded everyone to work in teams—one driver, someone to handle cell phone communications and anyone else to be lookouts.

Vanessa Beem had pictures of Birdie from the wedding. She and Cory passed them out as the pastor continued.

"Remember, we're helping the police. If you see her; just call 9-1-1 and then call my office. We'll search for two hours and meet back here."

Not for the first time, he felt the absence of the Mothers Board. They were the mortar that held River Jordan together.

Not only would they have had a plan in place to handle a missing person, but Mother Jessup would have had food cooking and coffee perking by now. He was gratified to see that Louisa Carlton and the Wilson sisters were taking care of those details. The scent of fresh coffee was already wafting through the building.

Darnell left the sanctuary and headed down to his office. He wanted to join the search, but there were other things he had to do first. A stop by the hospital to check on Tiffany and the reverend, to the jail to see if he could help Steve and Kendrick and there were two shut-ins to visit.

"Then, I should probably get back here to make sure everything's okay," he said, not realizing he had spoken aloud.

"He's finally snapped." Chess stepped in and startling the pastor. She smiled, "Talking to yourself is the first sign."

"Sometimes talking to yourself is the best conversation you have all day." He smiled back as he removed his tie and rolled up his sleeves. He looked around the office and sighed. Ordinarily, he would have begun straightening the cluttered desk as soon as she entered his office. *We're past that now*, he thought, pleased by the realization.

Chess tilted her head—an unspoken question.

"I don't have time to go home and change." He pulled gym shoes from the closet. This is the best I can do to be comfortable with what looks like another long day. I'm going to need a vacation very soon."

"What can I do to help?" Chess asked. "I can join the search or stay here or..."

"Or you could come with me, please." As soon as he'd said it, Darnell realized how much he preferred that option.

Dude, slow down! Darnell the Cool admonished. *You'll scare the girl to death with that needy act.*

"Um, I mean you could handle phone duty. It would help me to stay in touch with everyone while I take care of the visits." He hoped he didn't sound as lame as he felt. Why was he making such a big deal of this? Chess was his friend; of course he liked spending time with her. Besides, he honestly could use the assistance.

Especially, wearing those jeans, quipped the Cool.

Crossing River Jordan

Vanessa rushed in before they made it out of the office. She shook her cell phone in a clenched fist. "It's Albert. Something's wrong. I have to go."

"I'll drive you," the pastor said. "Where's Cory? Does he know?" His calm blanketed the room. There was no space for panic.

"I let him go with a group of teens. They were going to search around Tuley Park. Just having fun, I know, but…" her voice faded as she realized that she was rambling.

Chess took Vanessa's hand and put it in Darnell's. "I'll find Cory and bring him to the hospital," Chess said. "You go to the reverend. Everything will be fine; you'll see.

■

The police station on 61st and Racine had been built in the late '60s and was of a modern cracker-box design. A low, sprawling brown brick rectangle, only two stories high. No one who wasn't a neighborhood local would know that there were four tiers of cells built below ground. Steve had spent few hours in one of those cells, but still wondered how anyone locked in could manage to stay sane, much less sleep as soundly as some men could, if the snores were any indication.

He was still in his tuxedo, although the guards had made him remove the yellow cummerbund and bow tie. *I'll bet I'm the best-dressed prisoner in here*, he thought and shook his head.

To calm himself, Steve began to pace and make plans. *I'll go running with Wisdom every morning. That boy has good stamina and he's got his Mama's stubbornness. He could be a good long distance runner.* Five steps and turn; five steps and turn. *I've got to get Knowledge into the workroom. He's good with his hands—took Aunt Daisy's vacuum apart in no time!*

Thinking of the boys, Steve surprised himself by smiling. *What am I worried about? I didn't do anything wrong and the Lord wouldn't give me so many to love and so much to do, only to take it all away.*

H stopped in mid-stride and slapped a palm to his forehead. "Hope! She's already so shy; she'll probably be afraid of me now!" He sank down on the hard metal bunk.

A low voice came from an adjoining cell. "Who's Hope?"

"She's my daughter, my little girl," Steve said with wonder in his voice. "I just got married..."

"Man, little girls love their daddies, no matter what. You just remember that you're the one who will show her how a man is s'posed to treat her."

Steve couldn't see his neighbor; the cells were separated by steel walls, painted a muddy green.

Walking toward the wall so he could hear better, Steve asked, "What do you mean?"

"She'll watch everything you do—how you treat her mama and other women, too. But mostly, she'll take her cue from you. If you think she's smart, she will, too. If you think she's pretty or funny or good, that's how she'll be. Show her who she is." The voice broke off and such a violent coughing spell followed that Steve was alarmed.

"You okay? You need me to call a guard?"

When he could speak again, the man rasped, "Naw, I'm a'ight. I gotta let go of them cigarettes!"

Steve slid to the floor, with his back against the wall. "You seem to know a lot about raising daughters."

"I ought to know—I got four girls. 'Course, I know more about *not* raising them. I spend too much time in places like this. Got me a little Russian problem."

"'Russian problem?'"

"Vodka, boy. My problem is I can't get enough of it!" He broke into gravelly laughter that brought on another bout of coughing. "My son had the same kinda problem, only his was English."

"Gin?" Steve asked.

The sound was a mixture of laughing and coughing. "That's right!"

The clanging of doors interrupted them. A guard unlocked the door to Steve's cell. "Let's go," was all he said.

Steve's stomach rolled itself into a knot. He wanted to ask where he was being taken, but didn't trust his voice not to betray his fear. Just before moving off down the corridor, Steve realized that he'd just gained comfort from someone he'd never even seen. He looked back over his shoulder and called, "What's your name?"

"Willis, Joe Willis. You just remember what I said."

Crossing River Jordan

Processing Steve's release didn't take very long. He hadn't been arrested, merely held for questioning. He'd only been put in a cell because the station was short handed. Every available cop was doing crowd control at the Alley Celebration, so there'd been no officer to sit with him in an interrogation room.

Watched by the releasing officer and the desk sergeants, Steve stood at the counter that spanned more than half of the station's reception area, shaking his personal belongings out of a large manila envelope. Every sound seemed magnified by the cavernous space and then he heard Keisha.

"Well, why is it taking so long?"

In moments, the room was filled with people. Keisha barreled into Steve, followed by Wisdom and Knowledge, who wrapped themselves around his legs. His parents were waiting to hug him. Daisy and Carl had the rest of the children. Pastor Darnell and Chess Allen brought up the rear.

It took Steve a moment to sort his emotions—he was glad to be released and no longer suspected of murder, but he wasn't happy about the children being there. He wavered, wanting to kiss Keisha's face off and yell at her for bringing the kids to a police station. They shouldn't have to see him like this.

His father had always been able to read him. Stepping out of the huddle of people, Mr. Kent announced loudly, "It was nice of the officers to let us get here before they thanked you."

No one got it. The desk sergeants and clerks looked truly bemused.

Mr. Kent rolled his eyes and blew an exasperated sigh. "The *children* will be so *proud* of their father when they hear how he helped the police..."

Detective Hines was just coming from the squad room and she caught on right away. She walked to the front of the counter and extended her hand to Steve. "Yes, we really appreciate your cooperation, Mr. Kent. Sorry we had to keep you away from the family for so long."

Now, everyone was on board. The officer who escorted them from the building squatted to eye-level with the two boys. "Your dad is one of the good guys. We're a lot closer to figuring this case out because of his help."

The boys glowed. Steve noticed that Hope was standing slightly behind Daisy. The little girl hadn't once raised her eyes to look at him. He heard Joe Willis' voice echoing in his mind: *show her who she is.*

Kneeling next to her, he peered up at the brass nameplate on the officer's uniform. "Officer Ambrose, I'd like you to meet my beautiful daughter, Hope."

All the horror of the past hours fell away from Steve when Hope stretched out her arms to hug her new dad.

In the middle of the reunion, Daisy and Carl exchanged strained whispers over the heads of the children. "I don't see him anywhere!" she cried.

"There's no reason for them to hold him," Carl said, craning his neck to look around the room. "Here, take Lucky and I'll go ask at the desk."

The baby thought it was a game. He laughed as Carl pried loose first one arm and then the other. Just as he was being handed to Daisy, the baby would lurch forward, throwing his arms around Carl's neck once more. By the time Daisy was able to get a firm hold on Tremain, Kendrick appeared in the reception area, escorted by a uniformed officer and Detective Lucas.

He had talked until he'd lost his voice. The detectives had asked him every possible question about Lynn, their marriage and breakup. The repetitive questions frustrated Kendrick. The cops didn't seem to understand that he could only talk about the woman he'd known *before*. Their marriage had been over for more than two years and he hadn't seen or heard from Lynn.

Repeated questioning was a technique used by every law enforcement agency because it worked. The guilty became exhausted, angry or confused and let something slip. The innocent were also exhausted and angry, but frequently came up with important information that they didn't know they had.

After nearly three hours of answering the same questions repeated in different forms, Kendrick yelled, "I told you, she didn't have any family after her parents died! Except that low-life cousin and she couldn't stand him."

The detective jumped up from his chair. "Cousin? What cousin?"

"Some small-time thug. Lynn hardly ever mentioned him; she didn't want anything to do with him."

"A name, Mr. Peak. We need a name."

Kendrick's head was pounding and he was aching for a drink of water, but he was too proud to ask for one. "Roach! No, that's not right. Spud. No, it was a bug—Spider!"

Looking up from his note taking, a young cop said, "A spider is not a bug. It's an arachnid."

The detective glared. "Really, Mallby? Could you focus?" He turned to Kendrick. "Mr. Peak, are you sure? Any chance that you might know a last name?"

23

Dee showered and dressed with blazing speed. She wore what she considered "work clothes": jeans, a plaid shirt and white leather tennis shoes. She jammed a White Sox cap on her head and moved toward the door. Javier was trying to convince Langston to stay behind.

"You're supposed to be recuperating. You can't go running around—you can't run anywhere!"

"I'm going with you." Langston concentrated on navigating Dee's throw rugs with his crutches.

"What if Ms. Streeter comes back here?" Javi asked.

Exasperated, Lang banged a crutch on the floor. "She didn't come here in the first place. I'm going!"

Dee found out that River Jordan was sending out a search party as Javier helped Langston settle into the back seat of her car. Daisy called with an update. First, she told Dee about the telephone tree and then came the good news.

"The police just released Steve and Kendrick! They seem to believe that Lynn is the connection between the murder and the attacks on Tiffany and Rev. Beem. I don't think that Kendrick and Steve are suspects any longer, thank the Lord!"

"You know how people in the church talk. Someone is sure to have mentioned Kendrick's interest in Tiffany. That could explain killing Uttley, but not the attacks," Dee was talking to herself more than to Daisy, thinking aloud. Lots of people had grudges against the former deacon and the police knew all about the pictures he'd had taken.

As if reading Dee's mind, Daisy said, "The more the cops learn about Uttley, the more people they'll have to talk to. This might never be over."

"Maybe the killer was looking for Uttley that night and Rev. Beem and Tiffany just got in the way." Dee was still trying to piece things together. "Look, I'll call you back in a while. We're following up Javier's lead."

Following up a lead. Another time, Dee would have loved using "cop talk." Now her every thought centered on her mother—had she eaten, had she slept? Was she cold or scared? Did she even realize that she was in danger? She couldn't allow herself to wonder if her mother was still alive.

Dee tuned back into the conversation just as Daisy was saying, "I can't believe Lynn could do any of this. She was such a sweet girl."

"Yeah, right," Dee said. "That's what they say about all the psychotic killers—'he was always so quiet; he kept to himself.' Meantime, the cops find eleven people buried under the concrete in the basement!"

Javier was still checking in with his sources in the department when Dee's phone chirped again. She'd never been able to tolerate the headsets and didn't believe in using a cell phone while driving. She tossed the phone to Langston, who was in mid-rant.

"Deanna Ramsey, slow this car down! You think they won't give you a ticket just because you're riding around with two cops? You're going to kill somebody!"

She looked in the rearview mirror and made face at him, but she did ease up on the accelerator. The car had been well above Lake Shore Drive's 45 mile an hour limit.

"Dee Ramsey's phone," was all Langston got to say. Javier and Dee could hear the voice squealing, even though they couldn't understand a word coming from the phone.

Langston sat straight up. "Don't go to 47th Street," he told Dee. "We're going to Washington Park. This is Bernard and he's looking right at your mother!"

■

Crossing River Jordan

Seeing Dee's mom where he least expected her to be caused Mr. Bernard to do something that he'd never done before. For the briefest of moments, he broke character and, in his normal voice, said, "I don't believe it!"

No one seemed to notice the mistake. As MC of the Swing dance competition, Mr. Bernard portrayed Blanche Calloway and was dressed in a slinky white halter-necked gown. For the performance, he'd sung many of her songs and several of her younger brother, Cab Calloway's, hits as well. He immediately raised his voice an octave and resumed singing, "Hi de hi de ho!"

The spectators and the dancers echoed the chorus of *Minnie the Moocher*. The band continued to swing and so did the dancers—including Birdie Lee Streeter. It had been all Lynn could do to keep up with her as Birdie moved toward the sounds. The music had attracted her, but the dancing captivated her completely.

The portable stage held an entire big band and the tallest girl singer Birdie had ever seen, but that girl could wail! Below the stage was a dance floor and it was jumping, with people of all ages doing dances that Birdie remembered well. Before Lynn could stop her, Birdie had latched on to a young man in a purple zoot suit and pulled him onto the floor.

"Let me show you how it's done, young blood!" She yelled, clapping her hands and scooting her narrow hips backwards.

"Go, granny, go!" her partner yelled back and feet flying, they took off for the middle of the crowded floor.

They attracted a lot of attention; dancers and spectators urging them on as they danced. In an amazing move, Birdie did a flying roll across her partner's back and he did the same to her. The crowd went wild and that was when Bernard realized that he wasn't merely *wishing* to see Birdie Lee—he was watching her upstage him! As soon as his song ended, he ducked backstage and grabbed his cell phone.

Lynn realized that there was no way she could get Birdie Lee to come with her without causing a massive commotion. She'd been dogged by the nagging feeling of time running out. She had to get to that hospital before it was too late.

That's it; that's all! Lynn threw up her hands. She couldn't take anymore of the crazy old woman. At least she wasn't leaving her stranded and alone. Someone in the huge crowd would make sure that Miss Grandma got home safely. Lynn turned her back on the dancers and melted into the throng. It would take two busses to get to St. Benedict's, so she decided to splurge on a cab.

  Just as the gray brick structure came into view, Lynn asked the driver to let her out. She was no longer worried about how to get in—the hospital was going to come and get her.

■

  The word went out on the speed of sound as one cell phone connected with another—Birdie Lee Streeter had been seen at the Alley Celebration! Bernard had given Langston the location, but the exact information never made it through the branches of the telephone tree. From all parts of the city, the River Jordan posse converged on the park, determined to search all 372 acres. Church members honked horns and waved to each other as they sped down streets and pulled into lines of cars near the park entrances.

  The rescuers immediately ran into problems because there was absolutely no parking anywhere near Washington Park. Searchers who had brought their dogs were turned away by police—no dogs allowed at the Celebration—but an explanation of what they were trying to do quickly got the cops involved.

  For about five minutes, Dee drove around trying to find a parking space. Finally, she groaned in frustration and pulled up onto a curb on 61st street as Langston clutched his cast and howled in pain.

  "Sorry! I'm so sorry," she told him, while jumping out of the car. "Javier, you park it! I've got to hurry!"

  "Dee, wait! Let Javi go with you," Langston pleaded, but she never stopped moving.

  "It's by the fountain," Langston said and then groaned again as the wheels bumped off the curb. "There's a stage set up by the Fountain of Time. That's where Bernard saw Ms. Streeter!"

  The dance competition was one of the most popular events at the Celebration. It was certainly well-attended and Dee was exhausted by the time she'd made her way into the midst of the crowd surrounding the stage and dance floor. Dee hardly noticed that people were waving to her and calling her name as she moved through the crowd. She was so focused on the stage that she never noticed that she was drawing a group behind her as word went out among the River Jordan searchers that Dee had been spotted.

She had tersely, but politely, refused several requests to dance when a large man about her age would not be denied. The man was a wall, decked out in a lemon yellow suit with purple suspenders and an orange bow tie. A hysterical giggle escaped Dee as she was reminded of a game she played as a child called "Fruit Basket Upset."

"C'mon, baby, let's do this thing!" he yelled, grabbing her wrist and hauling her to his barrel chest.

Dee hopped and skipped, pulled along by her partner. All of her dance moves were calculated responses to his jumps and kicks; she was desperately trying to stay out of his way and save her shins. He finally spun her away so he could do a Lindy Rock step and she found herself eye to silk-covered chest with Mr. Bernard.

With a wireless microphone, Bernard sang Blanche Calloway's *Catch On* as he waded into the throng of dancers and spectators. The call and response song soon had everyone joining in. Javier appeared on the other side of Dee. A natural performer, he took Dee's right hand, Bernard took the left and they formed a chorus line, high kicking back to the stage. As Bernard finished the song, Javi sang along and hit a high note at the end that drove the audience into a frenzy. Dee couldn't think of anything else to do; she dropped to one knee and did "jazz hands" to the wild applause. They slipped backstage as soon as they could.

Bernard took off the wavy brunette wig and fanned himself with it. He smiled at Javier. "I heard you sing at the church once and I've got to say, you're in the wrong line of work. You know Blanche Calloway's work?"

"I know she was the first woman to lead an all-male band back in the 1930s. I was just faking the song."

"Well, anytime you want to work, I could get you a gig just like that!" Bernard snapped an impeccably manicured hand.

Rubbing her knees, Dee had finally regained her breath. She her head at the two men talking show business and blew an exasperated sigh. "My mother?"

"Is right down there!" Bernard made a sweeping gesture toward the pro-am dance contest that was taking place just to the right of the stage.

"Where? I don't see her." Dee peered into the frantically whirling dance.

"I saw her dancing down there just before I came to get you. You can't miss her ; she's been wearing those youngsters out. Just look for the big red hat. I have to ask her how she's keeping that thing on."

Dee started down the stairs, still unable to pick Birdie Lee out of the crowd.

"A big red hat, you said? That big red hat?" Javier pointed.

Birdie Lee was on the move again! The hat and its wearer were on their way out of the 55th street exit.

"Go, go!" Bernard busily adjusted his wig. "I've got to finish here. Call me when you catch up with her."

Dee had made it to the bottom of the stairs when Javi sped past. "Call Lang. I parked near there. Maybe he can spot her coming out of the park."

Dee resented taking the time to stop and use her phone, but she also knew that she could never have kept up with the young detective. She'd already lost sight of him. She relayed the information to Langston and then hobbled toward the exit as fast as her aching knees would let her go.

■

As they moved closer to St. Benedict's, the idea had come to Lynn full-blown, like a scene from a movie. She had the taxi drop her off at Food for You, a small store on 63rd street, less than a mile from the hospital. All she'd had to do was create a convincing scene at the grocery store.

As she approached the refrigerated fresh meat case, Lynn faked an asthma attack. She wheezed, coughed and staggered. Preparing for the action that would really sell the performance, a coughing spell caused her to collapse onto the saran-wrapped packages of meat.

Crossing River Jordan

Concerned onlookers and good Samaritans rushed to get help. Her actions covered by her body, Lynn unwrapped a package and took a huge bite of raw liver. She quickly pushed the open package beneath the others in the case. Now she was bleeding from her mouth as she crumpled to the floor.

Holding the raw meat in her mouth was so disgusting that she truly began to feel sick. Retching and writhing on the floor, Lynn looked up at the horrified faces surrounding her. *Great*, she thought happily. *This will do it!*

Outside, the sound of a siren grew louder. One employee tried clearing the onlookers away; no one moved. They all shouted ideas for what should be done to help.

"Put something in her mouth so she won't swallow her tongue," a young woman insisted, but the frothing, bloody mess Lynn was producing was too intimidating.

"Roll her on her side," an older man offered. Before anyone could try, the EMTs arrived with a gurney. With practiced speed, they performed a series of preliminary tests, picked Lynn up and moved her into the ambulance.

At that moment, Lynn couldn't enjoy a sense of accomplishment. No longer simply pretending to be ill, she felt like she was going to die. Lynn had forced herself to swallow the chunk of liver before it could be discovered by the emergency team. She had never felt so awful in her entire life. She hoped she didn't die before she got to finish her work.

The ambulance sped her to St. Benedict's emergency room. She by-passed triage and was taken right to an examination room. Lynn couldn't believe how well her plan was working and good fortune continued to smile on her.

In the brief time that she was left alone while the medical personnel conferred, she slipped away in search of the nearest restroom. She was a mess and needed to change clothes. Fortunately, no one had taken her personal belongings away. She was grateful; because of Birdie Lee and her "junk shopping," Lynn had a clean shirt.

The next step would be finding Beem's room. A phone call from a "concerned relative" would take care of that. She hoped he was awake. She wanted him to see who was delivering his justice.

■

"Pneumonia is a serious diagnosis, but it's not always a death sentence," the doctor told Vanessa. "The reverend is a strong man and he's taken good care of himself. This is a setback, nothing more."

"But he was getting better." Cory couldn't understand. He was shaken by the sight of his forceful, active father lying still and connected to tubes and beeping monitors. He held his mother's hand and his glance scanned the room, taking in everything except the reverend.

"We believe this was caused by the flour he inhaled. It's a complication, but your dad is responding well. Don't worry; we're keeping a close eye on him." He checked something on the chart and left the room.

Darnell and Chess had been standing quietly in the background while the doctor answered questions. The pastor sensed that Cory needed some time away and said, "Cory, I'm going to look in on Tiffany. Would you come with me? I bet she'd be glad to see a new face." Both mother and son looked grateful for the suggestion.

"I can stay, if you want," Chess offered.

Vanessa, shook her head. "Thank you, but I'd like to spend some time alone with Albert. There are some things I need to say, whether he can hear them now or not."

Darnell had a feeling that this new "Steel Vanessa" wanted to give Rev. Beem the pep talk she had been rehearsing. He ushered everyone out and closed the door.

The visitors stepped across the hall. Tiffany's door was open.

"Wow," Chess said. "You look wonderful!" She couldn't help making a mental comparison to how weak and wan Rev. Beem appeared.

Sitting up in bed, Tiffany was the picture of health. Even the bruising around her neck was fading. She self-consciously patted her hair. Just that morning, a hospital volunteer had taken the time to do her hair and give her a lipstick and mascara. She was delighted when Kendrick had walked in and given her a wolf whistle. She hoped the sight of her on the floor of the River Jordan kitchen would be wiped from his mind forever.

Crossing River Jordan

Kendrick told the story of his adventures with Dee and the police as Tiffany listened, eyes wide. He'd managed to tell his story without mentioning Frank Willis, even once. He wasn't sure how she would react—would she jump up and run screaming from the hospital? Would she again decide to take Tremain and leave?

"I'm ready to get out of here," Tiffany assured them. "I feel fine and I'm sure someone else could use this bed."

"Deacon Uttley probably could have used it, but it's too late now." Cory, who had no love for the late former deacon, thought he was being witty.

Tiffany's head jerked up. "What do you mean? What happened to him?"

"Shut up, Cory!" Kendrick snarled, furious that fear had filled Tiffany's eyes again. The boy took a step back as if he'd been slapped.

"I'm sorry, Cory." Kendrick apologized immediately. "She doesn't know. I didn't want to upset her." *It's not the kid's fault that you were being too cowardly to treat Tiffany like an adult.*

Tiffany waved her arms in the air. "Hello, I'm right here, Kendrick. What haven't you told me?" She began to cough.

"Do you need some water?" Pastor Darnell asked and Tiffany shook her head. "Do you want us to leave?"

Kendrick had never been so glad to have visitors. Whatever Tiffany's reaction, he didn't have to deal with it alone. He wouldn't leave anything out this time, even the parts about Willis. "No, I probably need you all to help me get things straight."

"You should start with the murder." Cory had recovered from his insult.

Tiffany's eyes grew wide again.

■

"I saw her!" Langston moved toward Dee and Javier as fast as he could swing his crutches. "I called her, but I guess she couldn't hear me."

"She was alone, right? She wasn't being taken away?" Dee prayed that her mother had some how gotten away from her kidnapper.

"She stopped on the corner, but I couldn't get to her fast enough!"

Dee stood on tiptoe to kiss Langston's cheek. She could feel his frustration; the broken leg made him feel helpless. A glance at the ground verified his words. A tiny pile of silver foil lifted and swirled in the airstream of the passing cars. She pointed it out to the detectives. "She waited right here to cross."

""Where could she have gone? We weren't that far behind her," Javier squinted in the sun's glare.

Dee scanned the buildings opposite them. At least there were only a few places she could have gone. They were looking at four businesses, a vacant lot and a church.

When the light changed, Javier said, "I'll take the laundromat; you check the nail shop." He looked at Langston, who was already fishing in his pocket for his phone.

"I'm calling it in and I'll wait here for the unit. There'll be cops all over the place in a few minutes," he assured Dee.

Having no luck with their first stops, Javier checked the Chinese restaurant while Dee found out that the copy shop had gone out of business. Together, they rounded the corner to the front of the church.

Dee began to smile. "That church has a red door. Mama couldn't resist it."

24

The little church was built of limestone that fairly glowed in the bright sunlight. Beneath an arch, the red double doors welcomed visitors. Javier pulled a gleaming brass handle and they stepped into the narthex. The church was lovingly cared for; the wainscoting of cherry wood was polished to a high gloss. They stood still for a moment, waiting for their eyes to adjust to the lower light.

Crossing a short hall to the sanctuary, Dee peeked in, but it was empty.

"I'll try to find the office," Dee said, turning to her right.

"I'll look down there," Javier said, moving toward a stairway on the left.

Then came a high-pitched scream, followed by a deeper yell.

Javier raced down the stairs, with Dee on his heels. The large room they rushed into was filled with a mass of figures, shrouded in black clothing and hoods, flowing toward them. Dee shrank back, horrified. They had run headlong into a nightmare!

"*Yame,*" called a woman from the front of the room, and the tide of motion stopped abruptly. "*Hajime!*"

Javier began to laugh as the karate students began a series of katas at their sensei's instruction. Carefully avoiding the flying hands and feet, Javi and Dee moved toward the instructor, edging along the perimeter of the room. They waited quietly, watching movements that appeared to be a choreographed routine.

After a few minutes, Dee realized that the students weren't all at the same level of expertise. Some moved looked like they were performing ballet; others were awkward and hesitant. A few were downright clumsy.

"*Yame. Rei.*" Again the students stopped immediately and then bowed in unison. The instructor clapped her hands. "Well done, everyone! Take a break; have something to drink."

Hoods were removed around the room, revealing men, women and children of all ages, shapes and sizes. The discipline of the exercising gone, they huddled in clumps, chatting and laughing. Only then did Dee notice the lone person dressed in a plain white karate uniform.

"Mama?" Dee couldn't believe what she was seeing.

Birdie Lee was using a hand to fan herself. "Woo wee, these things are hot! She brushed imaginary dust off the front of her pants. "How do you like my *gi*? That's what this outfit is called. They didn't have no colors, only black or white, but I can get me a red belt."

Laughing and crying, Dee ran to hug her mother. "I was so worried about you. Everyone's been looking for you!"

Birdie shook her off. "Girl, it's too hot for all that. What's wrong with you, anyway?"

Dee looked around and saw Javier on his way up the stairs. He gave her a big grin and a "thumbs up."

"Mama, nobody's known where you were for three days..." Dee began, but Birdie Lee interrupted.

"I knew where I was! I'm a grown woman; I don't need you to worry about my business, Deanna Ramsey!"

"Deanna? You're Ms. Streeter's daughter?" At first glance, the karate instructor looked like a teenager with an athletic build and her hair was pulled back in a functional pony-tail. She came closer, extending her hand. Dee could then see that she was a mature adult, with faint traces of crow's feet at the corners of her warm brown eyes.

"Hi, I'm Karen Rodgers, the sensei of this *dojo*."

"*Dojo* means school," Birdie Lee explained, proudly. "Hey, show me how to do that." She joined a group practicing kicks.

Dee met the woman's firm grip with her own. "I'm sorry; I thought this was a church."

"Most of the time, it is and then I'm Rev. Karen Rodgers. Twice a week, down here, we're God's Hands Shotokan Karate Dojo and I become sensei. We're doing a dress rehearsal for our ninja demonstration; that's why they're wearing black. Usually they'd all be dressed like Ms. Streeter."

They moved to a long table in the corner of the room. As Dee joined Rev. Rodgers in pouring small cups of juice for the students, she took care to keep her mother always in sight.

Rev. Rodgers was saying, "I'm delighted that you want to join us. We have a few seniors, but your mother would be our oldest student. I told her that she wouldn't have to buy a *gi*; the young folks grow out of them so fast; we always have a few extras."

"What?" Dee was distracted by the sight of Birdie Lee attempting a back-kick. Two young men, each holding one of Birdie's extended arms, kept her from falling flat on her face.

"Your mother came in saying that you had dropped her off, but you'd forgotten the exercise clothes. She said that you'd be right back and take care of signing you both up for the class then. She was so eager to get started."

"There's been a misunderstanding. My mother is as crazy as bubblegum shoes." Dee found herself telling a complete stranger about her mother's mental condition and how hard it was to cope with her.

Crossing River Jordan

Dee dropped her head. "Oh, Rev. Rodgers, I'm so sorry about this. My mother has been missing for three days. The police have her listed as a missing person. People have been running all over the city looking for her!"

To punctuate the point, Javi came thundering down the stairs accompanied by two uniformed officers. Dee waved them over.

"Rev. Karen Rodgers, this is my friend, Detective Javier Solis and these are…"

"Officers Stevens and Russell," Javi finished. "They're here, officially, to escort you and Ms. Streeter to the station."

"Not before she goes to the hospital. She's nearly 80 years old and she's been God knows where with God knows who for three days. She's got to see a doctor!" Dee stood with her legs spread and fists clenched, gearing up for a fight.

"Of course, she does." Javier stepped in front of Dee. "The officers will follow us to St. Benedict's and when a doctor gives us the okay, we'll all go to the station.

"I'll walk you out," Rev. Rodgers said, linking her arm with Dee's. "When the dust settles and you have some time, give me a call. I know a little bit about relatives with that 'bubblegum shoes' problem."

Birdie Lee was not happy about having her karate lesson interrupted. She fussed and fumed as Dee helped her collect her belongings and she refused to change clothes. "Sensei said I could *have* it. I told you I'm getting a red belt for it. Then I'll look sharp!"

Fixing Dee with a slit-eyed glare, Birdie Lee wouldn't walk with her daughter or answer any questions about where she'd been. Dee wasn't sure if her mother even knew how long she had been gone. Birdie didn't loosen up until she saw Langston leaning against Javier's car.

"Oh, it's a double date! Well, I can't go out looking like this. I have to get pretty first."

She took an appraising look Javier as he helped into the front seat and adjusted her seatbelt. "He's sure good-looking Deanna, but I told you, I don't want to be no bobcat. I can't date these youngsters."

"Well, Ms. Streeter, that's going to break a lot of hearts," Langston said, settled in the back seat with his arm around Dee.

She slapped his hand, whispering, "Don't encourage her."

Javier pulled in behind the squad car.

Turning to Javier, Birdie said, "Turn on some music, so I can get down and do my thing!"

Then she recalled her anger and twisted in her seat to give Dee the stink-eye. She muttered, "Always ruining my fun; you better get you some business."

Two blocks later, she'd fallen asleep.

■

"You're a little dehydrated and you need some rest, but otherwise, you're just fine, Ms. Streeter," the doctor sat on a stool, entering notes on a hand-held computer. "Your blood pressure is a little elevated, but still in the normal range."

All Birdie Lee heard was, "You're fine."

"Men been telling me I was fine my whole life, young blood. I'm sorry; I can't date nobody young enough to be my grandson. Don't you worry; there's always some girl looking to marry a doctor. You'll find somebody soon."

The doctor coughed into his fist, hiding a bark of laughter. He turned to Dee and lowered his voice. "Of course, she should be seen by her regular physician. And, if she's not already, she should be taking a multi-vitamin. It's good that you're taking care of her."

Dee felt a stab of guilt. She had *not* been taking care of Birdie Lee, not really. Her mother was so headstrong and could be so vicious. Dee had always chosen the path of least resistance, but it seemed to be time for that to change.

Langston and Javier were waiting with the other cops in the cafeteria. Checking her watch, Dee decided that they had a few minutes to spare. She wanted to check on Tiffany and Rev. Beem. As the elevator took them to the sixth floor, Dee inhaled and took the plunge.

"MamaIwantyoutocomelivewithme."

The sentence *whooshed* out of her so quickly that Birdie Lee didn't understand a word.

"What?"

Dee tried again. "I want you to come live with me."

It was the biggest lie Dee had ever told in her life and saying it had made her miserable. Dee wanted many things: quiet time, a chance to travel, a cure for arthritis, world peace. Throughout her life, she had wanted so much more. In fact, the last thing she had ever wanted was to live with Birdie Lee Streeter, but her mother needed to be looked after. There was no one else to do it.

Birdie looked at her and shook her head. "You just want to get in my business and take my money."

"Mama, I send you money."

"Well, you should. I'm your mama."

"I think it would be better if you lived closer, so I could help you more."

"I don't need no help. I can take care of myself!"

Unwilling to give up, Dee said, "That's true, but I could use your help at the church. A lot of the seniors could use someone like you to show them how to take care of themselves."

"So, you want me to come live with you so you can work me to death?" Birdie's voice rose, just as the elevator doors opened.

They stepped out into a corridor filled with stares. Hugely embarrassed, Dee drew a deep breath, squared her shoulders and put on her best "Queen."

"Come, Mama. We must get on with our visiting." She stepped smartly past the nurses' station, hoping that no one would "shush" Birdie Lee. That never turned out well.

They stopped briefly in the reverend's room.

"I hate hospitals," Birdie announced, dropping into a chair. "They kill people in hospitals."

"Mama, that's not true," Dee said. Her mind wasn't on Birdie; she was checking the monitor and looking at the IV.

"You don't tell me! Back home in Three Rivers, Mr. Wilson went in the hospital for a broken hip and he stayed in there four weeks. Two years later, he was stone cold dead!"

Mama, he was 97 years old!"

Birdie was off on another tangent. "Why do they have that bag on his head? Don't they know you can die if your head's in a plastic bag? I better get that thing off..."

Dee tuned back in to her mother just in time to intercept Birdie's reach. "No, Mama, the tent is *helping* Rev. Beem breathe."

Thinking, *I better get her out of here*, Dee said, "Let's go see how Tiffany is doing."

They entered to a burst of laughter. Kendrick was finishing a re-enactment of being questioned by the police.

"You sound like you were scared," Corey scoffed, with 14 year old bravado.

"Man, I was terrified. All the cops were like seven feet tall and weighed about 275, even the women," Kendrick joked.

Everyone, except the patient, surrounded Birdie Lee and she basked in the attention. Even Corey showed a moment of unguarded happiness before recovering his teenaged cool. Questions erupted, but Birdie ignored them all.

"Butterbean!" Birdie greeted Kendrick, joyfully. "Boy, what are you doing in a hospital? You're not sick are you?"

Kendrick gave her a peck on the cheek and a big hug. "Miss Grandma, we were very worried about you. Where have you been?"

"I've been learning me some Karate; see my *gi*?" Birdie did a slow turn. Kendrick looked over her head, sending Dee an unspoken question.

Later, she mouthed.

Birdie peered at Tiffany. "You don't look too sick to me. You better get out of this place before they give you some kind of disease."

"That's a good idea, Ms. Streeter," Tiffany said. "I'm leaving as soon as the doctors say I can."

"I got some candy in my purse," Birdie turned her attention to Corey. "You doin' good in school?"

"We're out of school for the summer, ma'am, but I did good this year." Vanessa's eyes snapped to her son. She couldn't remember ever hearing him call anyone "ma'am" before. Something about Birdie Lee brought out the old-fashioned boy in almost every male.

"Deanna, what did you do with my bag?" If Birdie Lee couldn't find something, it must be her daughter's fault.

"You wouldn't let me carry your bag, Mama. Did you leave it in Rev. Beem's room?"

"Probably. You pulled me out of there so fast, I must have forgot it."

Dee had taken two steps toward the door when Birdie grabbed her arm. "I can get it myself. You just want to go through my purse when I'm not looking!"

Dee sighed and followed her mother.

25

All that time spent with crazy Miss Grandma had burned through the money Lynn had taken from Spider. She was still free and zeroing in on her target, so the old woman may have been a good luck charm of sorts. In her mind's eye, she saw Beem with a large red 'X' on his chest, sniveling and backing away from her. She was an exterminator, ridding the world of parasites.

If Lynn hadn't been so low on funds she would never have stolen flowers from the hospital chapel. Until she made it to the elevator, she expected to hear "Stop, thief!" but she arrived on the sixth floor with no problems.

The basket of carnations and Peruvian lilies was heavier than it appeared; no way could she move swiftly down the corridor. She was forced to walk slowly and deliberately—*I'm sad and worried. I'm just a sorrowful family member bringing some flowers to my poor sick uncle.* She held the flowers close to her chest so no one could see that she wasn't wearing one of the stick-on visitors' passes distributed by the hospital receptionists.

At first, she walked past his room. That was surveillance. She was surprised to see Beem encased in the oxygen tent and pleased to see that he was alone in his room. A few steps down, there was a crowd gathered in a room across the corridor. A burst of laughter slowed her as she passed.

She nearly froze when she spotted Auntie Dee and Miss Grandma in the room with Kendrick. How had the old woman known to come to St. Benedict's? Lynn's thoughts raced as she tried to remember if she had let any of her plan slip. She couldn't have—she'd been making things up as she went along. She ordered herself to move, not to make a scene.

Lynn didn't even recognize Tiffany; there hadn't been enough light in the church kitchen that night for her to get a good look at her other victim. What almost made her drop the basket was the sight of Kendrick sitting on the bed with his arm around another woman. She felt heat rise from the center of her body. Her breath caught in her throat.

She was tempted to run into that room and slam the basket down on Kendrick's head. She could hardly make her feet move; every muscle tensed with the strain of the battle she fought with herself. Then, as suddenly as it began, the battle ended.

She didn't want to kill Kendrick. He had hurt her by cheating on her, but he wasn't evil. He was a good father to the children, their children. She had loved him once, but that seemed very long ago.

More importantly, he wasn't her Mission. She had to get a grip on herself—so close to achieving her goal, she had nearly blown the whole thing! Lynn realized that she had broken out in a cold sweat. She stopped in a restroom to regroup and splash cool water on her face.

Passing the room on her way back, she made sure to block her face with the flowers. Vanessa Beem and her boy were also in the room. She'd never liked Corey Beem; he had always been such a brat. She didn't know the other two people and she didn't care who they were. The most important thing was that Beem was alone and she had just thought of a perfectly simple plan.

Lynn kept walking to the end of the hall, which curved behind the nurses' station, forming an 'L.' She found an empty room and checked the closet to make sure that the room hadn't been assigned. She didn't want to be surprised by anyone wheeling a patient in.

Removing some of the florist moss from the flower basket, Lynn used it as kindling to start a fire in the wastebasket. She fed it tissue and paper towels. Closing the door behind her, she rushed to the nurses' station.

"I'm not sure, but I think I smelled smoke down there." Lynn pointed.

A nurse went to check, but didn't go far. Wisps of gray smoke seeped from beneath the door.

The staff hurried to implement the proper procedures. Lynn's fire didn't create the chaos that she had expected, but it did provide the distraction that she needed. She slipped into Rev. Beem's room and unplugged the monitor. Pushing the oxygen tent out of her way, she snatched the pillow from beneath Beem's head. His eyes opened instantly.

Lynn bared her teeth in a triumphant grin, straddled his chest and mashed the pillow down on the reverend's face. He thrashed and bucked. His hands flailed wildly and then he found her wrists. He was stronger than she expected, nearly able to pull her hands away from the pillow.

Lynn threw her weight forward, her arms trembled with the strain. She could feel Beem growing weaker, but she could also hear the sounds in the hall coming closer to the room. Maybe the staff was evacuating patients from the floor. Someone could be there any second. No, she couldn't fail again!

The bathroom door opened. Dee was saying, "No, I don't understand why you had to wash your purse out. Mama, who does that?"

Birdie Lee stepped out, still stuffing paper towels into the dripping bag. "Lynn, get down from there; that ain't right! You two can't be doing that stuff all out in public like that!"

Yelling for help, Dee ran to the door, but her voice was swallowed by the ruckus in the hall. She grabbed a chair, moving toward Lynn like an old-fashion lion tamer.

"Mama, go get Kendrick!"

"The hell I will," Birdie snapped, turning back to Lynn. "Girl, I told you to get down from there!"

Birdie rushed to the bed and jumped on Lynn's back. They tumbled to the floor, with Birdie on the bottom.

Seeing her little mother crushed beneath the larger woman, Dee lost hold of logic and swung the chair down on Lynn's back as hard as she could. Lynn screeched wordlessly. She had her hands pressed against Birdie's scrawny chest. Dee raised the chair again and then she realized what she was seeing: Lynn was trying to pull away, but Birdie Lee was clinging to her—holding on with all her might!

"Mama, let go," Dee pleaded, trying to pull her mother's hands away. The three women wrestled on the floor until Dee was able to pull Birdie away. Though Dee had hurt her with the chair, Lynn had risen to one knee and was trying to stand up. Birdie Lee stumbled to the door and pulled it closed.

"Mama, just let her go, "Dee begged. "The police will catch up with her downstairs."

Grasping the door handle with both hands, Birdie Lee leaned forward and kicked back. Her foot connected with

Lynn's head, sending it into the wall. Lynn slumped to the floor.

"That was my back-kick," Birdie announced.

Dee wrapped her mother in a hug.

Birdie shrugged her off, fanning the air with one hand. "Get off me. It's too hot for all that."

■

Various versions of Lynn's capture had swept the church within hours. The stories ran the gamut—from Lynn's wielding a bloody ax and hostages being taken to Birdie Lee's pulling a Chuck Norris on three men and saving Lynn's life. The truth was often lost in translation.

In fact, it hadn't taken the hospital staff long to realize that the fire was small and easily contained. Rather than evacuating rooms, they had called the fire department and moved to see that everyone was safely *inside* their rooms. They had insisted that no one go out into the corridors to leave the way clear. They'd seen Rev. Beem with his visitor, a young woman, standing beside his bed and then hurried to look in on other patients.

While Dee and Birdie struggled with Lynn, Javier and the officers were being kept out of the building while firefighters verified that everything was safe on the sixth floor. By the time they arrived in the room, Kendrick and Pastor Darnell stood guard as hospital staff worked on the unconscious Lynn.

The doctor tending to the reverend pronounced that Lynn had caused a minor setback, but, thanks to Birdie Lee, Rev. Beem would make it. Vanessa had hardly left his side after the second attempt on her husband's life. She wasn't sure how, but she promised the Lord that Albert would get that second chance with his family.

26

The Mothers Board had insisted on giving a reception for the newlyweds. Mother Jessup decided that it should be a cookout held at her home. No one argued with Mother Jessup. As if it understood its job on this special evening, her backyard was bursting with beauty. The purple clematis had outgrown its trellis and snaked along the fence, twining with red and yellow trumpet vines. The window boxes overflowed with pink and white wave petunias. Her bird house now had a companion, which had been handmade in Haiti.

The yard was fairly bursting with people, too.

The children were scattered all over the yard, lying on blankets or being held in laps. They had played and eaten and eaten and played until they could hardly move. Adults settled in to talk, as they always did when a party wound down. Seated on the wrap-around porch, they admired the great ball of orange slowly sinking on the western horizon.

The church family had so much to share, there was no way it would all be said at one gathering.

"It's still a sad situation," Mother Alma was saying. "So much is being done to help, but there's still so much to do."

"The people are amazing, though," Terri Blue added. "They're strong and hopeful. We had a great time playing with the Haitian musicians."

"We're going to join the other churches and see to it that more donations are sent," said the usually quiet Rita Thompson, who had been deeply inspired by the trip. Her husband, Henry, nodded his agreement and patted her hand.

"We won't be going away again any time soon, that's for sure," Mother Jessup joked, shaking her head. "You all get in too much trouble when we're not around."

Couples sat together, soothing sleepy children. Keisha and Steve had enjoyed a brief honeymoon, but there was simply too much waiting for them at home. They were anxious to start their life together.

"It's time, Pastor," Mother Jessup said.

Darnell smiled at Chess as he stood and cleared his throat. "I need a drum roll please."

Terri obligingly drummed on the porch floor.

"After many secret meetings and hushed discussions, we finally made a decision on a gift for Steve and Keisha—for the entire Kent family actually."

Steve and Keisha looked around, bewildered by all of the knowing smiles and grins.

The pastor reached into his pocket and came out with a set of keys. He held them up for everyone to see. "The keys to your new home. Well, not exactly new. Steve will only be moving a few yards away from where he already lives."

The pastor's announcement was greeted by blank faces. Keisha and Steve still didn't understand.

"The senior minister's residence!" Carl couldn't stand the suspense any longer.

"But, but..." Steve couldn't formulate his thoughts. Keisha began to cry.

"No buts, Steve Kent. We all agreed. Even Rev. Beem." Deacon Thompson grinned. "We need you too much to have you living far away from those old buildings."

Kendrick and Tiffany watched from a corner of the porch. They sat on the floor; Kensha and Tremain napped soundly on the glider behind them. Steve had broken into a dance, waltzing around with Hope standing on his feet.

"Sorry to have to share your favorite niece?" Tiffany teased.

"She's my only niece and no, I think it's just great."

He looked at Tiffany from the corner of his eye. "Speaking of sharing, have you thought any more about Frank Willis?" Kendrick felt her body tense and squeezed her hand.

"No, I haven't. I know he wants to see me to apologize. He said it's 'making amends' and it's one of the 12 steps. I just don't see why that can't happen on the phone."

"I'll go with you, if you decide to meet with him, but..." he left the sentence unfinished.

His stomach did flips every time he thought about Frank Willis. The man ran a profitable business. He seemed to be making a successful recovery from alcoholism. What if Tiffany chose to go back to him? After all, they had a child together.

She took his hand and kissed it. "I'm right where I want to be, Kendrick. I haven't even decided to meet with Frank myself, much less tell him that he fathered a child."

Kendrick figured he might as well relax and let the Frank Willis matter go. For now.

Dee and Daisy had already begun cleaning up.

"Why wouldn't she let us get her that dishwasher a few years back?" Daisy groused. "Oh, yeah, 'I wouldn't have one of them new-fangled contraptions chewing up my good china.' Wasn't that how it went?"

Looking out on the backyard, Dee smiled as she turned from the window. "You should have had Javier do the voice. He's so much better than you. You should see him out there with Mama. She's trying to teach him the Lindy."

Daisy took a quick look and cracked up. "He looks like a grasshopper on a hot skillet! His date is doing much better with Mr. Bernard, though. Is she a cop, too?"

"No, she's a civilian. She works at the station, though. They make a cute couple, don't you think?"

"Speaking of couples, when are you going to admit that you and Langston are one?"

"We're just friends, Daisy Franklin." Dee flicked her sister with a towel.

They worked in companionable silence for a few minutes and then Daisy asked, "What are you going to do about Miss Mama?"

Dee blew a frustrated sigh. "I swear, I don't know. She's so stubborn and *so* crazy. I don't know which is worse. She doesn't want to live with me as much as I don't want her to, but I know she needs looking after."

"I know you don't want to, but it may be time to have her declared incompetent."

I don't know if I can..."

"Deanna Ramsey, there is no psychiatrist in the world who wouldn't declare your mother to be as crazy as a June bug in July!"

They were startled by the door bell.

"I don't know who that could be," Dee said. "It seems that everyone we know is out back already." Daisy followed Dee to the door.

It had gotten much darker outside. After turning on the front porch light, Dee peeked out of the window. The young lady who stood in the glow could have been dropped from a Hollywood soundstage. Her almond-shaped eyes were framed by thick lashes, black hair fell in waves around her oval face and her lush lips were parted in a nervous smile. She was modestly dressed, but it was easy to see that even her curves had curves.

Dee and Daisy looked at each other and Daisy said, "Wow."

"May I help you?" Dee asked, finally opening the door.

"I'm sorry to come so late. My plane has only just arrived." She had a slight accent, but Dee couldn't place it. "I called River Jordan church yesterday and a young man told me that I should come to this address." She held a wrinkled piece of paper in her hand.

In unison, the sisters said, "Cory Beem!"

"We have *got* to keep that boy away from the phones," Dee said.

Dee led the way through the house as she spoke. "We're all in the backyard."

"We're Keisha's aunts—I'm Daisy and this is Deanna. You must be one of Steve's friends. Or are you a relative?" Daisy thought she knew all of Keisha's friends. There hadn't been many; the young mother simply hadn't had time.

As they stepped onto the back porch, the young lady peered into the purple twilight. Steve and a few other men were setting up mosquito-repellant lanterns around the yard.

Eagerly glancing from one person to another, the young visitor said, "My name is Katelyn Smith and I've come here to meet my father."

■ ■ ■ ■

Made in the USA
Monee, IL
16 January 2023